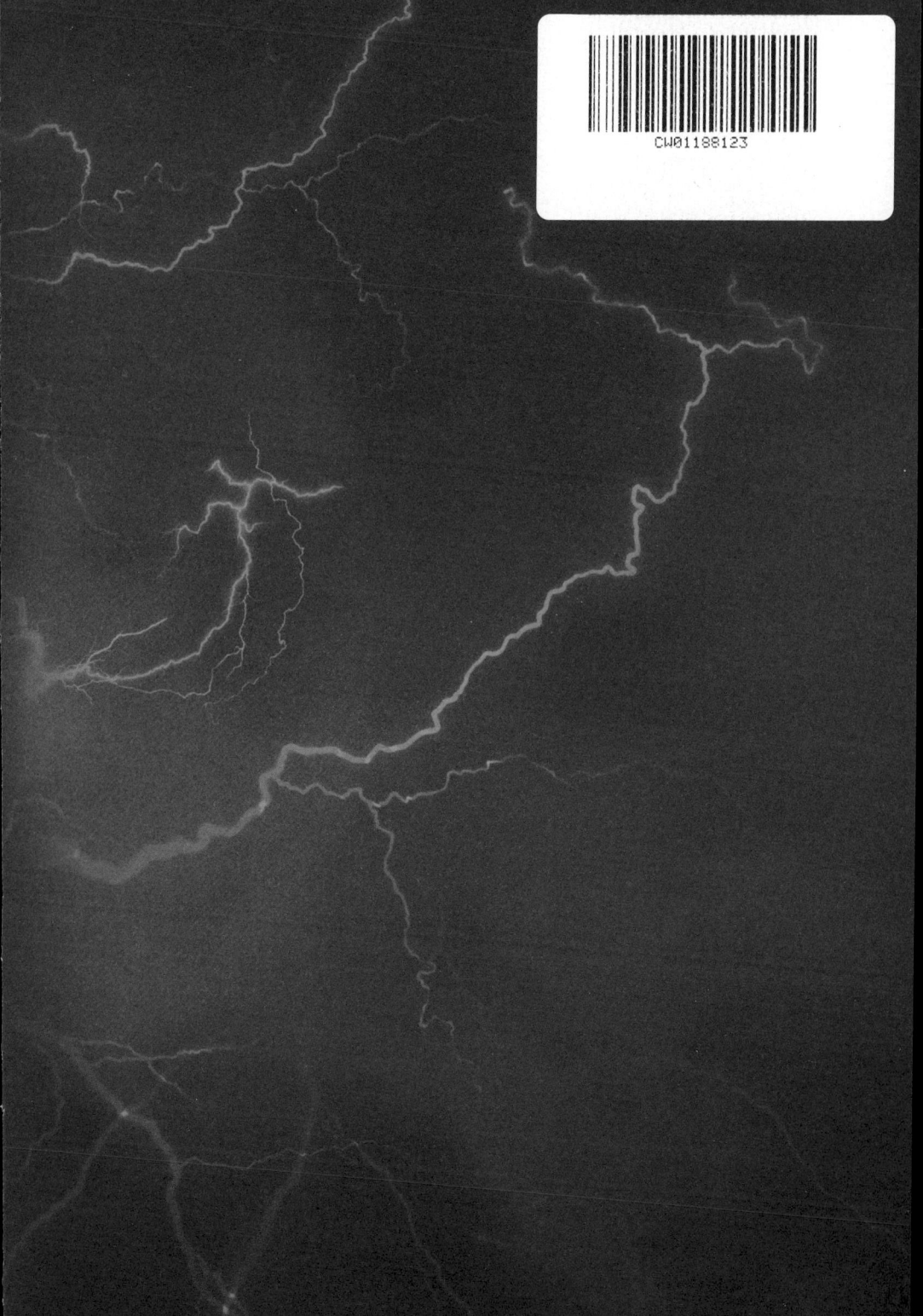

MARVEL

A NOVEL OF THE MARVEL UNIVERSE

ORIGINAL SIN

NOVELS OF THE MARVEL UNIVERSE BY TITAN BOOKS

Ant-Man: Natural Enemy by Jason Starr
Avengers: Everybody Wants to Rule the World by Dan Abnett
Avengers: Infinity by James A. Moore
Black Panther: Panther's Rage by Sheree Renée Thomas
Black Panther: Tales of Wakanda by Jesse J. Holland
Black Panther: Who is the Black Panther? by Jesse J. Holland
Captain America: Dark Design by Stefan Petrucha
Captain Marvel: Liberation Run by Tess Sharpe
Civil War by Stuart Moore
Deadpool: Paws by Stefan Petrucha
Morbius: The Living Vampire – Blood Ties by Brendan Deneen
Spider-Man: Forever Young by Stefan Petrucha
Spider-Man: Kraven's Last Hunt by Neil Kleid
Spider-Man: The Darkest Hours Omnibus by Jim Butcher, Keith R.A. DeCandido, and Christopher L. Bennett
Spider-Man: The Venom Factor Omnibus by Diane Duane
Thanos: Death Sentence by Stuart Moore
Venom: Lethal Protector by James R. Tuck
Wolverine: Weapon X Omnibus by Marc Cerasini, David Alan Mack and Hugh Matthews
X-Men: Days of Future Past by Alex Irvine
X-Men: The Dark Phoenix Saga by Stuart Moore
X-Men: The Mutant Empire Omnibus by Christopher Golden
X-Men & The Avengers: The Gamma Quest Omnibus by Greg Cox

ALSO FROM TITAN AND TITAN BOOKS

Marvel Contest of Champions: The Art of the Battlerealm by Paul Davies
Marvel's Guardians of the Galaxy: No Guts, No Glory by M.K. England
Marvel's Spider-Man: The Art of the Game by Paul Davies
Obsessed with Marvel by Peter Sanderson and Marc Sumerak
Spider-Man: Into the Spider-Verse – The Art of the Movie by Ramin Zahed
Spider-Man: Hostile Takeover by David Liss
Spider-Man: Miles Morales – Wings of Fury by Brittney Morris
The Art of Iron Man (10th Anniversary Edition) by John Rhett Thomas
The Marvel Vault by Matthew K. Manning, Peter Sanderson, and Roy Thomas
Ant-Man and the Wasp: The Official Movie Special
Avengers: Endgame – The Official Movie Special
Avengers: Infinity War – The Official Movie Special
Black Panther: The Official Movie Companion
Black Panther: The Official Movie Special
Captain Marvel: The Official Movie Special
Marvel Studios: The First Ten Years
Marvel's Black Widow: The Official Movie Special
Spider-Man: Far From Home – The Official Movie Special
Spider-Man: Into the Spider-Verse – The Official Movie Special
Thor: Ragnarok – The Official Movie Special

A NOVEL OF THE MARVEL UNIVERSE

ORIGINAL SIN

ADAPTED FROM THE GRAPHIC NOVEL BY
JASON AARON AND MIKE DEODATO JR.

GAVIN SMITH

TITAN BOOKS

MARVEL

MARVEL'S ORIGINAL SIN PROSE NOVEL
Print edition ISBN: 9781803361956
E-book edition ISBN: 9781803361963

Published by Titan Books
A division of Titan Publishing Group Ltd
144 Southwark Street, London SE1 0UP
www.titanbooks.com

First hardback edition: October 2022
10 9 8 7 6 5 4 3 2 1

This is a work of fiction. All of the characters, organizations, and events portrayed in this novel are either products of the author's imagination or are used fictitiously. Any resemblance to actual persons, living or dead (except for satirical purposes), is entirely coincidental.

FOR MARVEL PUBLISHING
Jeff Youngquist, VP Production and Special Projects
Sarah Singer, Associate Editor, Special Projects
Jeremy West, Manager, Licensed Publishing
Sven Larsen, VP, Licensed Publishing
David Gabriel, SVP of Sales & Marketing, Publishing
C.B. Cebulski, Editor in Chief

Special thanks to Tom Brevoort

MARVEL

© 2022 MARVEL

Gavin Smith asserts the moral right to be identified as the author of this work.

Cover Art by Mark Brooks.

No part of this publication may be reproduced, stored in a retrieval system, or transmitted, in any form or by any means without the prior written permission of the publisher, nor be otherwise circulated in any form of binding or cover other than that in which it is published and without a similar condition being imposed on the subsequent purchaser.

A CIP catalogue record for this title is available from the British Library.

Printed and bound by CPI Group (UK) Ltd, Croydon, CR0 4YY.

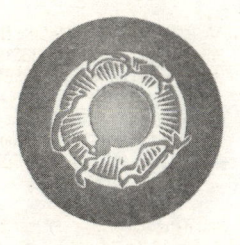

This is for Lou, Alex, Vicki, Mark, Sara, Sarah, Trev, Chris and, of course, Yvonne for giving me something to look forward to during lockdown.

PROLOGUE

IN THE Blue Area of the main satellite of the third planet orbiting the star known as Sol is a vast and majestic citadel. The citadel's technology is far in advance of even that of the greatest geniuses amongst the nearly hairless mammals that dominate said third planet. The technology is, in fact, more sophisticated than that of most species native to this particular galaxy—and even most species native to this particular universe. Technology sophisticated enough to make the sole inhabitant of the citadel, a visitor to this system himself, a god if he had so chosen. Instead of capitalizing on his technological power, however, he just watches events unfold. Seeing them from every possible perspective, every eventuality, every outcome, what is and all the might-have-beens, all the what-ifs. Nothing escapes his sight.

Except today.

THE TWO intruders to the Blue Area of the Moon wore space suits of no little sophistication to survive the vacuum of space. A camera drone, released by one of the intruders, sped across the blue-tinged lunar wasteland toward the alien citadel. Unchallenged, the drone made it inside the structure, moving between huge machines whose purpose the intruders could only guess at, through vast halls that echoed somehow, despite the silence, and finally into a circular chamber. There, the citadel's only inhabitant floated above the floor in meditative repose. The humanoid wore a simple, yet elegant robe. He was a giant in comparison to the intruders, whose space-suited forms resembled the rough shape and size of the third planet's hairless mammals. His pupils were white light: burning like a main sequence star through the void of his sclera and, for the moment, completely unseeing. He did not even notice the camera drone orbiting his vast bald cranium.

On the lunar surface, the first intruder viewed the feed from the drone on a tablet and watched the burning eyes flickering.

"Are we sure on our intel here? He really won't know?" the second intruder asked. He was not an individual given to nerves, but it was no easy thing to look at something that radiated such obvious power.

"Positive," the first intruder said, eyes still on the tablet. The alien hadn't so much as flinched at the drone's approach. "As long as we stick to our schedule"—numbers ticked down in the head-up-displays projected onto their suits' helmets—"we should be in and out before he's cognizant again."

Should.

"Before he's what?" the second intruder demanded as they approached the outer wall of the citadel.

"See for yourself." The first intruder showed his companion the tablet screen: the alien in meditative repose.

"Wait... what is he doing?"

The first intruder turned and pushed against the wall of the citadel. The technology in the space suit, while not nearly as advanced as the tech in the citadel, had been stolen or looted from many different species, from many different places and all of it was far in advance of the tech from the third planet. The suits' phase generators allowed both intruders to push through the wall of the citadel and into the interior. Had the alien been awake, his omnipercipience would have meant that he could have alerted the citadel's defenses to the intruders and their trespass would have been much more difficult.

"Watchers slip into a fugue state every three years for exactly forty-two minutes," the first intruder said. "We think they're uploading memories to their collective. The end result is the same: forty-two completely unobserved minutes."

They were moving through architecture scaled not just for a different-sized being, but for one who perceived things differently to the intruders. Supports, internal buttresses, and items that could have been furniture, art or machinery protruded from unexpected angles. The colors in the architecture stretched into strange new spectrums, giving the intruders the feeling of walking through the most excessive of psychedelic album covers from the 1960s.

"This is amazing," the second intruder said, wonder in his voice, "I never imagined I'd see any of this firsthand."

They moved into the meditative chamber as quietly as they could in their bulky space suits, as though stealth would make a difference at this moment. The alien, the Watcher, silent, unseeing, huge, his sheer physicality a definite and palpable presence, like gravity.

"So bizarre. He's a giant but it's hard to focus on him. Like my mind keeps trying to make me look away… make me forget I saw him," the second intruder muttered.

"That's their secret. Well, one of their secrets."

The second intruder stopped and stared at the Watcher through the polarized visor of his space suit.

"Terrifying when you can focus. So vast, powerful, ugly." The awe in his voice was gone now, replaced by something else. After all, fear and hatred frequently go hand in hand.

The first intruder stopped for a moment as well, also looking up at the unseeing Watcher.

"There's a theory they aren't a race of beings at all. That they're infinite aspects of one powerful entity," the first intruder said. "A being who experiences time and space in a way we can't even begin to comprehend."

"You believe that?" the second intruder asked. They were moving again, through halls of polished metal, their forms reflecting and distorting as though in a funhouse.

The intruders came to a high chamber with a curving wall, a cracked black mirror in which lay multiple realities, a fragmented always-changing map of a Multiverse of possibilities.

"We're standing before a wall of memories and windows into alternate universes," the first intruder said. "Where the Watchers are concerned, I'll believe anything." The camera drone returned to the first intruder, sinking into the machinery protruding from the back of their space suit. "We have twenty-five minutes before our extraction, so let's get to work. You tackle his most recent scans; I'll find his archives."

The first intruder's suit's propulsion system carried him out of the chamber, leaving the second intruder alone before a darkened Multiverse.

Schemata provided by one of the suit's more intuitive diagnostic systems cascaded down the inside of the suit's visor, the projected information displaying how the second intruder could access the recent scans. Looking around, he found what he was pretty sure was a control panel and activated it.

"Right, let's see what you've been recording lately, you omnipresent sonuva…"

Images played across the black mirror. Some showed beings with special powers far in excess of the majority of those who inhabited the third planet. Other images were of distant places and strange other realms. His suit recorded it all.

"Have you found anything yet?" the first intruder asked over the commlink.

"I'm not certain. He's been studying far space and other dimensions," the second intruder replied. "But there's no indication if these are events already happening or things in the future. Do we know how far ahead he can look?"

"No. Like I said, he may not even see it as the future."

"Right. Because he perceives every divergent possibility. What must his mind be like to contain all that?" The second intruder had to resist the urge to look behind him toward the meditation chamber. The Watcher may have been to all intents and purposes... *inert*, but somehow the alien's presence was tangible.

"There's a reason the leader says he's the most powerful creature in existence," the first intruder said. The second intruder knew it wasn't the kind of statement that the leader made lightly.

The second intruder couldn't help himself. He moved back through the shining metallic hall and looked back at the meditation chamber. Peeking through an archway at the Watcher. It felt transgressive, voyeur-on-voyeur.

"Imagine getting just one glimpse into that memory stream he's linked to. What you'd see... our knowledge of his insights..." the second intruder mused, not even really talking to the first intruder. There was a hunger in his voice.

"Don't even consider getting near him, Andrew." The first intruder's voice had an edge to it. It shook the second intruder, Andrew, out of his reverie. "Even if we could tap into his upload, you'd just lose your mind."

"Right, of course you're right," Andrew said, forcing himself to move again. It wouldn't just be a case of losing his mind: it would fracture into countless tiny fragments. Most minds in the universe just weren't built to perceive all the possibilities of reality simultaneously. Any mind not specifically evolved, either technologically or otherwise, would be driven irrevocably insane. Then again, did they even know enough about the Watcher to know that he wasn't insane? "How's it going in the archives? Any luck?" he asked as he made his way back to the black mirror.

"Nothing so far," the first intruder told him, "but we've still got a little time. I'm not giving up, that's for sure."

Andrew made it back to the black mirror and started working the controls again.

"Good, I'll scan more recent entries while you keep digging," he said. "See if I can find a link between them."

The images he was watching came to a seemingly inevitable point, a single coalescence of possibilities.

"That can't be," Andrew said. "That hasn't happened."

He was watching the Earth fall—an apocalypse playing out in front of him, bodies piled high in the street, craters where once stood cities, continents burning, the fall of gods and heroes, and above it all, against a sky of fire, the shape of a familiar enemy: the artificial intelligence, Ultron.

"It's sick, he's watching a disaster in our future. Something he could change, something he could stop!" Andrew cried as the first intruder floated back into the black mirror chamber.

"Now you know why the Unseen exists, my friend," the first intruder said grimly. He left it unsaid that this was the very reason that they had come to the citadel. "Come on. He's going to wake up any moment now."

Andrew stared a moment longer at the scenes unfolding in front of him before turning and following the first intruder. They ran through the hall as fast as their servo-assisted suits would allow. They sped past the levitating form of the insensate Watcher.

"We've spent enough time in this monster's keep for one lifetime," the first intruder said.

○────○

"HOW DO they—or it, if there's really only one of them—how do they not see that it's evil to stand by and do nothing?" Andrew asked as they bounced across the lunar surface. The gravity was now back to 0.166 g outside the bawn of the Watcher's citadel.

"Time and tides, Andrew. We're nothing but ants to them. For now at least."

Andrew checked the countdown. They had less than thirty seconds left. Thirty seconds before the Watcher awoke.

"Activating the extraction point. Stand back," the first intruder said.

The quantum bridge appeared, forming a curving tunnel from a glowing green grid. More looted tech.

"Did you find it?" Andrew asked. "Did you get what we came for?"

"Yes. Total mission success." The first intruder seemed pleased with the mission but it didn't make sense to Andrew. If this Watcher was omnipercipient, then what difference did it make sneaking away before he awoke? He would know what they had done as soon as he was conscious. He would still be able to see them, unless the Unseen somehow… Andrew smiled. He guessed it was in the name. He leaped into the quantum bridge.

"Now, when the time comes," the first intruder said to himself before following Andrew into the tunnel, "the Unseen will be able to kill the Watcher. All his secrets will be ours."

Then the Watcher was on his own once more.

THE WATCHER stood on the barren lunar surface. The impossibly ancient alien stared out into the void. Except it wasn't the void. It was information, every particle pregnant with possibility. It was his sacred cosmic duty to bear witness to each interconnecting strand branching out to form a possible event, a possible future. His responsibility was to act as a living record to Earth's chaotic and oft-interfered-with evolution.

And. He. Has. Seen. It. All.

He had walked beyond his own blue realm and into the stark majesty of the empty lunar landscape. It was something he did every subjective morning, if his duties did not keep him, to watch the planetary sunrise. To see the majesty of the star peeking round from behind the blue-marble-like world, so small from this perspective, so insignificant on a cosmic scale—and yet somehow always involved in significant events, somehow punching far above its weight.

The Watcher had seen all the beauty and horror that a planet like Earth had to offer. He had seen more births and more deaths than he could easily count. More war than any other living thing. He had seen colossal events rock the world and echo through history, and watched the quietest moments that changed humanity forever without them even noticing. He'd watched atrocities perpetuated on the subatomic scale and acts of love waged across the heavens. He knew humanity's greatest secrets: their struggles, successes, and their sins.

The Watcher had seen all that there ever was and yet, with each new day, he found himself full of anticipation over what he might see next. His sense of wonder did not just stem from the great events of the mighty, the events that shook the very pillars of the Earth; in fact, in some ways such days were the least of it. Instead, a newborn's first breath, the caress of a lover, tears wrought of remembrance in the twilight of a life. Each and every moment was utterly unique, something he had never seen before. He knew that those few humans who knew him considered him voyeuristic, but did they even truly appreciate their own lives, moment-to-moment, in the way he did? The few who knew him thought his life one of solitude, of isolation: not understanding that he was only alone with all of seething humanity in all their filth and splendor.

AS THE Watcher made his way home, he saw the cosmos played out in light against hues of darkness across the sky. He could perhaps perceive too much. The ability to focus only on every living possibility of just one world was a welcome respite to the celestial mechanics of even this galaxy, let alone the entire universe, and his earthly slice of the Multiverse was more than enough for him.

Returning to his citadel, machines older than the Sun and infinitely more powerful came to life all around him. They were useful to his work, a focus, yet it had always been more than mere technology that led him to where he needed to be. To see what must be seen. It was something innate, a feeling, a sense for where and when the world was on the verge of change. He let that feeling carry him to where had had to be, to bear witness as he must. He gave himself to the feeling. Let it transport him.

Today, however, as he walked through dark halls of silent, ancient machinery, today he knew that, for the first time in a long time, he wouldn't be going anywhere. He knew what he would be watching and where he would be watching it. For a moment he felt a twinge of the emotion he had seen on the face of so many others. For just a moment Uatu, the Watcher, knew fear. He would not run. He would not forsake his duty. He would watch without flinching, even though he must participate, however reactively, however passive that participation must be, because some things cannot go unseen.

Standing under the vast dome of the citadel's central tower, Uatu sensed these new interlopers before he saw them. They came with a not-insignificant amount of their own power. He supposed it was inevitable. For a very short amount of time, as he measured it, the Earth had been engaged in an arms race. Each generation of enhanced human more powerful than the previous. Sooner or later someone was going to come for the technological bounty, the power that he represented.

But he was Uatu. He was the Watcher and he would keep his eyes open wide… until he could see no more.

He turned to face the direction from which they approached.

"I see you," he said.

Then the dome exploded.

CHAPTER ONE

MEAT NIGHT

"THAT'S IT, I'm tapping out. One more bite and I'm liable to explode," Steve said.

From the outside the diner didn't look like much, though it was nicely situated just off the river and surrounded by the hills of the Hudson Valley. If the staff were impressed at their clientele and the Avengers Quinjet in the car park, then they were handling it well—and by well, Nick Fury thought, he meant unobtrusively. Something all four of them sat round the table appreciated.

"You're liable to get stabbed, you let that meat go to waste, Rogers. It's 'meat night.' Stop worrying about your damn figure," Logan said.

Fury liked the short Canadian berserker but it hadn't always been so. He'd been on the wrong end of the fast-healing mutant's adamantium claws on more than one occasion. Like him or not, Logan's presence always made Fury feel like he was in a room with a wild animal. A Wolverine. He guessed that was the point. Logan was the only one still eating, shoveling extremely rare meat into his mouth with gusto. Fury was full. He tried not to eat until he became too uncomfortable these days. Infinity Formula or not, time was as inevitable as cholesterol and he'd put away a lot of meat.

"This is good steak, but the best meat is from an animal you hunt and kill yourself," Natasha Romanov said. The Black Widow, spy, Avenger, ex-KGB assassin, the only woman at the table and the only person at the table that didn't have some kind of super-power. Even if Fury's own "super-power" had just been to live too long. "Next time it's meat night, I'm taking us to hunt bear." She emphasized what was left of her Russian accent as she said this. Fury suspected she didn't even realize that she was doing it, just subconsciously telling the story in the most effective way possible. He could spot the reflexes of a master spy. After all, he'd been in charge of the best as head of the Strategic Hazard Intervention Espionage Logistics Division, or S.H.I.E.L.D. as it was more commonly known. That was all behind him now, however, he was retired and just about managing to convince himself that he was enjoying it. That said, he had retired from *directing* S.H.I.E.L.D., not from meddling.

"I've eaten bear before, Natasha," Logan said. "No bear in the world tastes like this ribeye."

"You haven't eaten Russian bear," Natasha said, with even more emphasis on her old accent. "If you had, you wouldn't be so short."

Fury smiled. He was leaning back in his seat, just enjoying the banter. Logan took the jibe in his stride, even if it wasn't a particularly long stride.

"It's a really good steak, Logan, but I'm stuffed. I'll have to get up at dawn just to run this off," Steve said. Captain America, a genuine hero. Fury knew this because Steve, one of his oldest friends, had never been comfortable with the role of hero. He saw it as a responsibility rather than something glorious. He was part of the reason Fury had become who he had become. In private moments, Fury was of the opinion that he was the reason that Captain America could, for the most part, keep his hands clean. In other words, he'd done the dirty work. They were two sides of the same coin. He was pretty sure that Steve wouldn't have seen it that way, however, and that was probably for the best. Their friendship had been strained, and even broken more than once, but now that Fury was "retired" Steve had relaxed a bit. Sometimes being around Steve still made you feel like you were sitting across from some god, and Fury had sat across the table from actual gods. It was never a comfortable feeling.

"When have you ever not gotten up at dawn just to run?" Logan asked Steve. Natasha laughed. Fury allowed himself a soft, low chuckle. He touched his eyepatch, a reflex: the phantom itches in his blind eye had stopped years ago. Logan was right. Every morning Steve got up, said his morning prayers, drank his milk and then went out for a run. Fury had seen the surveillance footage.

"Tell us, old man Rogers, what was the best steak you ever had?" Natasha teased. It seemed like it was "pick on the old guy" time. Though Steve was only the second oldest, possibly the third if some of the things Fury had heard about Logan were true.

"The best steak? I don't know guys, maybe—" Steve started.

Fury decided to help him out.

"Christmas, 1944," he said leaning forward. "Bastogne."

It went quiet round the table. Three people with their own, very impressive, life stories stopped and listened as Fury spoke. Maybe it was respect, maybe they were just used to it because he'd called the shots when they'd worked together previously, or maybe they were just humoring some old retiree. He still appreciated it.

"We'd been under siege for almost a week, when out of nowhere, a cow comes running into the midst of a firefight. Once it went down, us and the Germans were basically fighting over who could get at it first." Fury paused, clasping his hands together as he let the memories of the camaraderie, of how shared suffering and loyalty had almost managed to hold the cold, hunger and fear at bay. There was just the slightest smile on Fury's face, though there had been little to smile about before they'd captured the cow—or even in the days that had followed.

"I don't think I've ever seen Bucky fight harder," Fury finally continued. "That night Bucky butchered it for us. God knows where an army brat who grew up in Virginia learned to butcher a cow. One of the guys from the 333rd had been a cowboy before the war. He fixed up a grill from a burned-out jeep." Fury could still remember just the slightest taste of gasoline in the charred meat. "It was the first food we'd had in months that hadn't come out of a can, and the last of anything we'd have for days. By the time we finished eating, I swear the whole damn cow was gone. Tip-to-tail. We gave the bones a proper military funeral."

They hadn't gotten into the fight over the cow but the prospect of eating it had provided significant motivation. Even then mankind could fly through the air, cure diseases, explore oceans and were getting closer to the stars than ever before. Two groups of regular guys, who under normal circumstances probably would've enjoyed a beer together, were killing each other over a cow. It was the absurdity of it. Except it wasn't over a cow. It had happened because some evil lunatic demagogue and his cronies had forced the world to dance to their tune.

Fury had been in worse fights, seen worse things. He had been a teenager when he'd signed up with the International Brigades to fight the fascists in Spain. He was a hard man. He had no illusions about what he was capable of even then—perhaps especially then. He had thought he had understood the threat fascism posed to the world when they had targeted civilians during the bombing of Guernica. None of it had prepared him for the camps, however. He'd had to force himself to look. That was when the true horror of the Nazis had become apparent to him. The camps had sealed his fate. Made him who he was. He knew then that he had to do everything he could to ensure that nothing like that ever happened again. He hadn't always been successful: he'd definitely made mistakes, and he'd backed the wrong side more than once, but he'd tried and that had to count for something.

Didn't it?

It had gone quiet. Natasha was looking at him with a raised eyebrow. Steve was watching him with no-little concern. Logan was still eating. Fury reminded himself to invite Steve to poker night with Dum-Dum and the guys.

"We slept like babes that night, even with the mortars falling around us. Least I did. And we fought like hell the next morning," he finished.

"Bastogne. I remember that. He's right, that was the best steak I ever had," Steve said. He was smiling. Fury suspected he'd only just remembered that day.

"That was the best steak anyone's ever had," Fury said leaning back from the table.

"Hard to top that," Logan said, though Fury was sure that he had similar stories. After all, he'd parachuted into Normandy with the Canuck 1st Parachute Battalion on D-Day, and they'd fought together in the Ardennes as well.

"It would have been better if it'd been a bear," Natasha said grinning.

Fury had to laugh.

Steve's phone started ringing. Fury wasn't sure if he was relieved or disappointed that he wasn't on call himself anymore.

"This is Rogers," Steve said, answering the call.

Logan was already helping himself to Steve's leftover steak. "He ain't gonna finish that damn steak, is he? Give it here."

There was a reason Logan was shaped like a barrel.

"Thor, slow down—say again?" Steve said into the phone. That got Fury's attention. He couldn't hear what Thor was saying but the tone of voice on the other end of the phone made him sound rattled. Fury knew that Thor was an emotional guy—he wore his heart on his sleeve—but the Norse God of Thunder was not easily rattled.

"I think we're going to need the check," Natasha called to the staff, playfulness gone. She was all business now. When he thought on it, Fury was astonished at how much she'd changed over the years. Once a stone-cold killer, after she'd defected—even after she'd broken the Red Room's conditioning—Fury had expected that she'd mostly work on the covert, black ops side of things, and remain one of his shadow warriors. Now she was an Avenger, a fully-fledged hero, much more like Steve than she'd like to admit, and Fury couldn't be happier about that.

"Are you sure? Is that even possible? Okay, calm down, we're on our way," Steve said into the phone. Fury didn't like the sound of an un-calm Thor at all, but he reminded himself that this wasn't his problem anymore.

The other three were on their feet.

"You guys go ahead. Go save the world. I'll handle the tab," Fury said. This was how he could help these days and he was fine with that. Or so he kept telling himself.

"Actually, you might want to come with us, Nick," Steve said.

Nick narrowed his one good eye. Of course he wanted to go with them, but this also felt like an old friend throwing him a bone.

"Sorry Steve, but you know I don't do that sort of thing anymore. That baton's been passed."

"I wouldn't ask, Nick, if it didn't sound like we might need you on this one," Steve said. Maybe it wasn't a bone after all.

"That bad a fire, huh? Where at?"

Natasha and Logan were just watching Steve.

"The Moon," Steve told him.

Fury gave this some thought.

"The Moon? Yeah, that's never good. All right, but I'm driving."

CHAPTER TWO

BLUE MOON

LETTING NICK drive had initially seemed like a mistake, and was definitely a manifestation of his old friend's desperate need to control things. They'd had to get the spacesuits from their own aircraft anyway. Steve had assumed that the Quinjet, which was capable of limited space travel, would be a better choice than a 1964 DeVille convertible, even if said coupé could fly. He was wrong. Five minutes later he was looking at the Blue Area of the Moon. He knew that S.H.I.E.L.D. had access to advanced technology but he'd barely been aware of any acceleration. He glanced over at Natasha and Logan, wondering briefly how Logan had got shotgun. They seemed to be business-as-usual, so Steve put his surprise at the coupé's capability down to his age. Then he saw the column of smoke rising within the citadel's self-generating atmosphere.

As Nick steered the coupé in high over the citadel, circling so they could get a look at the damage, Steve saw the ruptured upper dome of the central tower. He was pretty sure that was where the Watcher actually lived. Everyone in the car was quiet. They'd all dealt with off-the-scale power before, but there was something deeply disquieting about an individual or a group capable of going after the Watcher. The Watcher was more like an act of nature than an actual person. Every time his attention was drawn to the Watcher's existence and omnipercipience, Steve felt a deeply uncomfortable itch in the back of his neck. He was wearing the latest iteration of his uniform. Once he'd been uneasy wearing the Stars & Stripes—too much responsibility, too much to try and live up to. At times like this, it was a comfort.

Natasha tapped him on the shoulder of his armored spacesuit and pointed back towards the Earth. It took a moment but he saw a speck of darkness against the Earth's blues, brown, greens and whites. The speck was ringed by the unmistakable aurora of a repulsor blast. Tony was joining them.

○――――○

IN HIS armor, winged helm, red cloak and hammer in hand, Thor looked every inch the Asgardian God of Thunder. Like Steve, he was one of the founding Avengers. They were all standing in the citadel at the base of the still-smoking tower, surrounded by huge monolithic machines whose purpose Steve couldn't even begin to fathom.

"I was flying through the cosmos," Thor told them, "on my way to Midgard, when something struck me in the face. It was blood. There was blood floating in space."

Steve could hear something in the Asgardian's voice. Not fear—it took a lot to frighten Thor—but he was not happy. Thor's apparent disquiet added to Steve's unease, but he knew he couldn't let that show. They would look to him for leadership. Even Nick, who was more a "behind the throne" kind of guy. Steve hadn't always been comfortable with the some of the actions Nick had deemed it necessary to take. Much to his relief, it hadn't been a source of friction since Nick had announced his retirement.

"Then I noticed the smoke in the Blue Area of the Moon, coming from the Watcher's Lair," Thor continued. "I came inside and found him thus."

Thor's disquiet was justified. The rest of them were staring at the body. Steve forced himself not to look. He wanted to get the timeline of events straight in his head first.

"I had Mjölnir circle the Moon many times. There was no one else to be found," Thor continued. "Whoever was here, whoever did this, they had already fled like craven trolls."

"Hold up. Let's not go making assumptions and calling anybody trolls, not until we've weighed all the options." Wearing his gold and black armor today, Tony Stark—corporate CEO, technologist, futurist, self-confessed genius, and Iron Man—was another of the founding Avengers. Steve knew that Tony's trademark flippancy was just his way of dealing with tricky situations. It wasn't always appropriate, however. "For all we know, this could've easily been some sort of accident. I mean, look around. I couldn't tell you what most of this stuff even does, and I'm the smartest guy I know. There could've easily been an explosion or—"

"Tony," Steve interrupted. As much as he could see Tony's point. He didn't want to deal with the reality of the situation either. He just didn't think they had much of a choice.

"Fine. I know what it looks like. I just don't want to say it, okay? Something this big? I mean, not until we know for sure," Tony finished.

"Then I'll say it," Nick said. "It doesn't take a super-genius to see what happened here."

Steve closed his eyes for a moment then turned with the others to face the body. The Watcher was lying amongst the debris of the citadel's central chamber, blood floating from several wounds in his head. An entry wound pierced the center of his forehead, but far more disturbing were the bloody gouges around the Watcher's eyes. Just for a moment, Steve found himself wondering if Galactus had turned serial killer. He guessed the floating blood that Thor had flown through was the result of a localized failure of whatever mechanism generated the citadel's artificial gravity, or even just the force of the inflicted trauma from whatever weapon had caused the wound. Though it would have to be a pretty powerful weapon to do that, even on the Moon.

"The Watcher was murdered," Nick said, giving words to the obvious. Steve, not for the first time, reflected that he missed the simplicity of punching Nazis. Still, obvious or not, they had to go through the motions. He let out a long sigh and forced himself to kneel by The Watcher's wrist. It was thicker than one of his thighs.

"Do we... check for a pulse? Did he even have a pulse? Do we know?" Steve knew it was fruitless, but felt he needed to check. Just in case.

"I'm getting no energy readings whatsoever from the body. I'd say that means he's almost certainly dead," Tony said, telling them what Steve was already pretty sure of.

"Yeah, there's that and the hole in his forehead," Logan pointed out, not terribly helpfully.

Thor was looking around in the rubble. It was almost as though the thunder god didn't want to look at the body. After all, if someone could kill the Watcher this easily...

Natasha studied the head wound while Fury examined the injuries around the Watcher's eyes. Somehow this ad-hoc murder investigation seemed too mundane for a being like the Watcher.

"Who or what is powerful enough to put a hole in a head that size?" Tony asked, an edge in his voice. "Thanos? The Red Skull and the Cosmic Cube?"

Steve tried not to flinch as he heard the Red Skull's name.

"It was a gun. Judging by the wound pattern. I should know. I've seen a lot of wounds," Natasha told them. Again it seemed so mundane, but now Natasha had said it out loud it also seemed so obvious. "If we're lucky, there's still a bullet lodged in his skull."

"What the hell kind of gun could do that?" Logan asked.

"The kind we need to find quickly," Steve told him.

"His eyes are gone." Everyone turned to look at Nick. He was leaning down next to the Watcher's huge dome-like head. "Both of them carved out post mortem, I'd say. What kind of person takes another man's eyes?"

Nick said out loud the thing that the rest of them hadn't wanted to acknowledge. It had been impossible to miss, but for an entity called the Watcher it wasn't only a mutilation: somehow it seemed like an attack on his identity, his core being, his existence. For Nick to say that, someone who'd seen and done what he had... Suddenly the idea of Galactus as a serial killer didn't seem so ridiculous. Steve told himself to get a grip. It was a problem. They'd work the problem. Find the solution.

"What is that? A sign? Did he see something he wasn't supposed to?" Natasha asked. If that was the case, it narrowed down the list of suspects to 7.753 billion, give or take. He saw everything. That was his job.

"'Tis madness, is what it is," Thor said, finally looking at the body again. Steve was inclined to agree, but such observations weren't getting them anywhere.

"Logan, any scents you can follow?" Steve asked.

Logan was already shaking his head.

"Nothing, Cap. Just us. Air's antiseptic. His crazy machines must keep the place scrubbed clean."

Besides, Steve thought, if they've got the tech to take down the Watcher, then they've got the tech to cover up their crime.

Tony's chest piece projected light over a hole torn in the central chamber's wall. Steve and the others, except for Nick who was still studying the empty eye sockets, turned to look.

"Speaking of machines, I don't think eyes were the only thing our killer took." Tony told them. "This damage isn't just from a fight. This place was ransacked, quickly and crudely. Looks to me like there are all sorts of items missing." The cavernous chamber on the other side of the rent looked sort of like some kind of storeroom. "Weapons, super-tech, who knows what we're talking about. I know just enough about the sort of things he kept here to be very afraid right now."

It seemed like a lot of trouble to go to for a smash-and-grab robbery. Again the mundaneness of the crime struck Steve as odd, particularly on such a scale of power.

"So… we've got a killer on the loose, armed with a gun that can kill a Watcher and now he's loaded with enough stolen super-tech to do God knows what." Steve just wanted to say it out loud to get it straight in his own head. This day just kept getting better and better.

"Don't forget about his eyes," Logan said helpfully.

"Now do you see why I asked you to come along, Nick?" Steve asked.

Nick stood up from where he'd been crouched by the Watcher's head. "You need to get S.H.I.E.L.D. on this, Cap. And S.W.O.R.D., and everyone else."

"We will," Steve assured him, "but for something this big we need to take point on it. Although… the Avengers aren't murder police."

"Neither am I."

Steve was pretty *sure* that the L in S.H.I.E.L.D. stood for Law Enforcement, or at least had done once; he'd lost track of the acronym sometime in the '90s. They weren't just about intelligence gathering and covert operations. Nick was a more than capable investigator.

"You're as close as I've got," Steve told him. He left it unsaid that, for something of this magnitude, the case didn't just have to be investigated—it had to be managed as well.

Nick turned and walked away from the body, gesturing for Steve to follow.

"Steve," Nick said over a private comms link between their two suits. Steve turned to face his old friend and Nick put a hand on his shoulder. "You realize the list of people who even knew the Watcher existed, let alone who could've done this, is extremely short—and not all the names on it are bad guys."

The first had occurred to Steve, the second not so much.

"This investigation could lead to some very dark places."

"Someone was murdered. All I care about is the truth." Steve knew what he sounded like when he said things like this, but it was the only way he knew how to do this work. The simpler, the more straightforward he kept it, the better. A murder was a murder was a murder. It didn't matter if happened on a battlefield in Europe, a backstreet in Brooklyn, or here on the Moon. "Will you help me find it?"

Nick didn't answer.

CHAPTER THREE

LAIRS

WE ALL have lairs. We call them different things: facilities, secret bases, hideouts, even homes—mostly because lair sounds too villainous. It is, however, accurate. It's where we plot, prepare, or even lick our wounds. Where those of us in this most rarefied of vocations almost feel safe (some of the time, at least).

T'Challa, sometimes King of Wakanda, the most advanced nation on Earth, and always protector of that East African nation as the Black Panther, had his lair deep beneath the Necropolis, the Wakandan City of the Dead. Mine was somewhere else.

He took my call. I knew he would. I could see a little of his lair on my screen. It was lit faintly in blue by T'Challa's own bank of monitors and the glowing, holographic representation of the Earth that floated above his workstation. It was a typically Wakandan mixture of advanced technology and ancient pillared architecture.

T'Challa was dressed in his Black Panther suit. He did not wear his mask, though he may as well have. Even I'd never been good at reading his expressions—or lack thereof.

"You may have heard. There's been a murder... on the Moon," I said by way of greeting.

"I've heard. There was an alert from Captain America just before you called. Let me guess, you know something he doesn't?" Was there just a touch of impatience in his voice? I suspected that he knew he was being gamed but that didn't mean he wasn't going to play. He wouldn't be able to help himself. Few of us could.

"I know that there are some jobs the Avengers just aren't cut out for. This is one of them," I told him. The important thing about any deception, after all, is to use as much truth as humanly possible.

"And what makes you think I am cut out for it?" he asked.

Because I know just what you're capable of when pushed, I didn't say out loud. Instead, I said "I think you're used to going places the Avengers wouldn't dare." Practically the same thing, perhaps a little less confrontational. Diplomacy was not something that came easy to me.

"I'm not sure that was meant as a compliment."

Sure, let's play around a bit.

"From me, take it as a compliment. Take a look at this." I sent over the information packet. It was full of various bits of sophisticated malware and viruses designed to try—the operative word—to penetrate the Black Panther's systems. It was futile. Wakanda's computer security was second to none. Still, I had to try—old habits die hard.

T'Challa opened the packet after it had been sanitized and started to review it, opening the audiovisual files first. He spent a few moments absorbing the films on a split screen.

"What is this? What did you just send to me?" His tone was neutral but the very fact he had to ask, that what he was watching was beyond the ken of even the Black Panther, was enough to make me smile.

"A trail," I told him. "One I've been following for a very long time. One that goes in many different directions but only leads to one place." He'd seen the hook already, so I had to offer him the bait. "To the Unseen. To the Original Sin."

I would've been disappointed if I'd expected some significant reaction. Instead T'Challa just made himself more comfortable in his seat. If anything, his expression was slightly pained.

"You're being cryptic," he said. He wasn't wrong, but I'd made sure that he'd heard references to the Unseen in various odd places in the preceding few years. I was playing a long game but time was running out. "I don't like cryptic," he continued. "This trail. You believe it leads to the person who killed the Watcher."

"I believe it leads to answers, yes." I knew it did.

"Then send this to the Avengers. I have my own country to protect." He said it as though our discussion was over. He reached for the key to sever the comms link.

"That's all I'm asking you to do. Look at the files I sent you. You'll see this threatens everyone," I told him.

He hesitated.

"I'm not interested in playing your games," he said. I suspected that wasn't entirely true. He wanted to play my game, just not on my terms. I sympathized. I would have felt the same way. "If the answers are all in these files, then why do you need me?"

"The answers aren't in the files. Only the questions that need to be asked and the places you must go in order to ask them."

He spent a few moments exploring the files further. The filenames would be enough but I saw his fingers dance over the keyboard. His eyes scanning text and images quickly, one hand under his chin.

"These are some interesting places." I could hear the intrigue in his voice. It must have been killing him to take what was so obviously bait. "I could never cover all of this alone."

"No, you most certainly couldn't," I agreed.

"Stop being coy. You've already put together a team," he said, tiring of the cat-and-mouse.

"I had some thoughts. I'm sending them to you now. I think you'll find it a lively little mix."

T'Challa stared at the screen.

"You'd better be joking."

Perhaps. The real question was whether T'Challa could figure out the punchline before he reached the end.

CHAPTER FOUR

THE TROUBLE WITH TEAM-UPS

EMMA FROST hadn't been able to sleep. One of the problems with being a telepath was that ghosts tended to leak from your sleeping lover's mind. Even if those ghosts sometimes didn't have the common courtesy to stay dead. Emma's telepathy was as disciplined as every other facet of her life, but that discipline slipped when she was trying to sleep. She was tired of waking up with the dead staring down at her as Scott thrashed in the grip of a nightmare.

That was why she had been curled on one of the chairs in the control room of the Alkali Lake Facility. A place once used to do experiments on her people, mutant-kind; a base for the Weapon X program, where Logan had been turned into the Wolverine, where *Homo superior* had been reduced to brainwashed slave-warriors for *Homo sapiens*. In the far north of the Canadian wilderness, the stark, austere, echoing corridors were not without their own ghosts.

Still, it was safe and it was secret. She knew she shouldn't think of the X-Men here as "kids" but to her they all were, much as the Hellions, her own ghosts, had been before them. The world could be a harsh place at the best of times, and if you were a mutant then it could be downright unforgiving. She couldn't face the prospect of any more ghosts. So when something threatened the safety and security of her wards, she was less than pleased.

He had called in the middle of the night. The conversation had left her with a cold, calm sense of rage. He hadn't quite threatened to expose their whereabouts to the authorities but he had only just stopped short of doing so.

"What are you thinking?" Scott Summers—Cyclops, leader of the X-Men, and her lover—asked. She had been aware of him standing in the shadows behind her during the tail end of the conversation. His question said it all. He never knew what she was thinking, whereas he may well have broadcast his own thoughts.

"I think it's an unfortunate part of the entitled patrician's psychological makeup that pushes them towards trying to manipulate people rather than asking nicely," Emma said, hiding her anger from him.

"And if he'd asked nicely?" Scott asked.

"This is none of our business," she said.

"Why you?"

"That's a good question," Emma mused. She honestly had no idea. They didn't, after all, move in the same circles. "I would imagine… I would hope that it's my skill set."

"What are you going to do?" He had moved out of the shadows, his hand on her shoulder. He was still covered in sweat from his nightmare. Once, such a thing would have revolted her. Had love changed her that much? The thought sounded sarcastic in her own head. How her old self would have scoffed at her now.

"Why, Scott darling," she rested her own hand over his, "I am of course going to armor up."

Everyone thought her armor—her diamond skin—was her secondary mutation. But that didn't protect her from the harm that mattered. It was her attitude. That was her true armor.

She would push down her resentment at dancing to someone else's tune, for the time being, and see where this led.

SO FAR it had mostly led to a distinct sense of irritation. With a gun to her head, Emma would have had to admit that being a villain was certainly easier. She knew that the vast majority of "villains" didn't tend to think of themselves as such. Everyone had a reason for what they did after all, and everyone thought they were in the right, regardless of the mental gymnastics performed to reach that conclusion. During her reign as White Queen of the Hellfire Club, however, she'd had absolutely no illusions as to what she was and she had come to terms with it. Perhaps that had made her change of heart all the more surprising. She suspected that she still had a villain's lack of patience, however.

Take her current situation: before her flitted a tiny, tiny man, in a ridiculous helmet, wearing the *de rigeur* spandex—yes, she knew it was actually made of unstable molecules but it still *looked* like spandex. The tiny man in question was using two winged ants as flying roller skates.

"Hey, eyes down here! You ready to get this team-up in gear?" he said.

His inane question was redolent of everything she despised about so-called super heroes. He should perhaps remember that insects were intrinsically annoying, hence how frequently they got swatted. Furthermore, this tiny man had broken their security. That put her students further at risk and that was something she could not tolerate.

"He shouldn't have sent you here. You can't know this location," she told him.

"Don't worry, with such a tiny brain, I forget things real easy."

That she could at least believe. She wondered what he'd look like with his posterior going through his face, having hit the windscreen of a Porsche being driven at speeds in excess of one hundred and fifty miles an hour. The mental image cheered her up a little.

"*Yes, I'll see that you do.*" *Decisions, decisions, decisions, do I mentally spay the little bug or just step on him?* The former was less likely to spoil a perfectly good pair of Louis Vuittons.

"So, your super-secret hideout with Cyclops is around here, huh?" the insect asked. "It's none of my business, I know, but considering you're still a wanted criminal our new boss must really have something on you to get you to agree to come along on this." He was hovering inches from her face. It was clear he was one of those people who thought that being irritating was somehow cute, interesting or a worthwhile substitute for a personality. He was also right about their employer having something on her. That didn't mean she had to put up with his "insight."

"One more word, Mr. Lang, and I will render you incapable of speech." The earth under her feet started to shake. *What even was the point of a "secret" base?* she asked herself.

"Alrighty then," the insect said, "I guess it's gonna be a long ride down."

As the Wakandan burrowing vehicle breached the rock, the craft's spinning drills helping claw its way to the surface, Emma reflected that once again the insect was correct—broken clock and all that.

She wished she'd been partnered with the Punisher. She suspected that she wouldn't have liked him any more than she liked the insect, but he was at least pleasingly direct—psychotic but to the point. Moreover, if she lost her temper with the Punisher and accidentally tore his heart out with her diamond nails, nobody would get too upset. Not that she minded upsetting people. It was just the inevitable whining that tended to follow bored her. *Why did I ever give up being a villain?* Something-something for the good of mutant-kind, something-something Scott Summers, something-something "What Would Professor X Do?"

○—————○

"**THAT'S IT.** I've told you about every last one of them," the weeping, bloodied and bruised gangland killer begged. He was tied to a chair in a pool of light in the otherwise dark warehouse. The air was hot and sticky. There was no breeze coming off the Pacific tonight. Frank Castle missed New York.

"You're lying," Frank said. He didn't think this was the case, but it never hurt to double check.

"I swear," he was begging now. "I'll take you to where they're buried. *Please...*" Frank gritted his teeth. Had this man's victims begged when he and his friends had gone to work on them? Their victims had been family members of people the gang couldn't otherwise touch. They had been innocents who hadn't even been involved with the people-trafficking operation.

"He's telling the truth."

Once upon a time Frank would have responded to a voice from the darkness with violence. Nowadays he knew enough that anyone who could sneak up on him like this clearly had some kind of super-power. Besides, he'd been told to expect some garishly costumed weirdo by one of the few people in the world he was prepared to listen to.

The new arrival walked out of the shadows, presumably having decided his entrance was suitably dramatic. Neatly trimmed beard, greying temples: he would have looked distinguished had he not been wearing hose and a blue tunic that wouldn't have been out of place at a Renaissance fair. In particular, the long red cloak with the high collar was an article of clothing that even the most-flamboyant '70s pimp would've been ashamed of. Though it did seem to be moving of its own accord. Doctor Stephen Strange, so-called Master of the Mystic Arts, the wizard of Greenwich Village. Frank may have had a white skull painted across his chest but that was just to draw attention to where he had the most body armor. This guy looked ridiculous. Frank hated team-ups.

"Believe me. I see things other men cannot," Strange said.

Not mirrors, apparently, Frank thought.

"I know he's telling the truth," Frank told him. "The first fifteen minutes were to make him talk. The last hour was because he deserved it." This wasn't true. He tortured for information or to discourage others; it always had to have a practical purpose. He wasn't a psychopath. If he lost his sense of empathy, he wouldn't know how best to hurt his prey. He was just an ordinary man, however, so when dealing with people who had special abilities he took every single psychological advantage he could get. If Strange's reputation was even close to the truth, then there was no way Frank would be able to frighten him. If, however, Strange thought he was unpredictable—crazed even—it might give him the edge if things went south.

"He's had enough and we need to be going," Strange said.

"When I'm finished." Frank needed to know the location of the mass grave, for the families if nothing else.

"You are finished." Strange raised his hand. There was a burst of coruscating energy and the gangland killer disappeared.

"What the hell?!" Frank growled. It was a power play. Strange was trying to establish who the big dog was.

"I sent him to a dimension ruled by beetles the size of Dobermans. Surely even you must approve," Strange said.

As entertaining as the gangland killer spending the rest of his life running and hiding from dog-sized beetles might have been, that wasn't the point. It was territorial aggression. Strange had messed with his prey. Frank stepped out of the light and moved to the crates full of his gear. He picked up the Barrett M82A1M. The .50 caliber gun was designated an anti-materiel weapon. The Punisher was one of the few shooters in the world who could use it like a conventional rifle, without requiring the use of the weapon's bipod or resting it on something. It was heavy, bulky and not nearly as accurate as Frank liked, particularly for long-range work. He hated using it like this, but when moving in these kinds of circles it was best to have something capable of bringing down big game. Besides, the rounds were big enough that they could pack a few surprises. Every edge...

"Get this straight. Doc, we're not friends. Do that again and I shoot your kneecaps off." He wouldn't be aiming at kneecaps if David Copperfield got out of hand. This guy could probably turn him into a fluffy white bunny if the whim took him. However, Strange would have to cast his spell, or whatever, faster than a steel-jacketed bullet travelling at 2,799 feet per second. Judging by the expression on his face, Frank was pretty sure that the wizard realized this. It appeared that boundaries and mutual understanding had been established. "C'mon, let's get this over with."

WHY DID people have to talk? Being in space was hard enough for this poor boy from Shelbyville, Indiana, without the incessant prattle. Bucky glanced over at the pilot of the spacecraft. He was dressed from head to foot in white, with a crescent moon on his chest and a featureless white mask under a white hooded cloak. Bucky had been trying to remember what he'd heard about Moon Knight over the years since he'd become, well, *self-aware* again. Mercenary, vigilante, cultist of some Egyptian god, avatar of same. A madman? It wasn't encouraging stuff.

"The Watcher, huh? Big bald guy who lived on the moon, right? Funny I never crossed paths with him. Or you either. Say what's your connection to our boss? And are all the crazy stories I hear about him true? I could've sworn the guy was dead at least—"

"Spector, shut the hell up." It had been like this since Moon Knight had picked him up. A ceaseless stream of consciousness. Marc Spector was seemingly oblivious to Bucky's own monosyllabic answers. Bucky tried to concentrate on the view. After all, how many people got to see the Earth from orbit? It should have been peaceful from up here. "And you need to slow down," he added. "We're supposed to pick up our other team member right around here." Bucky was intrigued to meet the third member of their team. He hadn't met that many aliens—least of all a daughter of Thanos.

He watched Moon Knight's fingers float over the controls. Felt the speed bleed off as the directional thrusters fired.

"Something tells me that's her," Moon Knight said nodding forwards.

Bucky turned away from Spector. The ship's running lights illuminated a figure in a sophisticated-looking space suit floating just in front of them. She wore two sheathed swords, crossed on her back. The space suit's propulsion system carried her towards the ship. Even in vacuum there was something about Gamora's movement that made Bucky think of an apex predator. If nothing else, this job was going to be interesting.

○━━━○

NO, THIS *isn't disconcerting at all.* Emma's thoughts dripped with sarcasm. Despite their vaunted technological superiority, it seemed that even Wakandan engineers couldn't make a vehicle that could drill through the very crust of the Earth itself *and* make for a smooth ride. It was the way the rocks around her glowed that worried her the most. She was trying to take her mind off it all by imagining the diamond-clawed evisceration of the individual that had, effectively, blackmailed her into this nonsense.

"Let me get this straight. We're looking for a killer at the center of the Earth?" Ant-Man asked.

She was interspersing fantasies of evisceration with fantasies of twisting a tiny Lang's head off. Sadly, he was full-sized at the moment and sat in front of her next to their pilot. The Black Panther was, if not more interesting, then at least less obviously irritating than Ant-Man. Though in truth she suspected hemorrhoids were less irritating than Lang.

"We're following a lead, Ant-Man," Black Panther said, "and trust me, ours isn't the strangest destination."

○━━━○

"YOUR PLANE or mine?" Frank knew just enough about magic to ask. They were moving through the alleyway at the back of the warehouse. Not looking at all conspicuous during the middle of the day, what with Frank carrying the huge anti-materiel rifle and Strange looking like a disco space tyrant.

"Plane?" Strange asked. "He didn't tell you the details, did he? Oh, this is going to be good."

Not for the first time, it occurred to Frank that being smug was more difficult with a sucking chest wound.

"Wait. Just where is it we're—" he started.

Los Angeles dissolved around him.

⊙─────⊙

THEY SEEMED to drift for a while after they had picked up Gamora, the ship floating ever closer to the Moon. Whether this was by accident or design, Bucky wasn't sure. Nor was he sure about this new alien. She looked like any other dame… woman, except for the green skin. He had kind of expected more.

Moon Knight's fingers were busily tapping away at the ship's control panel.

"Course laid in," he finally said. "Here we go, boys and girls."

"Do we know what sort of resistance to expect once we arrive?" Gamora asked. "Do we have backup we can call if we need it?"

Bucky used the question as an excuse to turn around in his seat and look at her again. Green skin or not, there was no denying that she was attractive.

"Lady, haven't you heard?" Bucky asked even as the ship accelerated, the engines' torches lighting up space behind them. "The Watcher's dead." Moon Knight brought them low over the surface of the Moon. "There's no one watching anymore." The tower of the Watcher's citadel looked like a broken finger. "We're on our own."

CHAPTER FIVE

NEW YORK REAL ESTATE

"**START WITH** the obvious. Our killer is no amateur," Fury said out loud to his watch. Recording his thoughts on what they had discovered so far. "You don't find your way to the Moon, into the Watcher's home, and put a bullet in the big guy's brain without knowing what the hell you're doing." He was standing in an apparently empty chamber by a huge window that looked out onto the blue-tinged lunar landscape. His Coupe DeVille looked a little incongruous parked just outside.

"It was a clean kill, neat. One shot," he continued, there was something about this one. Not just the magnitude of it—the level of power involved—but an itch at the back of his neck. Old instincts honed over eighty years were telling him that something didn't feel right about this, besides the obvious. "This was no panicked shaky hand. This was someone who didn't hesitate to pull the trigger. Our killer has killed before." It might have been self-evident; you didn't play in these leagues without being very accomplished. Even so, it was worth recording.

"Nick?" Steve called. "You say something?"

Fury stopped the recording.

"Nothing. What did S.H.I.E.L.D. say?" he asked as his old friend joined him by the window. To the others he was Captain America, unshakeable and in control. Fury, however, knew him well enough to know that Steve was more than a little troubled by the Watcher's murder. He couldn't say he blamed him.

"They're working with S.W.O.R.D., poring through spaceflight records and looking for any available satellite surveillance footage of the Moon. I've sent Stark to help," Steve told him. Fury nodded. "I've also assured them that the scene is secure, so Thor and Wolverine are on patrol."

Fury knew this last task was busywork. Without a way to track the shooter, Logan was superfluous and, despite Thor's many qualities, a crime scene investigator he was not.

"Did you tell them I was here?" Fury asked, meaning S.H.I.E.L.D. It wasn't so much that he was on bad terms with his old agency, though things were a little strained, more that he didn't want to step on any toes. No, that wasn't true, he'd stamp on toes if he thought it would get the job done. But he didn't want to be seen to be standing on anybody's toes, for the time being at least. Besides, eighty-or-so years of professional paranoia meant he couldn't rule them out as suspects just yet. S.H.I.E.L.D. had the resources, after all, as did S.W.O.R.D. Steve had been right to inform them, however, and not just because of Avengers protocols. If neither agency were involved, then they could be very helpful.

"No, I didn't know if you still were," Steve said.

"Good. I don't know if I am either." All the old instincts were firing up. He knew he should step back but the problem needed working and he wouldn't be Nick Fury if he'd been capable of ignoring this kind of thing.

"Well, maybe this will help you make up your mind." Steve held out an evidence baggie. It held fragments of some kind of luminous green metal.

"Widow dug these fragments out of the Watcher's skull," Steve continued. "We think it's a bullet."

Fury leaned in for a closer look. They were definitely bullet fragments.

"It's glowing green," he said.

"Yeah," Steve agreed, "and I've learned to get real uneasy around things that glow green."

"We're going to want to talk to Banner as soon as—" Fury started.

"Hold that thought," Steve said, putting his hand to his ear.

Fury smiled humorlessly. He knew a lot of old timers who hadn't managed to quite get used to that voice in the ear.

"Call coming in from the FF," Steve told him, meaning the Fantastic Four. "Sounds like we may have found our first suspect."

Both of them turned and headed back the way they came. They made for the car, calling for Logan and Natasha to join them as they did so.

○─────○

THE DEVILLE'S autopilot was doing the driving while Fury tried to patch the feed from one of the Fantastic Four's satellites through to the flying car's dashboard monitor. They hit the Earth's atmosphere and the DeVille was surrounded by fire, leaving a tail like a comet. As they plunged through the atmosphere, Fury managed to get a picture. All four of them stared at the flickering screen.

Ben Grimm, the Fantastic Four's rock-skinned strongman, known as the Thing, was getting punched. Again. The creature doing the punching looked like some kind of heavily muscled golem. Its face was blank except for a Cyclops-esque visor. Fury recognized the creature whaling on Grimm but couldn't bring its name to mind. The device in the golem's hand gave him further pause for thought. He couldn't make it out clearly due to all the movement, but he was pretty sure that it was one of the missing items taken from the Watcher's ransacked citadel.

Having successfully completed re-entry, the DeVille was falling more or less gracefully towards America. Fury glanced over at Steve. He was similarly grim-faced watching the feed from the FF's satellite.

Judging by the destruction around them, the fight had been going on for some time. Midtown was in ruins, again. The street was so covered in wreckage, Fury couldn't even see the road. There was a burning yellow cab embedded in a pile of broken masonry.

Fury was aware of Logan baring his teeth, but if this golem was making Ben Grimm's day difficult then Fury doubted if Logan would even be able to hurt the creature. It wouldn't stop him from trying, though. Fury knew firsthand just how much Wolverine relished a fight.

The creature drove Grimm down into the street in an explosion of rubble. Fury exchanged a look with Steve. They both knew that Grimm was incredibly strong and that his rock-like skin was resistant to a great deal of damage. Fury willed Grimm to get up. He started to do so. Slowly. Then the golem hit Grimm with some sort of energy beam, sending him flying through the debris and throwing up a wake of bricks, beams, and lumps of concrete. Fury saw survivors fleeing the battle, desperate to get away.

He willed the car to go faster. On the screen, a much smaller figure swung through the air towards Grimm. Spider-Man. Steve was leaning in from the back seat, adjusting the monitor, seeing if he could enhance the sound now that they were into the atmosphere.

"Whoa!" Spider-Man said. "That's one of the Mindless Ones. Super-strong extra-dimensional monster dudes."

Mindless Ones! That was their name! Fury thought.

"I've fought these guys before. They're no joke," Spider-Man continued.

"Ya don't say?" Grimm said shaking off lumps of concrete after finally managing to push himself back up onto his feet. He was massive in comparison to Spider-Man, but still not as big as the Mindless One closing in on them both.

Suddenly Grimm clutched his head, crying out, visibly in pain.

"Don't seem so mindless to me!" Grimm managed.

"Something's wrong. They're not supposed to be telepathic," Spider-Man said while hanging off a steel support sticking out of what was left of a building.

It was clear to Fury that the so-called Mindless One had just transmitted something telepathically, but detecting what it had sent was well beyond even the FF's tech. Grimm was right: telepathy seemed at odds with their name and now that Fury was paying more attention to the Mindless One it seemed agitated—upset, even. He glanced up from the monitor and out the windscreen. He could now just about make out Manhattan against the Eastern Seaboard.

"Natasha, have you still got all your S.H.I.E.L.D. clearances?" Fury asked. He glanced back at her.

She nodded, not taking her eyes off the fight. He knew she would be planning what to do if it was still happening when they got down to street level. She was looking for weaknesses in the Mindless One.

"Contact the *Iliad*, see if Psi-Division has got any minds pointing at Midtown, let them know the Avengers are en route," Fury told her.

Natasha didn't even acknowledge him. She just started talking into her communicator. It would be better coming from her rather than a meddling ex-director.

"That ain't even our biggest problem," Grimm said to Spider-Man as Fury turned back to the monitor. Grimm was wading through the rubble towards the apparently not-so Mindless One. "Did ya see what he's got in his—"

"Knowing is pain," Natasha said. It took Fury a moment to work out she was relaying what the S.H.I.E.L.D. telepaths of Psi-Division were picking up from the Mindless One.

Back in Midtown the Mindless One swiped at the ground, sending a wave of broken concrete hurtling towards Grimm.

"Make I not know again," Natasha relayed.

Spider-Man leaped into the air, shooting webs and swinging out of harm's way.

"Its grammar's not up to much," Logan muttered.

Grimm emerged from the dust and debris.

"You asked for it, pal," he said, throwing a haymaker with his right that would have given the Hulk pause.

Spider-Man swung around the Mindless One spraying web from his wrist shooters, wrapping the creature up as Grimm kept it on the ropes, swinging again and again like some punch-drunk palooka.

"Get him down! Fast!" Grimm shouted. "And watch his hands!"

If Grimm, a long-standing member of the Fantastic Four, was worried about whatever bit of tech the Mindless One was carrying, then so was Fury.

The Mindless One tore through Spider-Man's restraining webs. It grabbed a car and clubbed Grimm with it. *He really was getting the worst of this*, Fury mused.

"No, you'll take I back. I, we never should have gone. We never should have gone to the Moon…" Natasha's voice trailed off as she said the last sentence. It was confirmation.

"The Moon?" Spider-Man said.

"The telepaths say that there's a lot of… mental static, I guess," Natasha told them. "It's getting more and more upset… hold on… The things we found there changed I." She concentrated, listening for a moment. "Changed us, are changing us. Making us see. The man on the Moon knew."

Then the Mindless One raised the device it held in its right hand and pointed it like a pistol at Spider-Man. It looked like a very high-tech staple gun. Grimm stepped in front of Spider-Man, hands raised. Fury could make out the tension even on Grimm's rock-like face.

"Making us know was his revenge," Natasha continued.

"Oh hell, that really is the Ultimate Nullifier," Grimm said down on the ground.

Fury swore. Steve didn't even pick him up on it.

"Unless it's named ironically, I'm guessing that's bad," Spider-Man said. Flippancy aside, Fury could hear the fear in his voice.

He didn't blame him. The Ultimate Nullifier was not ironically named. Fury knew it from documents filed in the Existential Threat-to-Everything section of S.H.I.E.L.D.'s files. A weapon that had once been in the possession of Galactus, it was capable of destroying anything it was focused on, from an individual to a universe. It wasn't surprising that Grimm was sweating concrete. It was pointed at him. Fury wondered if he would have stepped in front of Spider-Man in the same situation. He wasn't so sure.

The DeVille's intelligent autopilot levelled the flying car out. Fury could clearly make out the Manhattan skyline now as they came in low across the Upper Bay.

"Look. We're not your enemies, fella," Grimm said through the monitor. "Whatever's wrong, we can help. Just put down the Nullifier."

The Mindless One just stood there pointing the device at Grimm. Judging by Spider-Man's and Grimm's body language, they were receiving another telepathic transmission.

"You can't change what I've seen, what I've done," Natasha said before pausing to listen again.

He wasn't sure if it was important, but it occurred to Fury that the Mindless One's grammar was improving.

"They say it's coming through more clearly. The creature is calmer." Fury knew why the Mindless One was calmer. It had made a decision. Natasha started relaying what the telepaths were picking up from the Mindless One again: "I was so content being a beast, being a mindless monster, before I knew the meaning of sin. But now sin is all I can see."

Even with one eye, Fury saw it coming.

"Better to see nothing at all," Natasha said.

On the ground, Spider-Man was moving, leaping towards the Mindless One, who put the Nullifier to his own head.

"No!" Grimm cried, reaching for the creature.

The feed cut.

Fury saw the explosion as they came in over the harbor. For a sickening moment, Fury thought it was a nuclear detonation. He was relieved when he realized that it was a conventional explosion, albeit large enough to rise over the surrounding skyscrapers. Moments later they heard the sound of the blast echoing over the water.

"Seriously," Logan said, "just knock down Manhattan and turn it into a huge gladiatorial arena." Crass, but that was how Logan handled things like this.

THEY FLEW between the concrete and steel towers. Fury was pretty sure that there wasn't a surviving window anywhere within ten blocks of the blast. The city was covered in sparkling fragments of broken glass.

Fury was relieved to see movement around the edge of the blast crater: Grimm sat up, pushing debris off himself, while Spider-Man tried to stagger to his feet. Grimm must have sheltered Spider-Man from the worst of the explosion with his own body for the web-slinger to survive a blast of that magnitude. Steve leaped out of the DeVille before Fury had even found a flattish patch amongst all the damage to land the car on.

"Ben! What happened? Is everybody all right?" Steve called as he landed amongst the wreckage.

"No," Grimm said, "not everybody."

Fury couldn't see the Mindless One or the Ultimate Nullifier.

He brought the car into land and saw that Logan and Natasha had already leaped out as well. They would be looking for survivors. Fury rolled his good eye. Super heroes never waited until the vehicle had stopped moving.

Climbing out of the car, he picked his way through the rubble. Powdered concrete dust in the air still filled the air. Fury made his way towards Steve, who was talking to Grimm and Spider-Man, glancing around at the mess the Mindless One had made of his hometown. He thought back to the murder committed on the Moon, his mind now made up.

"The Ultimate Nullifier?" Steve was saying. Fury finally spotted the device: it was lying on the ground, next to the forearm and hand of the Mindless One—all that was left of the creature. "Nobody touch it until we can get some sort of containment team down here."

Fury missed a device of that nature being someone else's problem. He wasn't sure he knew of any humans he trusted enough to look after such a weapon. Himself included.

"Cap, what the hell's going on?" Grimm asked. "Is it true what I've heard? Is the big bald guy really dead?"

Grimm was one of the most decent people Fury knew, and therefore utterly unsuited for the world they all lived in.

"Ben—" Steve started.

"I'm gonna need you and everybody else to take a big step back, Grimm," Fury said, emerging from the cloud of powdered concrete filling the air. "This is officially a crime scene and I'm in charge." He was in this now and this was the only way he knew how to do things. "We have a murderer to track down. Let's get to work."

CHAPTER SIX

EYES

I!!!

                                                  I!!!

                          I!!!

                                                              I!!!

                                    I!!!

          I!!!

The thoughts that the Mindless Ones projected were at least drowning out her own internal monologue. Her thoughts normally sounded a little like the buzzing of insects with high-pitched drills for proboscises, or screaming in languages normally unheard on Earth. Oubliette's childhood had been… difficult, or blissful, depending on your opinions on mass murder and parents breeding their children as perfect weapons.

    Speaking of her parent, he didn't seem at all well. She hadn't decided how she felt about that… probably opportunistic. Under normal circumstances her father was one of the most powerful people in the world. His cosmically charged super-powers meant he didn't think twice about going toe-to-toe with the likes of Thor or Captain Marvel. Not only that, but he held vast wealth and global influence amongst governments, the military-industrial complex, and even the various agencies that attempted to govern superhuman affairs. He wielded power from the shadows, from behind numerous thrones. His ego was as monstrous as any tyrant's, but his confidence was such that it didn't need to be constantly on display to the world at large. He was largely unknown, which Oubliette supposed worked in her favor as far as usurpation was concerned.

Her father had always claimed that he could turn any situation to his advantage—it was why those who knew he existed called him Doctor Midas—except he hadn't been able to turn this situation to his advantage. Not yet, anyway.

His bulk was lying on a reinforced operating table underneath a sheet of tarpaulin. His flesh rippling with the changes that exposure to the very powerful and very alien technology had wrought in it. It was… *interesting*, seeing her father brought so low. Oubliette suspected that she could have enjoyed the situation more had the Mindless Ones' telepathic suffering not been quite so self-involved. She didn't like so-called self-awareness in other life forms at the best of times, let alone in those that were supposed to serve her and her daddy.

"I can't control them anymore," she told her current, and hopefully very temporary, partner in crime. She had forced him to wear a hood over what passed for his head. "We lost one today." The only illumination in the large loft space came, ironically, from moonlight shining through the skylight. As the Mindless Ones writhed on the floor, the sight of the Moon clearly exacerbated the situation. They seemed afraid of it. "They are changing too fast."

"As are we," her partner in crime said. He sounded different. Still ever-so-less-than-sane, but less like a whipped dog crawling in its master's shadow. She had preferred him when he existed in fear. At least he was keeping to the shadows. Regardless of his newfound confidence, the hood didn't cut out the squishing noise he made when he talked. She had never squeezed a pimple, but she did wonder if his "head" would burst like one if the correct pressure were applied. He was holding a bloodied rag that contained a spherical object roughly the same size as a bowling bowl.

"The things we stole, they're somehow evolving us. They're opening our eyes. Aren't they?" she asked. *Was it cruel to refer to eyes in the plural?* She hoped so. This technological bleed into her consciousness was making her mind race in ways she hadn't experienced since she had been with Noh-Varr on his ship. She could feel her own awareness expanding until she understood the evolutionary changes going on within her own body. She was surpassing even her daddy's ridiculous expectations. She was capable of such things now; she sighed as she contemplated the artistry of genocide.

"Yes," her temporary partner in crime said, answering the question that she'd already moved on from. He unwrapped the bloody rags to reveal a huge, gouged-out, blue eye. "But it's not *our* eyes I'm most interested in opening."

Something was whispering terrible, beautiful secrets to her, about her. Things that she had never known, did not want to know. She found herself shivering with pleasure at the awful things she was learning.

CHAPTER SEVEN

IN THE BOWELS OF THE EARTH

THE MOLOIDS reminded Emma of the fairy stories of goblins she had heard in her childhood. There were three of them: hairless, wiry, clad only in loincloths and—most bizarre of all—wearing glasses that looked like the old-fashioned 3D glasses you used to get at cinemas. She suspected that the eyewear was designed to cut down on the glare from the lights that she, Black Panther and Ant-Man had brought with them to illuminate the vast natural cavern.

There were three of the creatures. *No, not creatures—people*, Emma corrected herself. Were they the root myth of stories about goblins, human encounters with Subterranea codified as cautionary tales? It was easy to telepathically focus on the Moloids. She could taste their fear in her mind and looked for a way to soothe it. She certainly didn't want to be the cause of their fear. Concentrating on the Moloids while trying to establish enough rapport for meaningful communication was taking her mind off the horror of the rest of the cavern.

"Are they thinking anything useful?" Black Panther asked.

"Terror," Emma told him. "Do you consider that useful?"

"In some situations, yes," he replied. He certainly wasn't wrong. Fear was another tool, another weapon in the arsenal.

"By the looks of this place, I'd say our killer would agree with you." She wasn't in a great hurry to closely inspect the bizarre charnel house they had found themselves in.

"No, Ms. Frost, our killer prefers to be invisible. This place was never meant to be found," he said as they both turned to look at the closest of the bizarre, giant corpses.

"Then how did we find it?" She was sure that he knew more than he was telling her. Whether this was by design or habit, it didn't matter. She didn't like being left in the dark, particularly after being coerced, to the point of blackmail, into joining a mission so very far outside of her comfort zone.

"Every murderer leaves a trail," Black Panther said with frustrating vagueness. "Lang?" he asked over comms. "Have you found the source of the radiation?" There was no immediate reply. "Lang?" This time more insistent. It seemed as though the Black Panther was not one given to patience, but then patience wasn't a quality that royalty was known for.

"Give me a minute, will ya?" Ant-Man's voice crackled over the comms link, presumably due to interference from said radiation. "Trying not to puke here."

Emma couldn't keep the smile from her face. His situation was disgusting, but also a little bit amusing. Now it was clear why Ant-Man was with them. It seemed there were perils to being that small.

She turned back to the Moloids. They were writhing in the light, clearly uncomfortable. She shone the flashlight in another direction and tried not to look at the new and alien corpse that her beam illuminated.

It's okay, relax your minds, she told them. *We're not here to hurt you, believe it or not. We're the good guys.*

Their replying thoughts came through all at once as a jumbled cacophony. She had to sift through it, trying to translate the unintelligible noise of non-human minds into a comprehensible signal. This wasn't a process without flaws, but she couldn't think of a single good reason to let the other two know that.

"All the Moloids know about this place," she said after a few moments of concentration, "is that every few months another body appears. That this has happened for as long as they can remember."

"Then it would appear that they have rather long memories," Black Panther said.

Looking out over the field of decaying monster corpses, the air ripe with the stink of putrefaction, Emma was in complete agreement. Some of the corpses could have been those of demons and monsters from mythology, while others were completely alien. They were in varying states of decay: some had been stripped to the bone; others, still rotting, could not have died more than mere weeks ago at most. The cavern went on for miles. It was a horrific sight—not to mention smell—but more than anything else, Emma, who thought of herself as having had a strange life, was taken aback by the bizarreness of it all.

"A graveyard of giants and monsters hidden away in the center of the Earth. We X-Men are pretty weird but I've never seen anything like this," she said as they wove their way through the piles of huge bodies towards Ant-Man's position, trying to avoid the fresher pools of ichorous discharge from the strange carrion littering the cavern. "What makes you so certain this is the same killer who murdered the Watcher?"

"The facts will make me certain, once we have them," Black Panther told her. It was clear that any certainty came from their employer, again confirming that he had been told more than she had.

"And then what?" she asked. She had nothing for or against the Watcher. He mostly sounded kind of redundant to her. Looking around this open grave of monsters, however, she wasn't sure that she would have liked to have met any of them. Admittedly, she knew from personal experience that not all those with unconventional appearances were awful. Beast and Nightcrawler, for example.

Had the Watcher been a threat to someone, like these creatures? Despite his appearance, had he been a monster himself? She suspected that if he had been a threat, it was the "watching" that had made him so. No one like an uninvited voyeur, after all.

She hadn't looked at any of the corpses too closely, mainly because she couldn't think of a good reason to subject herself to such unpleasantness, but a number of them seemed to have entry wounds. Entry wounds big enough for a man the size of an insect to fit into. They approached the monstrous corpse that Ant-Man was examining from the inside. Emma could see the light of his miniaturized flashlight glowing from within the corpse's wound and she had to admit that she was still amused.

"Then we see where else this trail will lead us," Black Panther said, answering her question. She really didn't like the vagueness, the cryptic nature of his replies. She understood the need for security but she also understood the value of intel. She didn't want to die, or even be mildly inconvenienced because one of her temporary colleagues wished to appear mysterious. She considered telepathically probing his mind. It would be considered an escalation, however, and there was a good chance he had some kind of defense. She decided against it for the moment but didn't rule it out for the future. Eventually, even the "super-est" of so-called heroes has to learn that trying to conceal information from a telepath is ultimately futile.

"Gotcha," Ant-Man suddenly said over comms. For such an unpleasant job, the insect sounded absurdly pleased with himself. It seemed that his necrotic explorations had proved fruitful.

CHAPTER EIGHT

MY BEST SUPERSPY LIFE

AS HE flew the DeVille across the Manhattan skyline, Nick Fury reflected on just how much he was enjoying being back living his best superspy life. He would never tell the others how much he loved the trappings: the flying cars, the jetpacks, and gizmos that James Bond would have given his left arm for. Still, back to the job at hand.

"Cap, I can't see anything out here. Give me a sitrep," he said. Glancing down, he could see the hole in the side of the glass and steel skyscraper, into which their target had entered. "Is the suspect still in sight?"

"Sort of—" Steve blurted out.

"Good god, this thing is fast," Natasha cut across him.

"Move! Get down!" Logan shouted over comms.

"Maybe go ahead and knock off for the day people, we might be a while," Spider-Man added to the comms chatter.

The chatter was accompanied by the sound of breaking glass, the destruction of office equipment and the cries of terrified civilians.

Fury was not impressed. Spider-Man he could understand, he was a civilian, and he knew Logan got excitable when his blood was up. He was disappointed in Natasha, however. There would have to be a discussion about comms discipline in the near future.

"We're right on top of him," Steve said. "Just tell me there's somebody watching the back door."

"Back door?" Fury asked. "You're on the forty-ninth floor. What back—"

Which was, of course, the exact moment at which the Mindless One burst through the skyscraper's reinforced glass. Nick yanked hard on the DeVille's steering wheel, sending the flying car veering downwards and positioning it underneath the plummeting creature. It was instinct more than anything. The Mindless One hit the back of the car, hard.

"Nick! The thing jumped! Does somebody have eyes on it?!" Steve shouted over comms.

"Only one eye, Cap." Fury glanced in the rearview mirror. "But yeah, I got a pretty good view."

The Mindless One was thrashing around, half in the back seat, half sprawled across the DeVille's long trunk. Fury could hear it screaming in his mind. He was pretty sure that he was about a moment away from having his head torn off. He gained altitude, trying to take the thing away from the city, heading towards the river.

"Backseat defenses engaging," the DeVille's on-board systems told him. Fury knew it had taken only milliseconds for the car's systems to kick in, but it had felt like a very long time. Tendrils of living memory metal sprouted all around the Mindless One, slithering around its thrashing bulk, tightening.

Let me go! it roared in Fury's head. *I must keep running! I must outrun my own mind before it drives me mad!*

Yeah, because you're completely sane, pal, Fury thought, though he didn't know if the telepathic broadcast was two-way or not.

"Backseat defenses failing," the DeVille calmly informed him as the enraged Mindless One tore through the tendrils.

Fury drew his pistol and used the rearview mirror to aim, firing bolt after bolt of superheated plasma into the creature.

"This is the most action that backseat's seen in a long time. You ready to confess back there, pal?" Running an interrogation during a gunfight while piloting a flying Cadillac: finally, proof that he could multitask. Though for all the damage the bolts of plasma were doing he may as well have been using a squirt gun. They were over downtown Manhattan now. Fury thought he could see Doc Strange's house.

The Mindless One pushed itself forward through the remaining living metal tendrils. It was practically breathing down Fury's neck—or would've been if it actually breathed.

Being on the Moon was the first time I ever knew sin. It seemed Fury was in for more mental babble. *One doesn't deserve to die for their original sin, do they?*

"Then you admit that you killed the Watcher?" Fury demanded. He suspected, however, that what he was dealing with was a panicked creature desperately trying to cope with a newfound self-awareness, rather than something capable of a cogent response to his questions. After all, nobody actually liked self-awareness.

I... I still can't bear to look at that eye.

He was pretty sure that the Mindless One wasn't talking about Fury's own remaining eye.

Why won't you let me keep running!!?!

"Be my guest, big fella," Fury told him. It was getting too hairy to remain in the car. He triggered the ejection seat. The Mindless One tore free of its restraints and took a swipe at him, only just missing.

"Seatback jetpack enabled," the DeVille announced sedately as the ejection seat fell away from underneath him and the jetpack ignited.

"Now let's go read this thing its damn rights," he muttered.

He sped after his own car. He could see the living metal tendrils still putting up a fight, the remaining few trying to get some purchase on the thrashing Mindless One. The DeVille was still on course for the East River. Fury drew up alongside the flying car, careful not to get too close to any flailing limbs.

"You got the right to go to hell," he shouted at the Mindless One. "Any questions?" He was more than a little pissed about his car.

I demand the right to ignorance! it cried out in his head. *I insist that you make me mindless again!*

"Defenses offline. Navigation offline." They weren't great last words for the DeVille.

"It's all right, Bettie. Hope you know you were always my favorite," he told the car. "Just close your eyes, old girl."

The plasma bolt hit Bettie in the engine and she died in an explosion in the sky above the Brooklyn Bridge. The wreckage hit the river, plasma fire burning under the water as she sank. Fury knew that it would continue to burn for a while. He was pretty sure he hadn't killed the Mindless One. He just hoped he'd messed it up enough that they could recover it for interrogation.

"Everybody seeing this?" he asked over comms. There was a plume of fire, smoke and steam rising from the river.

"Please tell me you left this one alive, Nick," Stark said, joining the comms conversation from Avengers Tower in Midtown. If Fury didn't know better, he would've assumed that Tony was enjoying the first, possibly second martini of the day.

"Better have," Fury said, coming in to land on the Manhattan-side tower of the Brooklyn Bridge.

"Reed just confirmed it," Stark said, meaning Reed Richards, member of the Fantastic Four. "That was the one and only Ultimate Nullifier that we recovered yesterday, which was previously seen in the possession of the big bald man on the Moon."

It wasn't ideal, Fury thought, but if someone absolutely had to have the Nullifier in their possession, then Reed was probably the best choice. He was, after all, a hell of lot smarter than Tony. The thought made him smile. "So, these so-called 'Mindless Ones' are looking more and more like suspect numero uno in the Watcher's murder," Stark continued. "We could really use Doctor Strange on this. These things are from his turf."

Doctor Strange was another one who could give Tony a run for his money in the smarts department. Fury wondered how much this conversation was costing Stark's ego. It wasn't so much that he wanted his friend taken down a peg or two. More that it was necessary for Tony to remember that he wasn't the smartest carbon-based life form in the universe every now and again. It gave the tech billionaire a much-needed sense of perspective.

"These mindless ones are other-dimensional beings, right?" Doctor Bruce Banner said across the comms link. Fury was glad to get his input but hoped that Banner's big, green and very angry alter ego wouldn't have to get involved. The situation was hard enough to control as it was. He was much happier with Banner back in the tower tapping away at his workstation. "If we get one in the lab, I bet I could isolate some sort of energy signature, so we could track any others that might be out there."

"Well, you aren't here for your rosy disposition, Doc," Stark said. Comms discipline.

This was good. This sounded to Fury like they were ready to stop reacting and seize the initiative.

"I want the strongest cell you have at the tower," Fury told them, looking south down the river and out into the harbor. The Statue of Liberty always looked so small from the bridge. "I want a reliable telepath standing by. And Doctor Strange." Tony was right. Of all the threats that Fury had faced over the years, the mystical ones had always been the most difficult for him to come to terms with. Strange played it mysterious, flouting his vaunted wisdom, but he knew what he was talking about.

"Vibranium cell's ready and waiting," Stark said. Vibranium was a good idea. It would deaden the kinetic energy of even the strongest bad guy. "Telepath en route from Westchester," Stark continued. "No word from Strange."

Strange being AWOL was not good. Events of cosmic import

were happening; not a great time for the Wizard of Bleecker Street to disappear on holiday.

"As for me," Stark continued with his report/monologue, "I've reviewed every second of space-based surveillance footage from the last three days. S.W.O.R.D. says there were no approved flights between the Earth and the Moon, but I found this. An unmarked ship leaving the Blue Area of the Moon, headed towards Earth."

Fury checked his watch, saw the footage that Stark was sharing, and clicked the display to enlarge the image as a holograph. The feed showed a compact, sleek ship, styled a little like an Italian sportscar. The tech looked highly sophisticated but human in design. There was something weird about the spacecraft's color.

"Tell me I'm crazy," Stark said, "but does it look like it's made of gold?"

Fury touched the image to still it and then manipulated it to enlarge the craft for a better look. Stark may have been crazy, but he was also right. It did look as though the spacecraft was made of gold. That rang a bell somewhere.

Something—no, *someone*—flew overhead. Fury looked up to see Thor hovering above him. He gestured that he was on comms and then pointed at the column of steam coming from the river. Thor nodded, took a deep breath and let Mjölnir drag him down into the depths of the river and the still-burning plasma flames.

Fury knew that all the Mindless Ones' ruckus meant that the city's heroes would be taking notice. The wider Avengers membership were already on alert, but independent heroes would be mobilizing themselves to protect the city as well. They would be ready to deal with any threats but sometimes just their presence on the streets could reassure people—

"Tony, do you think maybe you should put some pants on?" Banner asked over comms.

Fury rolled an eye, reflecting that said reassurance was probably all the better because the average citizen didn't know what goofs some of these people were.

"We're hunting a murderer here, Bruce," Stark responded with mock severity, "and you're talking about pants. Let's try and be professional."

Thor burst out of the water near the tower that Fury was perched on, rising up until they were level. He was carrying the dripping Mindless One, the living metal tendrils still trying to restrain it despite having been severed from dear, departed Bettie. Fury nodded to Thor.

"Mindless One in custody," he said over comms, cutting through the prattle.

"Copy that," Stark said, all business now. "What's its mood?"

Fury studied the Mindless One. The creature wasn't resisting but seemed to be racked with spasms. It took Fury a moment to work out what was happening.

"I think it's crying," he said.

There was a moment of silence on the comms. Fury gestured vaguely in the direction of Midtown and Avengers Tower. Thor nodded and pointed his hammer north before taking off.

"Then it's ready to crack," Stark said, perhaps a little optimistically. The Mindless One may have given all indications of being ready to crack if it was human. Fury's worry was whether there would be enough common ground between the extradimensional creature's newfound self-awareness and human consciousness to get any useable intel. "Your interrogation cell is ready and waiting, Colonel Fury," Stark added.

Fury kicked off the tower, jetpack igniting as he followed Thor and their prisoner uptown.

"Now," said Stark, clearly enjoying the sound of his own voice, "would someone please tell me where the hell Doctor Strange is?"

CHAPTER NINE

FRANK HATES MAGIC

FRANK HATED magic. Not as much as he hated human traffickers, but it was a close-run thing. He hated being subject to it, being transported somewhere without his express permission and seemingly powerless to do anything about it. It was a problem. Strange was a threat to him, no doubt. He could kill the wizard if he had to, put two in the back of his head when Strange wasn't paying attention, but that would just leave Frank stuck here—wherever *here* was.

They were standing on what looked like a giant branch-like nerve, part of a larger system of "nerves" connected to cyst-like moons and tendrils of long cilia, waving in an unfelt wind. All was suspended in a void of fluorescing twilight, where areas of darkness seemed to have a life of their own, animate and flickering in Frank's periphery. His skin crawled like it had in-country, moments before walking into a night ambush. He liked it here almost as little as he liked magic. This was not a place for humans, and he was feeling so very, very human. He readied the Barrett, straining against its bulk as he hefted it like any ordinary assault rifle despite the weapon's weight.

"We shouldn't be out in the open like this," he said, the surrounding twilight deadened the sound of his voice. His senses weren't working correctly. He fought against a feeling of vertigo and nausea as he picked up a scent that he had never smelled before and that he couldn't begin to describe.

"This is a realm of man-eating shadows. Believe me, Castle, in the open is the only safe place to be," Strange said. He was looking around, surveying this alien realm as though he owned it—which, for all Frank knew, he did. Though Frank had to admit a realm of man-eating shadows would be a good place to get rid of bodies on the rare occasion he didn't want them found.

"I thought we were supposed to be hunting a murderer," Frank growled, still checking all around them, expecting a threat.

"We are." Strange was sitting in a cross-legged position now, floating three feet off the ground, concentrating, making complex gestures with his hands. None of which made Frank feel any more relaxed.

"Then that must mean we're bait. I don't like being bait." He *really* felt like bait.

Strange's forehead started to glow with an eerie red light. Golden birds with wings of fire appeared in the twilight gloom, circling the pair. Frank almost started shooting.

"Put your gun down," Strange told him. "We're not bait. See those birds? I conjured them. They can smell murder victims from worlds away. If there are corpses here, they'll find them."

Frank didn't find this as reassuring as Strange seemed to think it was. The birds shot away from them at astonishing speed, leaving trails of golden fire in the fluorescent gloom.

"Murder-sniffing birds. Why the hell do you need me, Strange?"

"If you remember, that wasn't up to me. You were chosen by— They've found something." Strange's eyes burned with the same golden fire as the birds' wings. Then the wizard was making more complex gestures. Frank realized he was casting a spell, though he felt foolish even thinking such a thing.

"No. Wait—" but it was too late and...

...they reappeared standing in a different part of this ganglionous realm.

"Next time I'll walk," Frank spat. He was getting sick of this. The ground had a crust, but under that crust it was soft underfoot. He looked down and then around. It took him a moment to conceptualize what he was standing on. It was a huge, featureless corpse. There was something half formed about it: the word protean swam up through his bruised memory, from something he'd read a long time ago. The corpse floated in the void. The nerve-like branches all around were more angular and less organic than their previous location. Small islands of rock orbited the body as though it had its own gravitational pull. It was clearly very dead, though it looked more calcified than rotten. They had found their victim.

Strange's murder-sniffing birds helped provide illumination as they flew around the body excitedly. There were other creatures here, creatures of teeth and tentacles, just as dead as the protean corpse.

"What a beast," Strange said looking down at the body. "King of the ancient world, eighty feet long." He almost sounded in awe of it.

Frank looked the body up and down.

"Eighty-five." Marine Scout Sniper school had taught him how to work out distances with some accuracy. "Been here for years."

He knelt on the creature. There were holes in its body, cracks in the calcified flesh spiderwebbing out from them.

"What are you doing?" Strange snapped.

"Looking for an exit wound," Frank told the sorcerer. He knew a gunshot wound when he saw one. He'd made enough.

"Don't be ridiculous. A thing like that couldn't be killed with a gun."

Frank ignored Strange and continued digging around in the large wound with his hands. It was wet inside. The fluid in the hole was the same color as blood but had a very different consistency.

"Give me a moment's quiet," Strange said, "and I'll divine what sort of spell it was that—"

"Well, now I know why I'm here," Frank said. He could feel something deep in the wound, though the green glow emanating from it wasn't filling him with joy. "You and your birds sniff out the bodies, Doc," he managed to get his hands around the object in the wound and yank hard, "and I'll find your damn killer for you."

He pulled the most perfectly preserved bullet he'd ever seen from the wound. Whatever substance it was made of was incredibly hard. It was a large caliber bullet, almost the size of a cannon shell. It also glowed bright green. Not good.

Frank knew that so-called super heroes hated him, thinking him little better than those he hunted. But they all came running when they needed him.

CHAPTER TEN

THE FUNDAMENTAL ELEMENTS OF A SMACKDOWN

ALWAYS IT *comes very slowly… the completed understanding of it. The repeating each one does to tell it the whole history of the being in each one. Always now I hear it, always now, slowly, I understand it. Sugar is not a vegetable.*

It had never made any sense to her either. Oubliette Midas had hunted vegetables as a child. She knew how ridiculous that sounded, but they were large, dangerous, ambulatory vegetables. They had been clones, genetically engineered from off-cuts of the Man-Thing. She had not hunted them for pleasure, as she might have liked, but rather because her father wanted her to know how to kill absolutely every kind of creature. It was why he had given her the sobriquet Exterminatrix—as though Oubliette wasn't bad enough. She hated her father so, and when she had the power to bend the Multiverse to her will, sugar most certainly would be considered a vegetable.

She had assumed that the Mindless One's ongoing broadcast of telepathic babble was going to get on her nerves. She had to admit it was distracting but only from the noise of her own unquiet mind. She had started to enjoy the stark terror that came with their burgeoning self-awareness. But a line had to be drawn somewhere.

"They're quoting Gertrude Stein now," Exterminatrix said. "I'm not sure how much more of this I can take." They were stood in the loft amongst some of her father's discarded tech. They had picked the loft space for its anonymity. It was big enough for the Mindless Ones to writhe in naked terror at their own emergent sense of self. Frankly she was dreading them discovering religion.

"They're evolving rapidly, as are we," their erstwhile ally said, his "head" still covered by the hood.

"Obviously. I haven't slept in three days, but I feel like I could wrestle a Mandroid," she replied. The changes she was experiencing wasn't the burgeoning manifestation of some low-rent super-power. Rather she was jumping several steps in human evolution: stronger, faster, tougher, smarter. *Homo omega*.

"That's good. You're going to need all that strength when they come."

In his hood he reminded her of a little action figure that she'd had as a child; a tiny fictional terrorist commander that she'd stolen from a boy she'd murdered during one of her more successful escape attempts. Her father had, of course, confiscated it from her after she had been recaptured. She wasn't allowed toys. Clubs and blades first, then she had handled her first gun when she was three years old before moving on to more sophisticated ways to hurt and kill.

Her ally was standing a little straighter since his trip to the Moon. She had noticed certain physiological changes, as well as the increased confidence and an increasingly misplaced trust in his own abject mediocrity. Though she had to admit he'd been right. The Moon had proven to be a treasure trove, albeit not without cost. She cast her eyes towards her father's bulk, still prone on the reinforced operating table.

"You should tell them to keep away from the windows," he said. Newfound confidence or not, there was still that unpleasant squishiness to his voice and the fact that all he did was stare at the huge eye he insisted on carrying with him at all times.

"I tell them lots of things." It was true. She whispered some of her desires to them, some of her fears but none of her secrets, because what did it matter? "But they don't listen." Though on several occasions she suspected that her whispers had only added to their sense of existential dread. "We lost another one today. Did you even notice? He tried to run on his own but the Avengers caught him." She was almost amused by this. There was a romantic futility in the situation that they had found themselves in. Had she been with Noh-Varr, she would have been happy to go out in a blaze of glory. This guy, less so. Besides, she didn't want her father to die until she could be the cause of his agonizing demise.

"Then they'll be coming sooner than I thought." He was right. Their actions had turned New York into an armed camp guarded by the most tedious, and most powerful, heroes. The sky was full of them and their vehicles. She wondered how the inhabitants of this city could look up and not feel their own oppression. Still, she knew firsthand that you could always find contentment in submission, if you so chose. It was always easier than thinking for yourself. The Mindless Ones were proof of that. On the plus side, at least they were quoting William Burroughs now. It was practically soothing.

"That's what I've been saying all along. But all you do is stroke that stupid eye," she told him. It seemed it was her fate to continually have to listen to men make what they thought were portentous statements when all they were doing was stating the bloody obvious.

He was staring down at the bowling ball-sized eye again.

"I don't know how to make it open," he squished. "I think there are things inside that want to get out."

"Ugghhh," her father groaned from the operating table. Even unconscious, he had presumably decided that he wasn't getting the attention he deserved. He was so needy like that.

"He sounds even worse today," she said. "Not to mention how he looks."

"He's changing," her ally said.

Ever since her father had bathed in cosmic rays, he had come to look like the Fantastic Four's Thing made from a softer clay. Now, his clay-like body rippled with protean potential. If she was the next several steps in human evolution, then her father had the potential to sublime to godlike power. It would only make his eventual usurpation all the sweeter. For now, however, he was just a liability, another burden to bear.

"He's dying and I don't know what to do," she said as her father groaned again. A vicious smile played across her face, but this wasn't the time for her to move against him. They had more pressing matters to deal with.

"If he's too weak to change, then we'll have to leave him behind."

Exterminatrix had one of her golden guns to his head before he'd finished the sentence. She felt a soft give under the hood as she pressed the barrel of her pistol against it.

"That's not going to happen." Not yet, anyway. Her father needed to experience his fall, appreciate her eventual and inevitable triumph.

"It will happen whether you shoot me or not, and you really shouldn't, you know," he told her, though she was tempted to squeeze the trigger just to see what it looked like. It was her vitreous sense of humor.

"ATTENTION MURDERERS AND MINDLESS ONES!" It appeared that the self-righteous had found them. The amplified voice sounded like an old business acquaintance of her father's.

Her ally had moved over to one of the large windows and was looking out at the brightly colored masses. According to the media, they were subject to one of the largest super-powered (wo)manhunts in the history of the city. Her ally was still stroking the eye in a way that was starting to disturb even her.

"Because you're going to need every last bullet," he said.

THROUGH THE reinforced plexiglass of the Quinjet's cockpit, Fury could make out another two Quinjets filled with more Avengers. The X-Men's Blackbird hovered in the air just below his own craft and there was a S.H.I.E.L.D. helicarrier standing by, ready to provide more fire support, aircraft, and boots on the ground if needed. Iron Man, Thor, Storm, Nova and Firestar were in the air; Iceman was surfing along on his precarious-looking ice sculptures; and those were just a few of the heavy hitters. Fury hoped it was enough, but he'd learned to be cautious.

He depressed the stud on the Quinjet's PA, his voice echoing across the city again.

"YOU ARE SURROUNDED BY EVERY HERO FROM ALL FIVE BOROUGHS OF NEW YORK CITY AND THEN SOME!" Gotta represent, he thought, allowing himself a grim smile. "I SUGGEST YOU SURRENDER QUICKLY! YOU HAVE UNTIL THE SOUND OF THUNDER TO COMPLY!"

"Or to make peace with your little mindless gods," Thor said. Fury shook his head. It was clear the points on improving comms discipline that he'd made at the pre-operation briefing had been ignored. Admittedly, when Thor was born, tactical communication had involved blowing horns and shouting a lot.

"That too," Tony added. Quipping seemed very important to these people.

"Guys, the energy we've been tracking is leaping off the charts here," Banner said. He was in the co-pilot's seat of the Quinjet, Fury was stood between him and Natasha, who was piloting the craft. The gamma-ray scientist was looking at the readout from the heavily modified spectrograph he'd installed in the Quinjet. "I'd say there were at least a dozen Mindless Ones inside that penthouse." There was an edge in Banner's voice. He was a scientist, an academic; Fury knew that when Banner wasn't the Hulk he was scared all the time. That was what made his actions all the more impressive. Banner's fear, even hatred, of his alter ego would not stop Fury from asking the scientist to manifest the Hulk if the situation warranted it—despite the potential for havoc that the green monster represented.

"Just one of those things levelled half the city. We need that building evacuated now," Fury said over comms.

"This is Rogers on the ground floor, we're evacuating as fast as Magik can teleport," Steve replied. The edge in his voice was the result of concern for the civilians inevitably put at risk when gods and monsters fought. Fury wondered what it was like for the average Joe when Captain America turned up at your doorstep with a teleporting mutant. Fury hadn't been an average Joe since he'd started wing walking. The war had been a leveler.

"Nick, look at the infrared. It's not just Mindless Ones up there," Natasha told him. "We've got other targets and what looks to me like a whole bunch of guns."

Nick leaned over to look at the IR sensor feed. As well as the relatively cold golem-shaped heat signatures of the Mindless Ones, there were two roughly human shapes, male and female, though the male had a weird-looking head. Both were burning much hotter than an average human. He'd seen it before: the revved-up human form. They'd been enhanced. There was a third non-Mindless One form; judging by its position, it was prostrate. It burned even hotter than the other two, bursting with energy, its form churning as though it were liquid encased in a vaguely humanoid form. Whatever else it was, Nick recognized power. He didn't like unknowns, but he'd erred on the side of caution. He'd brought everyone.

○──────○

EXTERMINATRIX DID not like to be hurried when choosing a weapon. There were so many factors: not just power but style, the ratio of suffering caused against instant death. What was she trying to say—what statement was she making? But needs must when you're literally waiting for the hammer to come down.

"Those people out there know what we did," she told the not-so-Mindless Ones as she stood in front of her wall of golden guns. "So aim for their faces." The pep talk was more for her sake than her "troops." She could hear them shuffling behind her, their glowing red mono-eyes reflected in gold. She knew they would follow her because death by super hero was the best way for the Mindless Ones to end their own existence. "And don't let their gushing blood slow you down."

She chose efficiency. The most damage she could do quickly at close quarters. The kind of weapons that would give even the likes of Thor pause for thought.

Then she turned and ran towards the window. She ran faster than she ever had before, a feral grin on her masked face, and leaped through the window into the air twelve stories above the ground. She dropped gracefully, leather coat billowing out around her, firing the two hugely destructive pistols in her hands into the target-rich environment. She was elegant, vicious death.

The Mindless Ones dropped through the sky after her, energy beams lancing from the slits in their heads.

Exterminatrix saw Nova tumble from the sky, hit by one of the Mindless Ones' energy blasts. She dropped past Thor, who ignored her, then one of the Mindless Ones collided with him, pounding on the Norse god as both of them plummeted streetwise.

It was clear to her that the "heroes" hadn't expected them to exit the loft in this direction. She landed on a Quinjet that had strayed too close to the building.

"Get him out of there!" she spat over comms, meaning her father. "Do you hear me?!" She pointed both pistols at the Quinjet's cockpit. The shocked expressions of those inside were beautiful. "We'll hold them off for as long as we can! Who knows"—she started firing bolts of plasma from one pistol, and molecularly hardened, electromagnetically propelled golden bullets from the other—"we might even kill a few." The front of the Quinjet burst into flames. "Tell my father I died gloriously. Tell him I made Thor bleed." *Why did it matter what her tyrant father thought of her?* was one of the many thoughts she was now capable of processing even while thoroughly enjoying the thrill of fighting for her life. She had always been a weapon: now she was an evolved one.

"You won't have to die once I figure out how to open it, you'll see," her ally responded. Even over comms his voice had a squishy quality. She assumed—no, hoped—he was helping her father down the concealed stairwell in the building.

"Damn you and that eye," she responded as she rode the spiraling, burning Quinjet through the air. "I hope it gives you cancer. Damn you for finding us in the first damn place!" She threw herself off the Quinjet into a backward somersault. The Mindless One was still beating on Thor; she shot the Asgardian in the back with a golden bullet. "Now shut up and run!"

The Hulk burst out of the Quinjet moments before it hit the ground and exploded. The huge green creature landed in the street at the same time as Oubliette. Her new physiology was more than capable of absorbing the impact. She assigned part of her hyper-consciousness to enjoying the feeling of power she was experiencing.

The Hulk put two people down on the ground. Exterminatrix recognized Nick Fury. His eyepatch made him imperfect, just as her own scarred face—the reason she wore a mask—made her imperfect. The other figure was the Black Widow. She was beautiful.

The Mindless Ones were emerging from the craters their impact had made in the street. She knew that Thor was in one of those craters. She had hoped he was dead, but her improved senses suggested otherwise. Disappointing.

"*Kill the pretty ones first!*" she cried, tailoring her own fury with her new emotional control, honing it like any other weapon. The Thing, Luke Cage, Wolverine, and another brown-haired X-Man she suspected was Kitty Pryde, with the Falcon in the air, had joined Fury, Black Widow and Hulk. She recognized most of them from her father's files. Her contempt for this assemblage of entitled, self-righteous, false power was most keenly aimed at Captain America, however. The anthropomorphic manifestation of everything wrong with the world in one package. He was an anachronism with no place in the modern world, let alone in the one she would build in her image.

The Hulk roared. The woman who may or may not have been Kitty Pryde said something that was presumably witty, but Exterminatrix couldn't hear anything over the screaming in her own head. She moved amongst the gunfire from Fury and the Widow as though dancing through raindrops. Captain America's shield flew past her, hitting one of the Mindless Ones in its face. Oubliette was already firing, her guns an extension of her will as she reached out to touch someone in the ruins of another New York street.

"Quite the turnout! I'm flattered! I just hope I've got enough bullets for all your faces!" She wanted to see Captain America's bloodied, fused skull hollowed out by superheated plasma.

THE ORB had to coax Doctor Midas up and onto his feet, and help his not-insubstantial bulk down the stairs from the loft they had been hiding in. Midas was weak but moving. He was, after all, nothing if not dedicated to his own survival. The Orb suspected that Midas's already extraordinary levels of power were making his evolutionary transition so difficult: even Midas's cosmically enhanced form was struggling to contain his newfound "gifts."

Midas was not the only one experiencing change. The Orb was a different person from the one that had approached Doctor Midas a few weeks ago. The technological bleed from the Watcher's cache of advanced super-tech that he'd been exposed to on the Moon was responsible for this transformation. Deep down he'd always known that he wasn't much of a villain. An odd appearance, a stolen repulsor pistol, and a deep and abiding hatred of Ghost Rider did not a super villain maketh. It was different now. The changes to his body and mind notwithstanding, he wanted more. He could feel it. He was on the cusp. It was difficult to describe. The Watcher's eye whispered to him in fractal images, ghost visions, fleeting and tantalizing. It was a hint, a promise of what lay ahead if he could just open the eye. If he could just bend it to his newfound will. He still wondered how Exterminatrix had forced him to wear the hood.

"I feel like my face is about to explode," Doctor Midas managed. His voice had a bubbly quality, as though his larynx was flooded. As the Orb supported him down the stairs, he could feel Doctor Midas's form flowing like a viscous, semi-liquid solid. The cracks in Midas's boulder-like face glowed with an inner energy, like neon.

"That's good," the Orb told him, "we might need you to do that." If nothing else the mental picture of such an occurrence was amusing. He could hear the sounds of the battle outside all too well. The building shook with noise.

"I hear you talking to that damn eye every night," Doctor Midas said. "You should get rid of it. It knows what we did."

The Orb was a little surprised to hear the fear in Midas's voice.

"It knows everything. That's the point," he explained.

○—○

WHERE HAD Spider-Man had come from and who was the fool in the red pajamas with the devil's horns and the club? Exterminatrix couldn't believe that he was trying to fight someone as evolved as she was with a club. Was there anything more telling? She was a new breed of human and he was facing her with a stick!

She was spinning, kicking, her foot making solid contact with Captain America's head, firing all the while, moving too quickly amongst them for them to catch as she shot the Hulk repeatedly in the face.

○—○

"IT'S SEEN the whole history of the world of us. It's seen all the secrets that are or ever were and I think they're all still inside it," the Orb continued. He didn't understand how Doctor Midas, someone who boasted of being able to turn every situation to his favor, couldn't see the potential for this. But then, the tyrannical had always feared knowledge. They shuffled the last few paces to the ground floor lobby.

"How do we get them out?" Doctor Midas asked.

"That's the question I've been asking every night."

"And what does it say?"

"It doesn't say anything. It's an eye, you idiot." Once he would've been too frightened, too in awe to speak like this to the likes of Doctor Midas. Now he just couldn't be bothered to explain the nuances of his relationship with the dead alien's ocular orb. How things had changed. "It just watches me."

It had gone suspiciously quiet outside. The Orb wondered: if Doctor Midas was so smart, then why was their great escape plan just to use the stairs?

THOR WAS up again, shrugging off Mindless Ones like they were kittens. Exterminatrix's visual processing was now so quick it looked as though he was leaping in slow motion through the air towards her, his hammer glowing, lightning playing around him.

A huge green fist flying towards her face.

It was inevitable, she thought, even as her consciousness fled, *if only she had killed a few of them.*

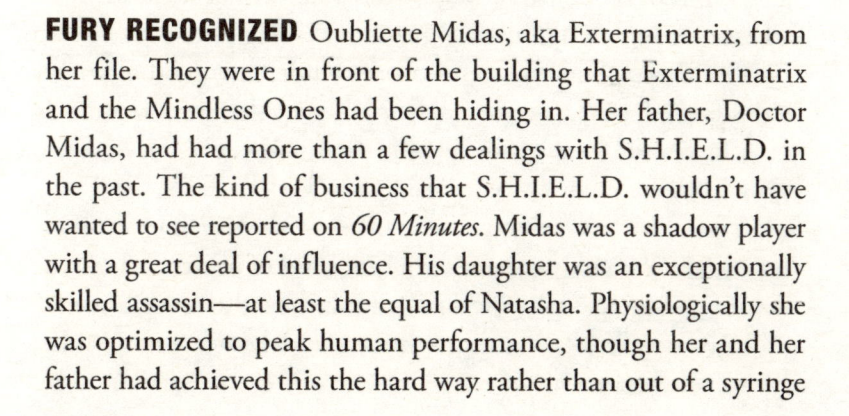

FURY RECOGNIZED Oubliette Midas, aka Exterminatrix, from her file. They were in front of the building that Exterminatrix and the Mindless Ones had been hiding in. Her father, Doctor Midas, had had more than a few dealings with S.H.I.E.L.D. in the past. The kind of business that S.H.I.E.L.D. wouldn't have wanted to see reported on *60 Minutes*. Midas was a shadow player with a great deal of influence. His daughter was an exceptionally skilled assassin—at least the equal of Natasha. Physiologically she was optimized to peak human performance, though her and her father had achieved this the hard way rather than out of a syringe like Steve. Maybe Fury had it wrong, but getting hit by Thor and the Hulk should have killed her, or at least broken every bone in her body. She was already conscious again. Natasha had Exterminatrix down on her knees in the rubble in restraints that the Thing would've struggled to break out of.

Exterminatrix was surrounded: Ben Grimm, whose rock-like presence Fury found a comfort as they stood amongst the dead and wounded Mindless Ones, Falcon, Luke Cage, Steve, Spider-Man—crouched on the Hulk's back—Kitty Pryde, Daredevil, Thor, and Iron Man. In the air there was Magik on one of her stepping discs; Nova, who had recovered from the hit he'd taken; Iceman skating in and Storm, the second of the gods present. It seemed overkill for one dominatrix.

Then the building's service door swung open and two figures staggered out into the partially destroyed street.

"Oh," the smaller of the two said. He wore a vaguely familiar red costume and a hood that covered his entire head. He was carrying something in his free hand, but Fury was distracted by the other, larger figure. For a moment Fury thought it could've been Ben Grimm, but the Thing was stood behind him. No, this was Doctor Midas, Oubliette's father, who'd bathed in cosmic rays to try and give himself all the powers of the Fantastic Four. Fury had once heard him referred to as Cosmic Man, though he thought that Doctor Midas sounded a lot better.

Fury looked back to the object the smaller of the two carried: a bloodshot sphere trailing nerve endings.

Well damn, Fury thought. That couldn't be good. Doctor Midas looked weak, spent.

"Oh yes, of course. You're still his, aren't you?" the hooded figure said, stepping away from Doctor Midas who swayed but didn't fall. He had put emphasis on the word "*his*." Fury had no idea who he was talking about. "You still want to be there when the world is changing." His voice had a squishy quality to it. "Like it is… right now. You still just want to watch." He didn't seem to be talking to them or Midas.

Is he talking to the eye? Fury was tense, ready to fire the moment either of them looked as though they were making a move.

Midas's head, the cracks in it like glowing fault lines, turned to look at the eye.

"I can feel it. It sees us, doesn't it?" His voice low but audible.

"Yes, it does," the hooded figure answered. "It sees all and everything, just like always, but now it also needs us to see." Then to the eye: "Thank you."

"Holy hell, they got the Watcher's eyeball. The sick bastards," Luke Cage said.

"Whatever the hell this is, it's finished," Nick called to them, "You're murderers and you're all going down." He was just glad that it was no longer his responsibility to stop Doctor Midas talking about his involvement with S.H.I.E.L.D.

"Put the eye down and step away," Steve ordered the masked figure.

"No, no, I don't think so. See, we're not the murderers you're looking for and this is not an eye anymore. It's a bomb," the hooded figure told them. Later, Fury would come to reflect that this was the time he should've shot the guy. The eye started to glow. "A bomb full of secrets. And what do bombs do?" He pulled the hood off. It was a significant anti-climax. Under the hood was a huge eyeball where a head should be. Fury vaguely remembered that this guy was a Z-list super villain called the Orb.

The wind picked up and lightning played all around the Watcher's eye, its nerve endings whipping around as though grasping for something.

"They go boom," the Orb said. Then he changed the world.

CHAPTER ELEVEN

INTERMISSION

SEVERAL WEEKS AGO

IT WAS *the quality of light he appreciated most. As though, if you were wealthy enough, you could turn the very air to gold. The Orb knew it was just a trick of the light, but it was still a good trick.*

"In my dreams... I'm on the Moon." Had he gone to the likes of Doctor Doom, the Orb was pretty sure he would have been killed outright for even suggesting a job based on his dreams.

"And there's a mansion there." Not that Doom would have taken the meeting.

"I walk inside it like I own it." But Midas recognized possibility. He had vision. "Like it knows me."

Midas was like a venture capitalist for the grandest of schemes. Doom, Strange, Druid—Midas was definitely the best of the doctors in the Orb's book. "I want to stay but I wake up and he's always there at the foot of my bed." That was how the Orb had found himself in the cathedral-like library/office of one of Midas's many domiciles. "He never speaks, he just... watches me." Here he was telling his story, his idea, to the man himself. "I thought he was part of the dream at first, but now I think that it's his house and he doesn't like that I can see it."

He was sat on the other side of the huge, polished desk. Midas. His bulk clad in golden armor, not dissimilar in style to Iron Man's, though he wore a smoking jacket over the armor. Sheer elegance! He was backlit, through a huge floor-to-ceiling window, by a beautiful, and of course, golden late summer sunset. His armor sparkled and glowed. The Orb would've blinked if his eye had a lid.

"That's what I do," the Orb continued. "I see things other people can't." He needed Midas to understand what they had in common. "And sometimes I steal eyeballs and roll around naked in them." Wait. Had he said that that aloud? "But mostly I see things." Phew, he was pretty sure that he'd gotten away with it. "For example, I can see that you've considered killing me at least seven different times since I came here—"

"Eight," Midas's terrifying daughter said. "Take off the mask." Though this was a problematic request.

"It's not a mask," the Orb attempted to demonstrate by taking hold of either side of his head-sized eyeball and trying to pull it off. Fluid moved around under the membrane.

"What do you mean it's not a mask?" Exterminatrix demanded. She leaned over the edge of her father's desk. "How are you talking if it's not a mask?"

It *was* a good question, the Orb reflected, as was *why have you decided to wear fetish gear to a business meeting?* He decided not push her on this point.

"It took me a long time to learn," the Orb explained. It was nice when people took an interest in his struggle after all. "I used to just make squishy noises and—"

"Never mind his damn face, Oubliette," Midas interrupted. It was no surprise that Midas's voice was that of a great man. Commanding, masculine, in control— everything the Orb wanted to be but so rarely felt. "The man you saw, what did he look like?"

"Big. Big and bald. I thought he was God at first but I don't think that God would dress like that," the Orb told them. He half expected to the see the huge, silent, brooding figure that haunted his waking moments standing behind Doctor Midas, staring at him disapprovingly. At least disapproval was a step up from disgust and loathing. People didn't cope well with the eye-for-a-head thing.

"And this place on the Moon?" There was just a touch of impatience in Midas's tone.

"Oh, it's wondrous, full of treasures. Full of things we can't begin to imagine. Secrets! The whole place is filled with secrets. More secrets than there are stars." He hoped he was communicating just how excited he was by the possibility of this joint venture. This was where he'd gone wrong in the past, like so many of his colleagues. Everyone wanted to be in charge: to be the big boss. The Orb knew he'd make a better advisor, a power behind the throne type. Like Gandalf. Leave the being in charge stuff to great men like Doctor Midas.

There were a few moments of silence. The Orb guessed that this was Doctor Midas considering the awesomeness of his idea. He was nervous. This was like a job interview.

"I have plenty of secrets already, and treasure enough for a thousand men. Why should I care about your dreams? Why are you here?"

Here it comes, the gamble, *the Orb thought as he pointed a white-gloved finger across the desk at Midas,* do-or-die Orby-baby. Had he seen far enough to ensnare Doctor Midas?

"Because you've seen him too, I can tell. You want to walk through the doors of that mansion the same as me and I'm the only man alive who can get you inside." The Orb hoped that was the case anyway.

Doctor Midas clasped his hands together. A soft neon glow came through the eye-slits of his armor's bullet-shaped helmet.

"So, what do you say, Doctor Midas? Do we have a deal? Shall we rob the Man in the Moon of all his secrets?" The Orb was suddenly feeling surprisingly confident.

"Let me shoot this fool in his big, stupid eye, father. Please?"

Exterminatrix was a bit of a buzzkill. She pushed herself off the desk and swished open her long leather coat to reveal one of her guns.

"Silence, girl." The great man hadn't even needed to snap at her. His authority was total. "He's called the Watcher, Mr Orb, and yes,

I've seen him. All men who change the world with their bare hands have seen the Watcher. I am such a man."

He's so cool, *thought the Orb.*

"Tell me though," Midas continued, *"if your power of sight is as you say… then where does he keep these secrets?"*

That was when the Orb knew he had him. Now to reel him in.

"Ah, isn't it obvious?" Don't push him Orby-baby, *he admonished himself.* "Close, very close. The Watcher keeps his secrets right where he can see them."

The Orb relaxed back into the antique chair. The thing was, it wasn't just a matter of the Watcher's secrets. It was everyone's secrets. That was the Man in the Moon's real treasure.

CHAPTER TWELVE

THE SECRET BOMB

THEY WERE engulfed in a swirling, nebulous blue light display. Bioelectricity flowed from the alien eye that the Orb held up high. Heroes fell like bowling pins as memories—secrets—were pushed into their minds.

○─────○

NOVA, SAM *Alexander, did not recognize the alien city nor the strange symbols painted in light that illuminated this down-at-heel metropolis. Nor did he recognize the various species of the few people on the refuse-strewn streets of this particular neighborhood. He did, however, recognize the man wearing the uniform of the Nova Corps: Jesse Alexander, Sam's absent father. He watched as his dad beat another member of the Corps bloody, kicking him into a side alley as a third Nova Corps member, a tall green alien with an elongated face, observed.*

Sam watched as though he was there, the exotic smells of the city, the clammy humidity on his skin different to the humidity on Earth. He watched helplessly as his father raised a weapon, some sort of futuristic handgun. The man his dad had beaten was on his feet again, his fists glowing. Everything seemed to slow down and Sam saw his father squeeze the weapon's trigger. He watched as his father murdered a fellow member of the Nova Corps, the blast from the weapon disintegrating the body, leaving little more than an outline in carbon dust on the ground. Then the dust was caught in the warm breeze and blown away. Sam felt culpable, as though the inherited memory meant he had inherited the guilt of the crime as well.

○――――○

BEN GRIMM *was on fire. He wanted to scream. Then he realized that not only was he not in any pain but he was exhilarated; he enjoyed the sensation as he flew through Reed Richard's extensive laboratory high up in the Baxter Building. He wasn't himself. Ben had never felt this free, this light, this untethered from the ground, but that was because this wasn't his memory. It was Johnny Storm's, the Human Torch's memory.*

Ben recognized the chamber in the center of the lab, however. He still felt the pang of that memory, the stab of hope betrayed. He couldn't recollect what Reed had called it but he had understood the basic underlying principle. Reed had intended to use the chamber to isolate and invert the changes that the cosmic radiation had wrought in Ben's form, turning him from the rock-like Thing back to a normal human being. It was a one-shot deal, however.

Ben-as-Johnny flew down to investigate. Ben watched helplessly, through Johnny's own eyes, as he hit the control to open the chamber and then flew inside, checking out the Thing-sized seat, making a comment about Ben's weight and then closing the door again. This was a part of that day that Ben hadn't known about. He remembered the rest, however.

He remembered the keen sting of hope, fool that he was. He remembered the gratitude he had felt to see that Johnny had come to wish him well despite their, at times, somewhat strained relationship. Then he remembered the pain in the chamber as though he had been taken apart molecule by molecule. This time he saw it from the outside, through Johnny's eyes, as a display of light and energy that did nothing to convey the agony of Ben's transformation.

And just for a moment it had worked. Just for a moment he had been human again, felt his own distantly remembered skin against the tips of fingers made of flesh and bone. Then the next transformation had kicked in. Then he had learned what real pain felt like. The kind of pain you could only experience if you were not limited by a normal human physiology. He had burst from the chamber more of a Thing than he had been when he had gone in. Caught in a cycle of transformation between rock and flesh, in agony as stone spikes grew through and out of his body.

Reed, with Johnny's help, finally managed to stabilize his form but Ben had become the Thing once more. He remembered how wretched he had felt. Now, seeing it through Johnny's eyes, he realized it was worse than even he had thought. Ben felt sick as Johnny confessed to Reed that he had messed with the chamber, thrown the calibration out. Reed had read him the riot act but in the end they kept Johnny's involvement from Ben. In the end his teammate had screwed him over. Taken away his chance to live a normal life. Johnny could never understand it—he loved being the Human Torch, even when it hurt people. He didn't want to be normal but it was all Ben wanted. It was everything and Johnny had prevented it, and worse, Reed, Ben's best friend had lied to keep his brother-in-law's secret. A two-for-one betrayal.

After years of holding Reed responsible, Ben decided he was going to share out some of the blame.

IT HIT Luke Cage in a storm of images. Little more than flashes; his cranium felt like it had been lit up from the inside. As though his skull must look like an X-ray burning through his skin.

He saw his father as a young man with a moustache and a full head of hair, long before what was left had turned white. He wore a black T-shirt and a leather coat, a .357 Magnum held out like he was on the cover of a pulp novel.

It was a moment before Luke recognized a younger Adam Brashear, the Blue Marvel himself.

Without all the dark clothes it was only the trademark stakes that gave away the near-ageless Blade. The vampire hunter's Afro was a statement.

Luke didn't recognize either of the women. One looked hard as nails, the other was a more glamorous-looking blonde, both beautiful.

Nor did he recognize the red-clad, semi-demonic-looking sorcerous type with the outrageous collar. Luke assumed he was the villain of the piece. There was something of the sorcerer about him.

The clothes, the style; the whole thing was like a montage from a '70s action flick had been thrust into his skull. It was little more than a collage of moving pictures; there was not much in the way of context but the connecting point between them all was his father. Even without context this would have been more than cool—his father running his own team of heroes in the '70s. There was just one problem: his father had made clear the disdain in which he held Luke's own vocation and lifestyle. He'd always had a difficult relationship with his father. Proof that he was a hypocrite only served to deepen the resentment.

―○――○―

SPIDER-MAN, PETER *Parker, was doubled over on the ground. The secret pushed into his head like a broken mirror, someone else's fractal memory tearing through the grey meat of his mind, filling his head, leaving little room for anything else other than blinding white light and lancing pain.*

He had never given much thought to the creature that had started it all. The spider that had taken him down the path that led to this very moment: fighting a gun-wielding dominatrix, extra-dimensional monstrosities and fractured memories given to him by a man with an eye where his head should be.

In a shard of memory, he saw the irradiated arachnid fall from his wrist, scuttle across the lab's tile floor and over a girl's foot. He tried to shout, to warn her, but this wasn't even his memory.

In another broken shard, he saw the same dark-haired girl accidentally terrorizing her parents because she could not control her newly developing powers. How could she? What even would her frame of reference for such a thing be?

Peter heard the girl's mother call her name.

Cindy. Cindy Moon.

Another shard and Peter remembered a man named Ezekiel training Cindy, helping her first control and then master her powers, becoming stronger. Perhaps too strong.

Peter wasn't sure what to make of him. Scientist, mystic, he claimed that he had been granted the powers of a spider spirit. He was promising Cindy Moon's parents that he could help them, that he was familiar with such things.

Another shard and Peter saw Ezekiel's realization that Cindy had become powerful enough to attract the attention of those who would prey on people like them. Monsters like Morlun, who hunted those with spider-like powers.

Another shard and he saw Ezekiel lock Cindy in a specially constructed room designed to shield her from predators. Peter knew that she was still there, even now, even though circumstances had changed. She had been kept locked away from the world.

He had no choice. He had to find her and free her.

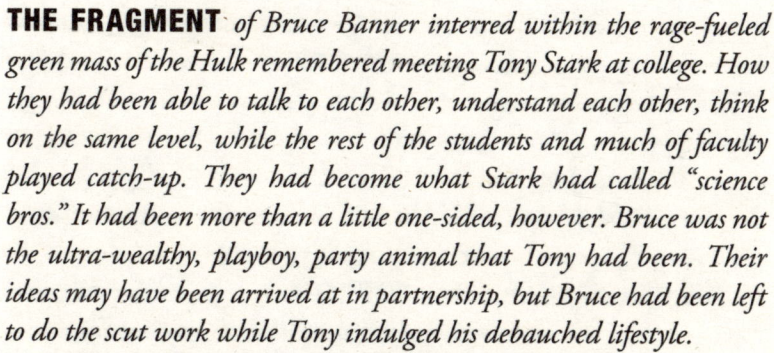

———◦———◦———

THE FRAGMENT of Bruce Banner interred within the rage-fueled green mass of the Hulk remembered meeting Tony Stark at college. How they had been able to talk to each other, understand each other, think on the same level, while the rest of the students and much of faculty played catch-up. They had become what Stark had called "science bros." It had been more than a little one-sided, however. Bruce was not the ultra-wealthy, playboy, party animal that Tony had been. Their ideas may have been arrived at in partnership, but Bruce had been left to do the scut work while Tony indulged his debauched lifestyle.

Bruce could well remember all this. Except this time, he was remembering it from Tony's perspective. This time he knew what Tony was thinking when he used to waltz out of the experimental energy lab, a girl on each arm. He was thinking that Bruce had it within in him to build a bomb, a weapon that his family's arms business could capitalize on.

Years after he had graduated from college and Tony had been expelled, Bruce could actually feel just how inebriated Tony had felt when he had crashed the meeting with General Ross. Thunderbolt Ross had been in charge of the Gamma Bomb project for the Pentagon. Tony had just wandered in, swilling martinis. Ostensibly he was there as moral support for his old college buddy. In practice he'd immediately made himself the center of attention. Just like he always had.

Then, of course, he'd started to interfere. He had pointed out to a room full of hawks that the bomb could be better. By better, of course, he meant it could cause more damage. Kill more people. Drunk, arms-dealing Tony was a different person to the sober Tony Stark who wore the Iron Man armor today, or so Bruce had hoped.

They'd had words. From his own memory and those of Tony's that had been forcibly shared with him, Bruce knew that they both regretted the things they had said.

Years later they would become colleagues again and then friends, old wounds healed over. Except what Bruce hadn't known was that, after the argument, an angry and even drunker Tony had hacked the schematics, changed the parameters on the gamma bomb's heat shields. Made the bomb more powerful.

It was typical Tony. He didn't think he was always right, he knew he was always right. That "knowledge"—coupled with a great deal of power, technical acumen and zero sense of responsibility—had made him dangerous.

It had been Tony's fault.

Tony Stark had sabotaged Bruce's Gamma Bomb experiment.

He hadn't meant to do it, but then again he never did.

Tony Stark had created the Hulk. He had kept it secret every day since. Every moment they had worked together, fought together.

Bruce became fury.

And the Hulk was a rage amplifier.

THE ONLY secret the bomb shared with Tony Stark, Iron Man, was the knowledge that Banner now knew that he had hacked the gamma bomb schematics. Tony decided that he needed to put some distance between himself and Banner, for the time being at least. Also, it might be worth readying some of his Hulk countermeasures. This was not good and would need to be handled very carefully, not just to avoid being beaten into a sack of boneless jelly wearing a tin suit, but for Banner's sake as well. Not that he'd see it that way.

BEING IN the blast radius of the secret bomb was perhaps easier for Thor Odinson, the Asgardian God of Thunder. Not only was his physical form and mind far stronger than the majority of mortals caught in the blast, but he had also experienced mystical visions before. Nevertheless, he staggered momentarily as memory after memory impacted his cerebellum.

At first he saw Ragnarok, the Twilight of the Gods, the inevitable apocalyptic end that must come to all creation. Then he saw this same war, shaking the very cosmos, being fought by his father as a young man. Young enough so as to tell Thor that this had happened at the very dawn of time itself.

It was as stirring to Thor's blood as it was terrible. He saw the Nine Realms torn asunder with fire and blood. No. Not the Nine Realms. Ten! It made no sense.

But there it was, a tenth realm fighting for its place amongst the branches of the great World Tree, Yggdrasil. A realm of ferocious, winged warrior women. At first Thor had thought them Valkyries but it was clear that they were something more than that.

He saw his mother, Freya, Queen of Asgard, in the throes of childbirth. She gave birth to a girl.

Great serpent's teeth! He had a sister!

Then the vision's assault speeded up. He saw the winged warrior women steal the child.

He saw a dagger fall. A spray of blood.

A young Odin racked by grief.

Then his father, alone in the harsh night of space. Odin glowed with light and power and fury. The Tenth Realm before him, an island amongst the cold stars.

Thor watched as Gungnir, his father's spear, fell as it was swung with all of Odin's might and magic, cutting the Tenth Realm away from the other nine, severing it from the branches of Yggdrasil.

○——————○

CAPTAIN AMERICA, Steve Rogers, saw his own greatest failure unroll in his mind's eye like an old movie. He hadn't understood everything that had been explained to him by Reed Richards, but he caught the gist: a collapsing alternate universe had collided with another, creating a crack in the Multiverse that had the potential to cause more collisions, and destroy more universes. The incursion point was Earth, because of course it was.

So all the great and "good" had gathered. They had called themselves the Illuminati without a trace of irony, perhaps unaware they were the living embodiment of every paranoid conspiracy theory the average person in the street had about "super heroes." They had met around a long table in a boardroom that may as well have been constructed from shadow. It was there this group of men, a number of whom had been born as normal humans just like Steve, took it upon themselves to decide the fate of not just their world but countless others.

In addition to their extraordinary abilities, they were amongst some of the smartest people in the world. They were acting in good faith and trying to do the right thing, at least as they saw it. And of course the same thing happened that happened every time a group of men decided that they knew better than everyone else and made a unilateral decision. They plotted atrocity and were in total agreement. They would build a weapon, destroy an entire other universe, every living thing in it, every iota of matter, every last drop of energy. The greatest act of villainy ever committed on Earth would be committed by some of its so-called greatest heroes.

And Steve knew it was his fault.

When T'Challa had first become aware of the threat, of the approaching multiversal incursion, it had been Steve who had desperately cast around for an alternative solution. They had risked using the Infinity Gauntlet, the power of the Infinity Gems, to stop the collision, to save both Earths and their respective universes. He wondered how he had ever forgotten—or rather been made to forget—such power. For a moment he'd had control over the heavens and the Earth, over the raw stuff of creation, over light and spirit and force and the minds of all, over reality itself from the birth of the universe to its cold death. He had done it and lived but in doing so he had destroyed all of the Infinity Gems, except the Time Gem, which had simply disappeared.

He had dealt with the symptom but not the cause, and now they had lost the means with which to prevent the next incursion.

It was then that he had known they would go through with it. The Illuminati would save this reality by killing another. His position weakened by his failure, Steve had argued. Finally he had delivered his ultimatum. He would not allow this to happen. That was when Doctor Strange had taken the memories of these events from him.

He had been betrayed by some of his closest friends—Tony's involvement particularly stung—and they had done so to commit an atrocity so vast in scale as to be barely quantifiable.

It was done now. A fait accompli. *That didn't mean it was over. There would be a reckoning. There had to be. Such a thing could not go unanswered but Steve had to deal with the current existential threat first.*

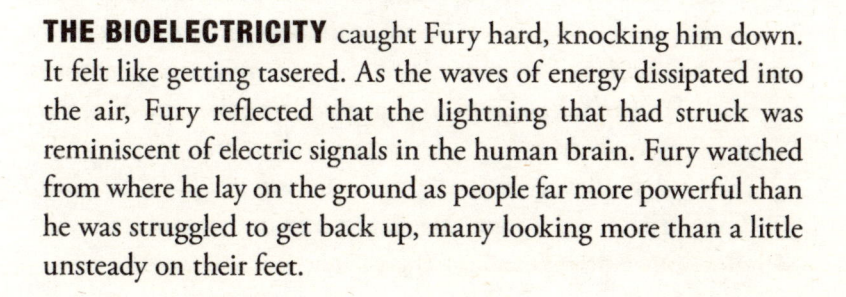

○──────○

THE BIOELECTRICITY caught Fury hard, knocking him down. It felt like getting tasered. As the waves of energy dissipated into the air, Fury reflected that the lightning that had struck was reminiscent of electric signals in the human brain. Fury watched from where he lay on the ground as people far more powerful than he was struggled to get back up, many looking more than a little unsteady on their feet.

"So many pretty little secrets. All now out in the wild. This will be fun to watch." The Orb wasn't even gloating. There was an almost scientific curiosity in his tone about what might happen next.

"What the hell does this mean?" Luke Cage muttered. "Why would…"

Iron Man took off without a word, his flying more than a little erratic.

"What just happened? Was I the only one who saw…? Who saw…? Oh no…" Spider-Man said as he staggered through the rubble.

Fury sat up, not entirely sure what was going on, trying to clear his thoughts through sheer willpower alone.

"By the spires of Asgard, I have a sister?!" Thor's voice broke through the confused babble of those around him.

Fury was aware of civilians further down the street, those that Steve and Magik had evacuated from the building. At first they appeared similarly dazed, but then he could hear shouts, arguing and the first inevitable punch was thrown.

"*Hulk*! *Smash*! *Stark*!" Hulk bellowed loud enough to kick up clouds of concrete dust then he leaped into the air after Iron Man. That wasn't good, but Fury knew that Tony could handle himself and had Hulk contingencies in place. He needed to concentrate on the matter at hand.

"Orb!" He recognized Midas's voice. "I don't know what the hell you just did but this is our chance! Move!"

Peering through the dust, Fury saw what he thought was Midas and the few remaining Mindless Ones making a break for it. Forcing himself to his feet, he made his way through the cloud expecting to find the Orb gone as well. Instead, as he emerged from the murk, he found the strange man just standing there holding the Watcher's eye.

"Put it down," Fury spat.

The Orb ignored him. He was watching Midas and the Mindless Ones disappear into the distance. Fury couldn't quite believe he was going to lose out on capturing them for the sake of a foot pursuit, but his priority had to be securing the eye. It had just incapacitated some of the more capable heroes in his Rolodex. Midas and his Mindless Ones could be dealt with later. He also suspected that Exterminatrix was long gone. He'd had better days. The Orb still hadn't moved.

"Put down the eye and put your hands on your head!" Fury shouted, his plasma pistol leveled at the odd figure. Fury was ready to turn the Orb's head/eye-thing into superheated steam if he so much as blinked. He wasn't sure what had happened here. From what he'd heard, what the Orb had said in the moments before he'd "detonated" the Watcher's eye, information had been forced into the heads of those in the blast radius. Unwanted information. Secrets. Given what Fury did—*had done*, he corrected—for a living, he saw this as an appalling violation. Secrets had been his bread and butter. "You're under arrest for murder."

"There's no need for that," the Orb told him calmly. "I'm not the one you're after. I want to know the next big secret. The same as you." It was said with such calm deliberation that Fury almost believed him despite the fact he was holding an eye carved from the Watcher's mutilated body. The Orb didn't put the eye down, but he did raise his hands. "I want to know who really murdered the Watcher. Because it certainly wasn't me."

CHAPTER THIRTEEN

FLESH SPELUNKING

EMMA WAS as much amused as she was disquieted. She was amused by Ant-Man having to crawl through bullet wounds to retrieve the mass of green glowing bullets—Black Panther was holding an evidence bag full of them. But she was still disquieted by the mass monster grave that was the cavern. She assumed that she had been brought along as a combat-capable telepath. Her job had been to communicate with the Moloids and now that was over she wanted to leave, but her compatriots were still intent on playing CSI Subterranea. She had never considered herself claustrophobic but during her time down here she had become very aware of the weight of the Earth above her. Also, had she known where she was going, she would have worn different shoes.

"I don't really think there's any question. They were all killed with the same gun," Ant-Man said, hefting another of the green glowing bullets, each larger than his tiny form, back towards where Emma was standing with Black Panther. They were close to one of the many stalagmites in the vast charnel cavern. She noted that

Black Panther was happy to let the tiny man come to him—royalty and all that.

"And the same gamma-irradiated bullets," Ant-Man added. Emma hadn't been in a hurry to touch them and Black Panther was being very careful in how he handled the bullets. She tried to remember if ants were naturally resistant to radiation. "But not all at the same time. I'd say the oldest corpses have been here for decades; the most recent, only a few years."

This was kind of obvious given the differing states of decay for each of the corpses, though it was difficult to be sure. Who really knew how monstrous physiologies worked? That said, it gave them an admittedly vague time frame to work with.

The green bullets made Emma nervous. If they were capable of doing that sort of damage to the monstrous big game all around her, then she suspected that they were capable of breaching her diamond skin.

"They're all creatures of the underworld. Some are familiar, some I've never seen before, which likely means no one has seen them before," Black Panther said. His words sounded arrogant to Emma, but she suspected that if half of what she'd heard about him was true, then it was probably simple fact.

"A bunch of dead monsters buried in the center of the Earth… What does that have to do with the Watcher being shot on the Moon?" She asked the question just to get thought processes rolling, regardless of how obvious it might sound. Assumptions of knowledge led to failure.

"Our killer has been at this for a very long time, right beneath our feet, which means they are quite skilled at staying hidden," Black Panther said. "Perhaps the Watcher died because he saw something he should not have."

"He saw the killer?" she asked.

"He was the Watcher. He saw everything. Even the Unseen."

Was "unseen" just a turn of phrase or did it have some kind of significance she was missing? Again, she couldn't shake the feeling that Black Panther knew more than he was saying. She was getting closer and closer to probing his thoughts telepathically, though she didn't relish the idea.

Looking around, Emma saw the Moloids crawling across the body of a vaguely humanoid monstrosity that had tentacles where a head should have been. *Was it so bad that such a creature was dead?* she asked herself. It could've been a gentle creature, helped shovel snow from its neighbor's drive, been kind to its mom… but it didn't really seem built that way.

Emma shivered. She couldn't shake the feeling that she was being watched, but that was impossible. The Watcher was dead.

FRANK WAS almost starting to like this dimension of gloom, despite the fact he couldn't shake the feeling that the shadows here were reacting to him somehow. He didn't think that boded well for his companion, whom he still hadn't warmed to. He hoped the whispers he heard in his head still belonged to his own mind.

"This one was shot from somewhere over there," Frank said, standing on yet another corpse of some extra-dimensional creature. It looked like a cross between a dragon from a kid's fairy tale and an insect. It was lying dead but preserved on one of the thick trunk-like nerve structures. He pointed out into the gloom at one of the distant floating rocks. There was a lot of guesswork involved—the gunshot wounds in dragon/insect things were presumably different to gunshot wounds in humans—but he was starting to get to grips with the differences and could make reasonably educated guesses at the distances involved. Also, it was where he would've shot from, and this shooter knew his business.

"Hard to tell in this place, but that looks to be almost four thousand yards away. Doesn't matter what kind of gun you've got, that's one hell of a shot." He pulled the Barrett up and looked through the scope at the distant rock. The more he looked at the rock, the more he liked it as the sniper's nest. Perhaps it was more like a hunter's hide. He lowered the oversized rifle. "There aren't many people alive who could make that shot. Not on Earth at least."

I'd say ten total. That includes me." He was reasonably sure, say ninety-five percent, that he hadn't done this.

"Common killers walking these sacred planes, I like this not," Strange said. Frank wondered if the anachronistic speech patterns had come before or after the wizard training. He suspected the latter.

"Funny. I can't tell if you're talking about the guy who did this, or me," Frank said. He wasn't enjoying that each statement coming out of Strange's mouth seemed like a passive-aggressive barb. Maybe he was getting sensitive in his old age; more likely it was just that other people were exhausting.

"Is there a difference?" Strange asked. If he meant it as an insult, he'd missed the mark. Whoever was killing these creatures was a good shot. There was nothing common about this killer. Hadn't Strange heard him when he'd said only nine other shooters?

"When I kill somebody, I don't hide it," Frank told him. *Unless I have good reason to do so*, he decided not to add.

"No, you most certainly do not," Strange said as though passing judgment.

Frank just stood and looked at him for a moment. There was nothing quite like getting crap from the guy you're trying to help. The way this guy dressed wasn't helping Frank take him seriously either.

"You can take me back to LA anytime you like, Doc," he said, poking Strange in the chest. "And then explain why to—"

"This place makes you uneasy," Strange said looking down at Frank's finger on his chest. It was clear where he thought the balance of power lay but if he was expecting obsequiousness from Frank then he was going to be sorely disappointed. "Good," Strange said, looking back up, having no problems meeting Frank's eyes. "I like you uneasy." He wasn't even bothering trying to mask his distaste now. "Ten people, you said." He turned and walked away along the nerve structure, his cloak billowing out of its own accord in the distinct lack of breeze. "Tell me, Castle," he threw over his shoulder. "Tell me every single name on that list."

"THIS IS a complete waste of time," Gamora said.

Bucky could see where she was coming from. Three very disparate people floating around near the galaxy's outer rim. It was like a bad joke. Told by nerds.

"There's nothing out here," Gamora persisted. Again she was right, which meant that they were missing something but he couldn't see what. Nothing in visual range, nothing on the long-distance scans. "Who was the fool who gave us these coordinates?"

"Someone who's not normally known for being a fool," Moon Knight said. He was defending their employer but Bucky could hear Spector becoming impatient as well. They had been following the vector they'd been provided for the better part of a day now. Loss of patience was understandable, though he couldn't shake the feeling that Gamora felt she had other more pressing concerns to attend to. Perhaps she did, but all the complaining was starting to rub Bucky up the wrong way.

"We should be back on Earth, searching for the Watcher's killer there. Turn the ship around, Moon Knight. I've had enough of this folly," Gamora said.

"No," Bucky said. He'd had enough as well. "We were told there was something here. So there is. Keep going, Spector." He wasn't hugely enamored with their current employer either but he had to admit they were competent.

"I don't remember agreeing to take orders from you, Winter Soldier," Gamora retorted and again she wasn't wrong. It was one of the problems with these kinds of missions: no clear chain of command and a lot of big egos. Bucky had always envied Steve's ability to manage the inherent problems of working with disparate and powerful people, except perhaps when working with Tony Stark, though even he'd come round in the end. It never worked as well when Bucky tried to do the same. He couldn't understand why others just didn't do their job, or why those same others seemed to sense something about him and wanted to keep him at arm's length.

"Then get out, Gamora," Bucky told her. He didn't necessarily disagree with anything she'd said and it wasn't ideal that certain elements of operational security meant that she had to be kept in the dark, but at the end of the day you're either part of the solution or part of the problem.

"Um, guys," Spector said, "technically it's my ship and I say—"

A number of thuds and the sound of scraping came from the hull of the ship. Not hard, but enough to get their attention.

"What the hell was that?" Bucky asked, suddenly tense. He'd come to the conclusion that he wasn't a natural space traveler.

"Something is hitting the ship's hull," Gamora said. Moon Knight having his own ship notwithstanding, Bucky was pretty sure that the green lady was the most seasoned space traveler out of the three of them. "Meteorites, most likely."

"Right," Spector said and then switched on the ship's powerful searchlights, illuminating the space directly in front of them as they heard more light impacts. "Except that these meteorites look an awful lot like a trail of shell casings floating in space."

Bucky stared out at the trail. There were thousands of the casings. Judging by their uniformity and positioning, it looked like the result of a significant, if one-sided, gunfight.

"I'd say we just found what we were looking for, people," Spector said.

The shell casings stretched out in a long irregular line, reminding Bucky of breadcrumbs.

"No," Bucky started, "what we're looking for…"

○━━━○

"**…IS WHATEVER** lies at the end of the trail."

Bucky had never been stupid. Perhaps a bit too enthusiastic about his work, but not stupid and he had the patience of a sniper. Unlike Gamora, who had the patience of a space viking. If I was disappointed in anyone—as I watched the surveillance feed from the camera and transmitter I'd had installed in Moon Knight's ship before I had dispatched them—it was Spector. Maybe it was who I'd teamed him up with, maybe it was the situation, or maybe it was just his reputed instability—though I'd seen no particular signs of it manifesting—but he was going to have to work much harder to impress me.

"Won't be long now," I said, touching the monitor screen to freeze the feed. I hadn't heard Andrew's approach; I'd just become aware of him. Not *all* my instincts were atrophying. He stood in the gloom behind me, in full uniform, anticipating my needs as ever. "We'll have visitors soon. Make sure everything's ready. Prepare for the worst."

"Yes sir. We always do," Andrew replied.

Yes we do, I mused, picking up one of the glowing, gamma-infused green rounds from the surface of my workstation.

"I'm afraid we're going to need a hell of lot more of these."

Andrew withdrew quietly and left me all alone, sitting amongst the machinery in the light of my monitor, alone with the world.

CHAPTER FOURTEEN

STAB COP, SMASH COP

THERE WAS a very definite noise that Logan's adamantium blades made when sliding in and out of their flesh sheaths.

"Hear that sound?" he asked.

Fury, surrounded by banks of monitors rising up around various workstations, was watching the interrogation of the Orb from the control room in Avengers Tower.

"That means you've got about three seconds to tell me what I wanna know," Logan continued. It was a crude threat, an even cruder technique—and it was a bluff. Once upon a time Fury knew it wouldn't have been. Logan had changed a lot in the many decades they'd known each other. A crude bluff or not, most people in close proximity to a claw-popping Wolverine tended to tell him what he wanted to know—and that was before you factored Hulk into the equation.

The Orb was sat on a bare bench in the holding cell, wearing sophisticated-looking manacles that covered both his hands. Hulk loomed over him, filling the small cell with the color green and a definite aura of impending loss of limbs. Fury didn't like being in enclosed spaces with Hulk, and he suspected that Logan wouldn't have been so keen if it wasn't for his unbreakable skeleton and lightning-fast regeneration. It was difficult to read a man whose head was one big eye, but the Orb didn't seem phased.

"A tortured schoolteacher and a deranged physicist," the Orb said. "Is this some sort of bizarre variation on the good cop, bad cop routine?" No, he wasn't bothered at all.

Fury had looked at the files that both S.H.I.E.L.D. and the Avengers had on the Orb. The psychometrics suggested that the ocular super villain should be sitting in a puddle of his own urine, telling Logan and Hulk everything he knew. Something had changed. This was not the same Orb.

"More like 'stab cop, smash cop.' Start talking, bub," Logan told him.

Hulk leaned in even closer to the Orb.

"Tell eyeball man to stop staring at Hulk!"

The problem with Hulk was that he might not be bluffing, or, depending on the variable level of Hulk-sentience, understand the concept of bluffing. Fury was worried that the Hulk was about to squeeze the Orb's head like a zit. The Hulk had not been happy after the eye-bomb had gone off. The last thing Fury needed was Hulk taking out his anger with Tony—sooner or later, everyone got angry with Tony—on what was, so far, their only significant lead. He had no idea what the beef was between Stark and Hulk, but it seemed prudent to keep them apart for the time being. There had been a distinct change in everyone who'd been caught up in the blast when the Watcher's eye had "detonated." They seemed distracted, preoccupied. Fury didn't like it, but he had to play the hand he was dealt.

"Two seconds," Logan growled, his claws already extended. Fury could see he wanted to use them. He wanted to cut the Orb just enough to get the information they needed; at one time, Logan would have actually done it and in other places—other times, really—Fury would've let him. They'd all changed for the better. Besides, it would've ended in an awkward conversation with Captain America that neither he nor Logan wanted to have. "Tell me what happened on the Moon. Tell me how you killed the Watcher."

It was too late. The Orb had called their bluff. Even so, Fury couldn't make the Orb, not even this new improved version, as the killer. As for Midas... That was S.H.I.E.L.D.'s can of worms as far as he was concerned. It wasn't his problem anymore. He'd inevitably get caught in the fallout, even though strictly speaking it hadn't been on his watch.

The Orb was just looking up at Logan as though he had not a care in the world. It was admittedly difficult for the Orb not to stare, but even then there weren't that many people prepared to go eyeball-to-eyeball with the Wolverine. It looked as though the Z-list super villain wasn't going to say anything. Fury opened his mouth to shut the interrogation down.

"I didn't come here to tell you anything," the Orb started. "You're not the one who can stop this. You want to know what happened? What is happening? Then put me in front of the man in charge. Bring me Nick Fury and I'll tell you everything."

Fury brought his hand up to his chin, thinking. So, the Orb thought Fury was the man who could "stop this," whatever this was. He was skeptical; however, he'd learned the hard way not to give villainous types what they wanted. Still—

"Cap to tower."

"This is Fury. Go ahead, Steve," Fury replied over the comms. He checked the position of Steve's transponder on the holographic topographical map projected over his workspace. Captain America was atop an apartment building five blocks south of their latest adventure in property damage. He could see Tony circling in the sky above.

"Trail's gone cold, no sign of Midas or his crew," Steve told him. Disappointing news, though not unexpected. "Stark says the energy signature we used to track the Mindless Ones is suddenly nowhere to be found. Midas must've caught on and figured out how to block it. We're back to square one." Fury smiled as the picture of Steve holding his hand to his ear as he they spoke over comms popped into his head. "Which means we're stretched pretty thin out here, Nick. If I'm going to have to canvass the entire planet, I'll need more bodies. Where the hell is everyone else?"

Fury raised an eyebrow. Steve had relaxed a lot as regards bad language. That said, it showed how frustrated he was that he'd said "hell." That was the thing about hero types. Everyone turned up for the big fight and then they went back to their own business. Still, Fury knew that the eye-bomb was a significant factor in the sudden drop off in available boots on the ground—or boots in the air, for that matter.

"It was a bomb full of secrets, Steve," Fury said. It seemed clear that it had affected his old friend, just as it had everyone else. "That's what the Orb unleashed on us today. The Orb. Still can't get over that part. Readings confirm that it's the Watcher's eye." He turned and looked down at the eye, laying on its bed of bloodied rags next to him. It was staring at Fury, but then he guessed it didn't have much of a choice in that. "The current theory, courtesy of Reed Richards, is that it acts as some sort of living storage device, recording everything the Watcher sees." Eye-to-eye, Fury couldn't look away from it. "The Orb was somehow able to access that info and basically throw our own secrets back at us like grenades. The good news is only those people in the immediate vicinity were affected. Bad news, half the team is suddenly out of action or barely functioning." With his chin resting on his hand, Fury found that he was somehow still stuck staring at the eye. "Thor, Spidey and Daredevil lit out right away and nobody's heard from them since. It's all I can do to keep Hulk from tearing Stark apart for some reason." And that could really be for any number of heinous activities on Tony's part, particularly anything from the time when he was still drinking. "I have no idea what sort of secrets people saw, but whatever they were it has thrown us into chaos. Which, I imagine, is exactly what the Orb was hoping for." It was a mess, and here he was sat on his throne-like Starktech chair staring at the Watcher's eye. He wasn't sure why, but he felt like the Fisher King.

"Is the Orb talking?" Steve asked. "Has he said anything?"

"Tell me, Steve, what did you see when the bomb exploded?" Fury asked.

Why didn't I just answer Steve's question? Fury wondered. He picked the eye up. It was surprisingly hard to the touch, like an ostrich's egg.

Steve didn't answer for a moment or two.

"That's not the mission right now, Nick," his old friend told him. Fury knew Steve well enough to know that whatever it had been had badly shaken him. "Call me when you've got more info. Cap signing off." The comms link went dead.

"See, even Captain America saw something—and Captain America doesn't have secrets." That wasn't completely true, but still. "But I do. More than I can count. So why didn't I see anything?" Fury asked the eye.

If Reed was right then the eye may have seen everything, recorded everything, knew everything. It remained silent. It was just an eye after all.

CHAPTER FIFTEEN

BRASS BREADCRUMBS

THE TRAIL of brass breadcrumbs had led them to another anticlimax. A barren planet, maybe a moon: Bucky didn't really know space stuff. He did know that he was wearing a space suit, but not digging doing so. Under the red-gold sky, the surface of the planet was a lifeless, cratered wasteland. There were a few low rocky hills and the blackened bare bones of spiked trees suggested that the planet had once been home to some kind of life. The shell casings notwithstanding, he half expected to find an alien goose to chase. He would be having words when they got back to Earth. *Did his current employer have a particular reason to keep him and Moon Knight off Earth?* It was solipsism, however. He knew he was competent, and good at what he did, but he couldn't imagine his absence would make that much of a difference; Gamora wasn't even Earth-based, and Moon Knight? He couldn't see it. So, for the time being he concentrated on looking around, on putting one foot in front of the other—which was trickier than it sounded because of the low gravity—and wishing that younger people were more taciturn.

"When you follow a trail of bullets through space. You expect to find, I don't know… something pretty crazy at the end of it," Spector said. Bucky wondered how practical attaching a cloak to a space suit was. "Some big, dead floating space god full of bullet holes. Maybe Galactus with a giant machine gun," he continued. Bucky wasn't sorry to miss this last suggestion. Galactus sounded way above his pay grade. "Instead we get a whole bunch of nothing. The bullet trail ends here but my ship's scanners show no life forms. Not even dead ones."

It was a fair point, even if it could have been communicated with significantly fewer words. *Had the shooter been using the world as target practice?* Bucky asked himself. That didn't make sense either. Worlds made pretty big targets; it wasn't like they were difficult to hit. It did make him look down at the ground, however. There were tiny craters everywhere.

"Radiation levels are extremely high." It appeared that Spector hadn't finished his monologue.

Bucky knelt to check out the craters.

"Did our killer wipe out an entire civilization? Is that what we're looking at here?" It seemed that Spector was planning to give voice to every single thought that ran through his grey matter.

As Bucky leaned in closer to one of craters, he could've sworn he saw a faint green glow. He drew his knife and used it to dig into the crater.

"There would still be ruins," Gamora said. As a daughter of Thanos she would know. Her father had certainly made enough ruins of his own. "Some signs of settlement. There is nothing here. Nothing but a dead world."

"Dead world," Bucky said to himself as he dug a surprisingly intact-looking green glowing bullet from the crater, except he was starting to suspect that it wasn't a crater at all.

"Look around you," Bucky said standing up and pointing at the small not-craters. "These are bullet holes. More bullets than I can count, all shot straight down into the dirt. Our killer was either a terrible shot or… oh hell, a damn good one." He imagined a figure in an armored space suit with some vast, rapid-fire, high-tech weapon just laying down round after round after round. They weren't craters. They were wounds. He turned to face the other two.

"We flew in from the planet's dark side, didn't we?" he asked Spector.

"Yeah, but what does that—" Spector started.

"Send up a camera, now." Bucky did not like where this was going. He didn't like the enormity of what he was suggesting, though he suspected that it was so huge as to be abstract to his very human brain. As Spector launched a disc drone into the air, the scale of the thing wasn't what bothered Bucky most. If he was right about what had happened here, there was a disturbing mix of old and new school about this. Incredible levels of technology appear to have been used to commit this crime but the way they had been utilized suggested, if not a limited imagination, then a limited frame of reference. It was like some kind of crazed stellar drive-by. It was so very human.

"I do not understand what you think you will find," Gamora said. "We have scanned the entire planet. There is nothing here."

"Nothing but a dead world, just like you said," Bucky told her. "A world surrounded by empty brass," he said, meaning the shell casings—though he doubted they were actually made of brass. "A world shot full of holes. Our killer doesn't miss. He never does." How could he with the level of technology on show? "Our bullets hit the ground because that's where he was aiming."

Spector opened up a holographic window to share the feed from the drone.

"We're looking for a corpse," Bucky added, quietly.

The world had a face. The face was screaming, locked in rictus. What they had taken for asteroids on the way in were in fact, blown-off chunks of planetary flesh.

"We're standing on it," Bucky finished. He had been right. He couldn't deal with the scale of this murder as anything other than an abstract. It was as high above his pay grade as a machine gun-toting Galactus or dead space gods. He suspected that Spector and Gamora were having similar problems in working through what had happened here. They were just staring at the holographic feed.

"A living world. Someone shot and killed a planet." Not surprisingly, Spector found his words first. "I'm gonna need a minute to process that." Though not silently, it seemed.

"I've seen worlds like this before," Gamora said. "Sentient ecosystems like Ego the living planet. The power it would take to slay one is almost unimaginable."

Bucky turned and walked away. It was certainly power that should have been way beyond anything a human could wield, short of a global cooperation to launch Earth's entire nuclear stockpile at something. He would have heard about such a thing, however, and that wasn't what had happened here. Everything about this pointed to a single shooter: a single shooter that could slay an entire world.

"Someone sure imagined it," Spector said, "Can't be many people in the known universe who could pull this off, am I right?"

Bucky knew he had trust issues—being experimented upon and then brainwashed into being an assassin will do that—but, paranoid or not, he could feel a web closing around him.

"I mean this sure has to narrow down our suspects?" Spector continued.

Bucky knew that if he was right about this being a human crime, then whomever was at the center of it had access to technology far in advance of the likes of Tony Stark or even Reed Richards. It also had to be someone capable of manipulating them all. To arrange for him to team up with people he didn't know and couldn't trust.

"It certainly does," Bucky said, agreeing with Spector as he pressed one of the buttons on his suit's wrist console. He wasn't going to kill Spector and Gamora, though part of him knew he should to save himself trouble further down the line. But without knowing whose strings they were dancing on—and he had his suspicions—he had to ditch them. It was a simple matter to remote access one of the smarter explosive devices he'd brought with him but left on the ship, because better to have and not need, and set the timer running.

"We need to get in touch with Black Panther. Tell him what we've found. This is some sort of cosmic killing spree we're looking at here. We're going to need to call in the... the... *everybody* on this." Spector sounded as though he was losing it. It made Bucky hesitate for a moment—but only a moment. If he was right, then the "everybody" Spector was talking about could already be compromised.

"Tell me again, Winter Soldier, exactly why was it we were sent here?" Gamora asked. He could hear the suspicion in her voice. Both she and Spector had been too intent on looking at the drone's feed to notice him walking away but Gamora was already turning. "And by whom? Who knew of this murder?"

Bucky triggered the teleport device he'd "borrowed" from the Avengers before Gamora had finished turning. He had taken the device because he hated going anywhere he didn't know how to get away from. No matter how angry they would be at his disappearing act, they would be even more angry when Spector's ship blew up. They might even start to suspect him: with his history of brainwashing, even he couldn't rule himself out as the shooter until he could rule himself out as the shooter, and he wasn't sure how to do that. If he was the killer, however, he was just a weapon and he was pretty sure he knew who was pulling the trigger. The person in question was not beyond implanting mind control contingencies in those they manipulated. To be on the safe side, Bucky decided to take a "murder first, seek corroborating evidence second" approach. After all he was an assassin, not a detective.

CHAPTER SIXTEEN

KILLER

FURY WAS still sat at his borrowed workstation in the Avengers Tower. He was still staring at the eye, lit only by the light of the monitors and wondering why the secret bomb hadn't affected him. He had so many secrets, he would have thought his presence would have significantly increased the "bomb's" blast radius.

What am I missing here? He knew this was getting him nowhere. Instead, he was just getting more and more frustrated.

Logan's grizzled image appeared on the largest of his screens.

"Fury, you better get in here. This eyeball guy's ready to start talking." If Logan was concerned about the sight of Fury handling the Watcher's gouged-out eyeball, he kept it to himself.

"Yes," Fury told Logan and then cut the vid-comms link with a touch of the holographic control panel. The screen blinked off. "That's what I'm afraid of." This last comment was much quieter. Talking out loud was a dangerous trait for a superspy, but it really helped his "process," as the younger ones called it. "An eye full of secrets," he paused just for a moment, "but last I checked the Watcher had two. So, who's got the other one?"

He was jolted out of his reverie by a flickering golden light from behind his chair.

"What the hell...?" Spinning around, he saw an armored figure—no, not armor, just a space suit with no helmet, almost a shadow against the slinky-like tube of golden light they were emerging from. The figure had a bulky rifle strapped across his back. Then Fury recognized him.

"Bucky? Where did you—"

Bucky genuinely gave him a chance. He hadn't stepped out of the teleporter's quantum tunnel, now collapsed, with a weapon in his hand. Fury could tell, however, that Bucky was about to reach for one. Fury made the decision to go for his own. He reached for the plasma pistol and had just about torn it from its holster but Fury was no match for one of the deadliest, if not *the* deadliest assassin of the Cold War. Not in a fair fight. It was one of the reasons Fury always tried to avoid fair fights.

Time slowed down. Fury saw the muzzle flash, then felt the sledgehammer blow to the chest. He fell back, it felt like his chest was on fire. The Watcher's eye went flying. He hit the ground. He became aware that he was no longer holding his pistol and that he was coughing up a lot of fluid.

"Bucky... why..." Fury desperately tried to reach for his plasma pistol. It was just a few inches away from his fingertips.

He fell into shadow as Bucky stood over him.

"No more hiding, Nick." Bucky raised his weapon and fired again, the muzzle flash throwing the tower's control room into harsh relief. Fury screamed as his hand was blown apart. "No more running from our sins."

Fury wanted to call out. Wanted Hulk and/or Logan to come running to his rescue. That was their job, right? Even if they had heard the shot, which was unlikely from where they were in the holding cell, even if Hulk tore through walls to get here, Fury knew they'd never reach him in time. Still, at least he knew who the killer was now.

"No more turning a blind eye," Bucky said, drawing what looked like a thin-bladed machete from a sheath.

Through the pain, Fury could just about make out Bucky's words but he had no idea what they meant. It sounded like Bucky had lost it. He'd been a teen soldier, fought in one of the most vicious wars the world had ever seen, been witness to the horrors of the Nazis. Stalinist Soviets had experimented on him, brainwashed him and sent him out to kill his own people. It had only been Steve vouching for his friend that had convinced a skeptical Fury not to have Bucky live out the rest of his life under comfortable house arrest after the Winter Soldier had been rescued and de-programmed. Fury had always thought, even during the war, that Bucky had liked the killing a little too much. Now it seemed the Winter Soldier had turned serial killer. Fury could imagine few situations more dangerous, particularly if Bucky was capable of hunting game as big as the likes of the Watcher.

All of this was going through his mind in what he knew were the last few moments of his life. Too little, too late, and nobody would ever know…

"Bucky," Fury managed. He thought about pleading with Bucky but it wasn't really how he was wired. Besides Fury had lived a long life full of lies, so he decided to tell the truth at this last moment. "I never liked you, you sonuva…" Then he coughed up more fluid.

"No more, Nick," Bucky said and raised the short sword.

The blade came down. The cybernetic strength of the Winter Soldier's bionic arm pushed through flesh, bone and sinew, severing Fury's spinal column.

Somehow Fury was still conscious. He was struck by the inane thought that he'd heard about this happening; that you were still aware for a few moments after your own decapitation.

As Bucky lifted his head up by the hair, Fury looked down at his own headless body. These final few moments seemed to stretch on and on. He was already dead, but he prayed for it to be over.

From his vantage point he could see Bucky holding the Watcher's eye in his other hand.

"No more secrets," Bucky said.

Fury welcomed the darkness as it claimed him.

CHAPTER SEVENTEEN

TOO LITTLE, TOO LATE...

FRANK DIDN'T have many friends before he became the Punisher. Regardless of the extent he went to ensure they weren't killed needlessly, it had never been a good idea to get too close to his men. At the end of the day the mission outweighed the cost, or so he had thought. Looking back now, the war had been a waste of resources and life. A war waged in bad faith, for the wrong reasons and fought, for the most part, by the reluctant.

His friends had been his wife and his kids. It was so difficult to remember now. It was so long ago. Another life. He had been another person—or at least he had convinced himself that had been the case. War, however, was a stain on the soul; he could never shake the feeling that Maria had sensed that about him. Realized that he had been damaged, though that could have happened even before the war. He was self-aware enough to know that he had embraced combat a little too readily. Perhaps he had thought that friends would come later, or perhaps the self-contained unit that was his family would have proved to be enough, but then they were taken. One bloodstained moment when the sound of bullets had echoed through New York's concrete canyons, when Central Park had become a war zone, when he had failed to protect his family...

He'd had few friends and nobody else whom he had trusted since Microchip—his confidante, quartermaster and technical support—had been killed. It was safer that way for all concerned. He made an exception for one of the few people he had come close to liking: someone he'd known since the war, someone who'd enabled him, and someone he'd worked with. Someone who was on the list of ten shooters, along with himself. The list that Frank had just related to Doc Strange.

Strange had an unerring ability to zero in on the most aggravating thing to say. With eight other names to choose from, of course Strange had picked on Frank's friend. In terms of power, the wizard may have been a magical nuclear bomb but now Frank had a very powerful rifle pointed at the wizard's face. Frank was moments away from finding out if Strange could cast faster than the time it took a .50 caliber bullet to turn his face into a bloody cavity. To give Strange credit, he was handling looking down the barrel of the Barrett quite well, which suggested that he at least had a contingency.

"You're talking crazy," Frank told him, "I suggest you stop." They were standing on the corpse of yet another extra-dimensional demon, its body lying on one of the vast, branching, nerve-like structures suspended in this realm's hungry void. The shadows shifted and crawled in time with Frank's anger, as though they were reaching for Strange. Frank knew that if he shot the wizard he was stranded here, but then you had to have faith in your convictions, right?

"I'm Doctor Strange. Crazy's sort of my second language but just because it sounds crazy doesn't mean I'm wrong."

If "crazy" was his second language then Frank suspected that narcissism was his third.

"You don't know what the hell you're talking about. That's why you're wrong," Frank spat. Even as he said it, he knew it wasn't exactly the world's greatest counterargument. Some of this was just territorialism. He didn't want people he didn't know— and didn't particularly like—talking crap about people he did know and who Frank came as close to liking as he ever did with anyone. Still, there had been eight other choices on that list. Why did Strange have to start pushing his buttons?

"You're the expert when it comes to mass murder, Frank. If you have a better explanation for what's going on around here, I'm all ears," Strange said. He may look convincingly heroic and mysterious with his self-billowing cloak, but Frank noticed that the wizard had actually taken a few steps back, and he was sure that he'd seen a few beads of sweat. Perhaps magic was not quite the protection against mass-meeting-explosive-chemical-reaction that Strange might otherwise have liked.

"Someone's been killing monsters in your backyard. Someone's been doing your job for you better than you and that pisses you off," Frank growled. That was the thing of it. What was the motive for the destruction of these creatures?

Frank was raised a Catholic—though he knew he was pretty far from God's grace nowadays—and these things looked like the illustration of demons from medieval bestiaries. Maybe he shouldn't judge by appearances, but it was difficult to imagine these monsters wishing anyone well before the mysterious shooter had put them down, and that was before you factored in their environment. This whole place felt somehow malevolent, which was perhaps why the realm seemed to be reacting so strongly to him. You couldn't come up in a place like this and think everything was sweetness, light and happy unicorns. Either the shooter was protecting someone or something from these creatures, they were hunting big game, or they were some kind of serial killer preying on demons. Of all the possible motives, killing to protect something seemed like the most likely explanation. Frank's understanding of Doctor Strange's bullshit job title as "Sorcerer Supreme" suggested that the shooter was indeed doing this clown's job.

"What pisses me off," Strange began, "is being lied to." And he did look pissed off. A vein was standing out on his forehead. This suggested to Frank that Strange was struggling to be as patient with him as he was with the wizard. Strange stabbed his finger past the barrel of the oversized rifle. Frank almost shot him. He couldn't be sure if Strange was casting a spell or if pointing was just the precursor to some kind of tirade. "Has it been so long since anyone dared to lie to the almighty Punisher that you've forgotten what it feels like? Or are you just too used to lying to yourself?"

That hit home.

"I bet this big guy we're standing on thought he couldn't die from a gunshot either, right up until the moment he did." It was face saving and Frank knew it. Strange was arrogant but he wasn't stupid. Frank's friend existed—even more than he himself did—in a world of shadows and lies. If anyone could pull this off, and manipulate both Strange and himself to dance on the end of their strings, it was Frank's "friend," the man who had sent them to this bizarre and godforsaken place.

Frank slung his rifle, taking some pleasure in watching Strange heave a sigh of relief. He knew he was being petty, but this tights-wearing medieval throwback was a major jerk.

"It would appear our mysterious killer has been very busy for a very long time and someone knew right where to send us to pick up his trail. All of us. We have not been told the whole truth," Strange said as he turned away from Frank, his cloak carrying him off the corpse of the latest dead demon and down onto the trunk-like nerve structure.

Frank clambered down off the corpse after him.

"You don't trust anybody else? Good," Frank told the wizard as they strode across the root/nerve structure. It was glowing with dots of bioluminescence that formed complicated spiral patterns—perhaps a defense against the hungry shadows. "You said *all of us.* Please don't tell me there's others?" He'd used what little patience he had for "team-ups" in not splattering Merlin junior's brains all over the void.

"Ha! If you thought this little team-up of ours was awkward, just wait until you meet the rest of the gang," Strange said over his shoulder.

Frank decided right there and then that if that duck-guy was there, he was going to put two into his beak just on general principle.

"Whatever, but right now that person you don't trust is exactly the one we need to be talking to," Frank said. It was as if both of them were afraid to say the name, because if Strange was right then the foundations of the world that they thought they lived in were about to crumble away.

It was time to go and see what Nick Fury had to say for himself.

CHAPTER EIGHTEEN

WALKIN' ON THE MOON

BUCKY STEPPED out of the golden slinky light of the collapsing quantum tunnel and onto the surface of the Blue Area of the Moon.

He knew he didn't have long. Literally everyone would come after him. There was a momentary pang as he thought about how Steve would feel when he found out that his best friend, strained though that friendship could be at times, had apparently killed one of his oldest friends. Even during the war, Steve had never really had the stomach for these kinds of operations. Nor did he have the gamesmanship, because Bucky knew that was what they were doing right now: playing someone else's sick game. You could complain about the rules or you could play better. What he was planning was more than a little risky but he intended to do the latter: he would outplay his opponent. He just had to stay several steps ahead of the "good guys." He knew the likes of Black Widow and Wolverine would be out for blood. He just didn't know what Steve would do. After all, even Captain America can only give so many second chances.

"Can't be far now," Bucky said, checking the motion detector on his personal scanner. Nothing. He shifted modes: no quantum disturbances that the handheld device could detect. This meant that nobody was following him using teleportation technology. Finally, he checked the signal trace he was running. Pay dirt. It was perhaps too easy—as though this puppet master wanted him to find it—but that was okay too. He would settle in at the destination. He could bide his time.

Standing on the surface of the Moon, one of the Watcher's eyeballs hanging from his belt next to his holster and Nick Fury's dripping severed head in his left hand, he decided it was time to bait his—admittedly rudimentary—trap. He activated the spacesuit's wrist comms.

"I know you're out here. I know you can hear me. I'm coming." He held Fury's severed head up so the built-in lens of the comms module could pick it up. "And I'm bringing a friend."

He took one last look around the blue lunar wasteland. He was a long way from Shelbyville, Indiana. Then he activated the teleportation device and was gone as though he had never existed.

CHAPTER NINETEEN

A MIND FULL OF CATS

EMMA FROST still wasn't loving the travel arrangements for this mission. She was even missing the X-Men's Blackbird. The Wakandan drilling machine was now swimming through molten rock. Emma wasn't sure if her discomfort was psychosomatic—all she could see outside was the white light of lava—or if she really was feeling the heat bleeding through the machine's hull. Still, she couldn't let on that she was nervous. Team-ups were like poker games. Never let them see you sweat, even if you are swimming through a lava field.

An incoming message icon blinked on her control panel. She clicked it and started reading.

"You guys seeing this?" she asked.

Ant-Man, now returned to his normal size, invaded her personal space by appearing over her shoulder and reading the message from her console despite the fact that he could have read it on his own. He still smelled faintly of subterranean carrion. "Avengers global alert," she continued for the benefit of Black Panther, whom she hoped was concentrating on piloting this infernal machine. "One suspect in custody. Multiple others at large." She rolled her eyes at "multiple others."

"Doctor Midas," Ant-Man said, reading off her screen, "I've heard of him. Super rich. Super weird. I maybe buy him for the Watcher job but not for the charnel house of dead monsters that we've just seen."

Except that "super rich, super weird" were red flags for her.

"Men that wealthy tend to get bored quite easily," she pointed out. She left it unsaid that sometimes they dress up like pussycats and fight crime. "Do you know what a very wealthy, very bored man is capable of?" She didn't even wait for an answer. "Absolutely anything, darling. Hunting underground monsters for sport? If only they were all so quaint."

She could tell Ant-Man was not convinced, but for all his intelligence and ability—and Emma had to concede he was as capable as he was irritating—his sensibilities were very proletarian. Black Panther knew exactly what she was talking about, however. Big game hunting underground monsters was no stretch with the right connections. Had she thought of it, she would have even considered it as an amusement for the club's members back when she had been the White Queen.

"In the Hellfire Club, I saw people used as poker chips by men with more money than—"

"Uh, T'Challa, we're coming up on the surface, you might want to slow down," Lang said. If anything, the drilling machine was speeding up. "T'Challa?"

The drilling machine burst through the surface in gouts of molten rock. Emma was pushed back into her seat and Lang hung on for dear life as rocket motors folded out from the body of the craft and ignited—turning the burrowing machine into a rocket.

"Expanding orbital scans. All Wakandan satellites at full capacity." The voice came from the vehicle itself. Whether it was an on-board artificial intelligence or part of a larger Wakandan AI hive mind, Emma didn't know. What she did know was that she was sick and tired of the mushroom treatment from Black Panther.

She had not wanted to do this but felt she'd had little choice. There was only so much thrashing around in the dark she was prepared to tolerate. It was undignified.

Emma steeled herself. She knew that she would be facing Wakandan-level anti-telepathy countermeasure technology, as well as T'Challa's own formidable mental discipline. She pushed in with her mind, visualizing her own not-inconsiderable telepathic power as a lance of white force penetrating T'Challa's cranium.

Well now, she thought at him, *and what is this we're up to all of a sudden, Mr. Tall, Dark and Mysteri*— Then she was screaming. Hands clutching her head as her mind was savaged.

"Best stay out of there, Ms. Frost," Black Panther told her.

"Your mind is like a bear trap," she spat, "wrapped in barbed wire… that someone set on fire." It was hyperbole. Probing his mind had had been like getting scratched, a lot, by a big cat. It wasn't just the tech built into his suit. Something ancient, primal and ferocious lived in his mind.

"What do you know that we don't, Panther?" Lang demanded. He sounded angry on her behalf. It would have been sweet had he not failed so utterly to endear himself to her since she had been manipulated into working with him. Besides, she was too busy trying to regain her composure and processing what she'd learned when her probe had, for a moment, slipped past Black Panther's defenses.

"Nothing," T'Challa said. "That's what worries me."

As they rocketed into the night sky, Emma knew he was telling the truth. T'Challa knew little more than they did. He had been playing poker as much as she had but he was disquieted, perhaps even frightened. He did not like how high the stakes were becoming. He did not like were this was going.

"Another alert coming in," Lang told them. He'd made it back to his seat and strapped himself in. The Moon was huge through the windscreen. Its silver light filled the cockpit, washing out all the other colors. "What the hell? This can't be right." Emma could hear it in Lang's voice, could practically taste his shock with her sensitive, recently lacerated, mind. "It says Nick Fury is dead."

Well that changes things, she decided. If nothing else, her already weird day was becoming more interesting.

CHAPTER TWENTY

AN ANGRY MUSTELID

THE INTER-DIMENSIONAL space between realms was red and you walked it like a path. It got you places quick, Frank conceded, but he still would've preferred a muscle car, an armored van or a Harley. On the bright side, however, at least he wasn't in a helo. He'd been in enough helicopter crashes to last a lifetime. The odd thing about the path that Strange had him walking was that, like an actual path, he could see ahead: see where they were going through the red-lit interspatial murk. It looked like some kind of control room. There was a headless body lying on the floor, the Hulk standing over it. Wolverine was kneeling down next to the body. His claws were popped, glinting in the weak light from the monitor screens and holographic displays.

Frank had Wolverine filed under "occasionally useful-if-difficult." However, the murderous mustelid's hypocrisy bothered him. He was every bit the killer Frank was—he was standing over a headless body, after all—but Wolverine liked to pretend his scat didn't stink.

Hulk, on the other hand, was walking collateral damage.

Frank exchanged a look with Strange. The wizard nodded. Frank swapped out the magazine on his Barrett for the special load rounds.

He could hear words coming from the control room. Faint, distant, but clear enough to get the meaning. As they got "closer," Frank started to suspect he knew who the body belonged to as well.

"...never liked him much when he was alive. Now how the hell did he even get—" Wolverine was saying.

Wolverine's words confirmed what Frank had suspected. Wolverine and Hulk were responsible for the corpse. It sounded personal.

Frank and Strange stepped off the red path and back into the real world. Wolverine and Hulk turned to face them. The control room looked like some kind of high-tech nest. Exactly the sort of thing Frank expected from "super hero" folks. They were the kind of people who'd never eaten MREs in a sewer.

"Um… this ain't what it looks like, fellas," Wolverine said—but his claws were still out. Frank suspected a stalling tactic. The Hulk was practically growling, his bulk coiled like a spring—a massive green spring—ready to pounce.

Frank didn't hesitate. The Barrett came up to his shoulder. Strange was already casting. Frank caught the wizard's glowing red eyes in his peripheral vision.

"Neither is this," Strange said. *It didn't even make any sense*, Frank thought.

"What the hell?" Wolverine sounded more surprised than anything. He was wrapped in glowing red bands of energy that lifted him off the floor. "Hulk smas—" The order to his big green companion was cut off in a grunt of pain as the bands gagged him as well.

Sure, you handle the angry weasel, I'll take on the fricking Hulk, Frank thought. He fired the Barrett from the shoulder six times in quick succession. The recoil shock absorber in the oversized rifle's butt did what it could, but he'd shot so rapidly the recoil was cumulative. He staggered back. One shot missed. It didn't matter that the Hulk was close enough that the other five hit. The Hulk even walked into them, barely reacting to the impact of the bullets, coming at Frank head on. After all, as far as he was concerned he was impervious to even .50 caliber fire. Frank let the rifle hang down his front on its sling, one hand still on the grip, the other reaching for one of his pouches.

"Was that supposed to hurt, little man?" the Hulk asked. All these super jerks did like their "puny human" speeches. Frank liked them as well. The longer Hulk was talking, the more time he wasn't pulling heads off.

"No," Frank said. He had his smartphone in his free hand. "But this might." He pressed send.

He had found the special rounds in the inventory of an arms dealer he'd killed. They were experimental bullets nicknamed "Splats." Starktech from back when Stark Industries had been an arms company. They were basically a concentrated form of plastic explosive mixed with a powerful adhesive that stuck to a target while the part of the Splat that was exposed to the air hardened to provide a degree of tamping. In effect, each Splat was a small but powerful shaped charge.

The Splats exploded and blew the Hulk through a wall. Strange brought his other hand up, made a few gestures and raised some kind of mystic shield to protect them from the back-blast that made it through the explosive's tamping. Frank was impressed with the special bullets, not least because they had given him an unobscured view of Midtown. It was nice to be home, though he was pretty sure that they were in Avengers Tower, which wasn't great.

He spent a disproportionate amount of time working out countermeasures for costumed clowns. Sooner or later someone always decided that he was the bad guy, rather than the symptom of a broken system that they were all part of. He liked the look of surprise on their faces when it didn't go their way. He liked to remind them of what normal humans were capable of. After all, he'd gone toe-to-toe with Doctor Doom as well. Still, it didn't always work out in his favor.

Any pleasure he had taken in putting the Hulk through a wall drained away as he kneeled by the headless corpse. The ID in the corpse's wallet told him what he'd already suspected. There was only ever going to be one guy dressed in a suit that Dean Martin would've been jealous of in this tower.

"No such thing as retired, is there, Nick?" he said quietly. They went all the way back to Frank's second and darkest tour of duty. He'd been a Marine Raider, in theory working for Marine Forces Special Operations Command—but in practice he had mostly been doing the CIA's Special Operations Group's bidding. He looked up at Wolverine, still suspended by Strange's magic. Frank felt disgusted. They had heard the mutant confess as they were inbound. He couldn't believe Wolverine would try and lie his way out of the murder. He could see where Fury and the mutant's paths would have crossed. He knew that Fury pissed people off, manipulated them, used them; hell, even Frank had once tried to kill him, though that had been a mistake. He didn't have a lot of time for Wolverine but he'd expected better. Still the list of possible shooters had diminished by one.

Wolverine was twitching in the red bands. Veins standing out, teeth grinding together, sweat running out from under his mask. He looked as though he could break through the magical energy with sheer determination and orneriness. If Wolverine got free he wouldn't make the same mistake that Hulk had. There would be no hesitation, just diced wizard and vigilante.

"Hulk may be an idiot, Strange, but that trick will only work once. Unless you got any more ideas, we had better move fast."

"Working on it," Strange said. One hand was pointed at Wolverine; Frank guessed the wizard had to maintain the spell. With his other hand Strange appeared to be conjuring more red light and shadow. His eyes were glowing again as he peered into the magical energy as though looking for something.

A cursory examination suggested the head had been cut off with a sharp blade; Wolverine's claws, that made sense. It didn't explain the gunshot wound to the chest, however, or the second gunshot wound that had blown Fury's hand off. It wasn't unknown for Wolverine to carry a gun, but it was certainly unusual. Frank glanced around, and the gun's whereabouts was not immediately apparent either. Nor was Fury's head. Frank wondered briefly if the Hulk had eaten it, but alarm bells were starting to ring. What if, despite the apparent admission that Frank had heard on their way in and their presence over the cooling body, Honey Badger and the Jolly Green Giant weren't actually the guilty parties?

"We should bring the body with us. It's worth a closer look," Frank said standing up.

"No, it isn't," Strange replied immediately.

Well thanks for giving it some consideration, Frank thought. He couldn't wait to get back to killing human traffickers. This team-up bull was always the same: ridiculous clothes and even more ridiculous egos.

Strange now had a floating, glowing eyeball in the middle of his forehead as he traced symbols of light in the air before him with more strange hand gestures.

"But there's something else here that certainly is," the wizard said, then the control room vanished and they were standing in a holding cell. In a moment of paranoia Frank thought it was a setup—that Strange and some of his super-pals had decided he was surplus to requirements and had just teleported him into a supermax prison somewhere. Then he saw the actual prisoner.

"Hello. Are you here to kill me?" The prisoner wore manacles that completely covered his hands and a ridiculous red costume with white booties. By far the strangest thing, however, was the massive eyeball the prisoner had for a head. Frank started reviewing all the decisions he'd made that had led him to this point.

"No," Strange said.

Frank suspected that the wizard was jumping to conclusions.

"Maybe," he offered instead.

"Get up, you're coming with us," Strange added.

That just about made sense to Frank in terms of how his day was going. Now eyeball-guy was part of the team.

"Someone stole my eye, didn't they?" eyeball-guy asked.

Really? Frank thought, the distaste he was experiencing written across his face.

"Looks like someone stole everything but your eye," Strange said. As he did so, floating lines of liquid light extended from the wizard's hands. There was a clicking noise from the manacles and they floated off eyeball-guy's hands.

"He did send you," eyeball-guy said, and by now Frank was assuming that "Eyeball Guy" was the punk's actual super-name. "I can tell, but not to kill me."

It was ridiculous because presumably all this guy could do was stare—maybe that was his super-power—but Frank was not enjoying the guy looking at him at all.

"The truth is you don't even know who you're working for. You haven't seen him. Not truly," eyeball-guy said.

Frank wasn't really sure how this guy was talking. He didn't like the squishy noise he made as he did so. The problem was that the person who'd asked him to do this favor, to work with Strange, who'd sent him on this ridiculous path, was lying in the control room of Avengers Tower about a head shorter than he had been this morning. Frank and Strange were working for themselves now.

"You haven't seen the Unseen," eyeball-guy continued. Frank was already done with this cryptic nonsense. "I have. I saw him… in the eye. I saw his sins. I saw when he… I didn't know one man could kill so many things."

Frank frowned, the look of distaste momentarily gone from his face. It sounded like eyeball-guy was talking about their shooter: the person responsible for all the inter-dimensional demon killings. He was implying that it was the shooter, this *Unseen*, pulling their strings. It made sense. Fury was no fool and if he had gotten on to the trail of this Unseen, it was likely the reason he was now dead. Wolverine hadn't seemed to like Nick and wasn't a particularly bright sea otter. It wouldn't take much for some criminal mastermind to manipulate him and the Hulk into doing their dirty work.

There was a roaring noise followed by the unmistakable sound of someone—something—smashing through steel supports and reinforced concrete. The whole building was shaking. Frank wondered why the Avengers hadn't Hulk-proofed their own building.

"The Hulk is in the building. We don't have time for this," he said, drawing one of his .45s and pushing it up against eyeball-guy's eye/head-thing for a little bit of extra-visceral vitreous persuasion. He didn't like the membranous give against his old .45's barrel. "Start making sense or we see what happens when you go blind."

"Castle—" Strange started but stopped, perhaps sensing that Frank was long since out of patience. In addition, the destructive sounds of the imminent Hulk suggested that they were quickly running out of time.

"I hear it calling me. The eye. It likes me. It likes the way I look at it," eyeball-guy said. It didn't make a lick of sense but Frank could hear the fear in his squishy voice now. He didn't think eyeball-guy was lying. "If I try real hard, if I listen with all my might... I think I could lead you to it."

Frank lowered his .45, re-holstering it, aware of Strange heaving another sigh of relief at this. Frank knew he had eyeball-guy's cooperation now.

"The only problem is it's going to want to show you the truth, and you're going to want to look, but believe me some things should never be seen."

Eyeball-guy wasn't wrong about that, but then it was a lesson Frank had learned on his first tour.

CHAPTER TWENTY-ONE

MASTER OF PUPPETS

"**TELEMETRY COMPLETE,**" the vehicle previously known as Black Panther's drilling machine told them. "New coordinates determined," the now-a-rocket-ship added.

What new coordinates? Emma wanted to know. She was standing in the cockpit between the seated Black Panther and Ant-Man. The former was piloting the ship. The latter was doing something technical-looking with a holographic control panel. She liked the view of the Earth from up here. The world was a living map of blues, greens and browns; above, the clouds formed ever-changing, ephemeral continents of their own. She was pretty sure she could see Wakanda from here.

"Whatever this signal is, it looks like you've been tracking it for quite some time," Ant-Man said to Black Panther.

"Mind telling us what hell is going on, Panther, or should we just start guessing?" Emma asked. She understood that the three of them didn't know each other and therefore couldn't trust each other. She even understood how T'Challa had no choice, given his position, but to play the alpha in any situation. She had, after all, met more than her fair share of men like him in the past. The mushroom treatment, however, was starting to feel more like showmanship than anything else. Once she could have easily eviscerated his brain but her powers were somewhat diminished these days. Even so, and even with his defenses and the spirit of the primal cat that lived in his head, if Black Panther didn't start playing straight with them she would find a way in. After all technology and mysticism could only get you so far.

It was a moment or two before Black Panther answered them. Emma suspected that he was deciding how much to tell them.

"I'm tracing a signal from a call I received. The call that led us to the center of the Earth." he finally said.

Emma could hear the tone of resignation in his voice. She suspected this was the unvarnished truth. She had no doubt T'Challa was a skilled diplomat but, despite what people thought, that did not mean he was a skilled liar. She knew liars. She had learned from the best.

The Wakandan rocket ship was still rising up into the night sky.

"That would mean—" she started as she became aware of light above them.

"That all this time we've been searching for something unseen without realizing that all we needed to do was open our eyes and look up," Black Panther finished.

Emma didn't know much about satellites but the one she was staring at looked sophisticated. As in, more sophisticated than the ship they were in. As in, a higher level of technology than Wakanda—the most technologically advanced place on Earth. It was formed of tech that looked like it could give the Kree a run for their money.

The satellite was a pillar spotted with engines and tanks. A ring—which she guessed was a habitation area—revolved around the central shaft of the pillar. Two massive rectangular sails, stretching out to obscure the heavens, topped the pillar. She guessed the sails collected solar energy and/or other forms of power from the cosmos.

"Satellite detected," the ship said. *Really?* Emma thought. "Registration not found. Launch history, undocumented. Point of origin, unknown," the ship continued in its soft Wakandan accent.

Black Panther brought the ship into land on a vertical pad on the main shaft underneath the ring. She had wanted to ask him if he was sure, but she was starting to suspect that coming here had been the point of the exercise. She did not like being played and they were definitely being played.

o——————o

EMMA WOULD have described the interior of the satellite as cavernous, which, given the amount of time she had just spent in an actual cavern, was more than a little tedious. She would have described the decor as alien-industrial. It was a strange mix of huge machines made of a black metal that she did not recognize—indeed, she struggled to guess their purpose at all—and very human-looking user interfaces. She suspected that the tech on show came from a number of different advanced alien cultures. In short, the tech in here had been salvaged or looted and then cobbled together in such a way that humans, or a species very like humans, could use. *Curiouser and curiouser.*

"I'm not sure what scares me most," Ant-Man said, "the fact that this satellite was so hard to find or so easy to break into."

Of course they hadn't broken in: they had been invited in. They were walking down a high-ceilinged hall somewhere in the satellite's habitation disc. Huge coils of concertinaed tubing hung overhead. Dials attached to the tubes were of a sufficient size to suggest: "here be giants."

"Emma, can't you use some of those mutant brain powers of yours to figure out if we're alone in here or not?" he added.

The sounds of their steps echoed with every footfall, except Black Panther's—his suit seemingly absorbing the sound.

"My powers aren't what they used to be, Ant-Man, but my common sense works just fine. No way are we alone," Emma told him. Besides, she'd tried. She had thought she'd detected something;

a mental presence, the fleeting, slippery essence of a human-like mind, but it was gone as soon as she thought she had sensed it. There was something eerie about the place. Sepulchral, even.

"We've just followed the trail of a murderer from ten miles beneath the Earth to thousands of miles above it," Emma said, turning towards Ant-Man as they walked. Black Panther moved ahead a little, his head on a swivel as he prowled. "If we can do that, you better believe that we're not the only ones."

"We were never alone," Black Panther said quietly. His voice didn't echo like Emma's and Ant-Man's had. "At the moment that is the only thing we know to be true. Even with the Watcher dead, someone is always watching." Then he stopped. Holding his hand up, head cocked as though he was listening for something.

Emma felt it as well. There was someone here, someone with them that hadn't been there a moment ago. The hairs on the back of her neck stood up. They were being watched. She reached out with her mind, quiet stealthy tendrils of thought. There were two of them. Her tendrils recoiled from one: she detected real power, significant mental defenses that tasted like magic. The other mind was a cold, merciless bruise, a pustule of horror that she didn't want to press too hard, lest it burst.

"Keep your hands and your feet where I can see them, Panther." A voice like gravel.

The three of them turned around. A tall, dark-haired, heavily built man, dressed in black, a white skull emblazoned on his chest, was pointing a rifle at them. The weapon was so large that it just screamed overcompensation to Emma. Frank Castle, the Punisher.

"You shrink, you die, Ant-Man. Believe me, I'm one hell of a shot. And Frost... don't even think about it."

Emma found herself smiling. A mortal man amongst the gods in this castle—*ha!*—in the sky. He didn't flinch, didn't give an inch. She suspected that pointing a gun at the Black Panther was a lesson in futility. She had heard, however, that the Punisher punched well above his weight. She was intrigued. Fortunately, he hadn't directly threatened her and as a result she wasn't going to mentally lobotomize him quite yet. She was, however, going to encase herself in diamond the first opportunity she got.

But where is the other one? she wondered.

"Put that away, Castle, you're embarrassing yourself," Black Panther growled.

The Punisher did not lower the weapon. Despite the rifle's ridiculous bulk, he had no problem holding it steady.

The second mind revealed himself. He stepped from the shadows, or rather the shadows receded around him. He wore a blue costume with a red cross motif and a high-collared red cloak that moved of its own accord. Tall, with a salt-and-pepper goatee, saturnine features and greying temples, there was definitely something of the silver fox about Doctor Strange. Emma decided that she preferred the minimalism of the Punisher's outfit. They were an odd couple, though.

"Believe me, T'Challa, you'd rather he twitch his finger than I twitch mine," Strange said. Despite the tedious alpha male nonsense, Emma had to admit that Strange was something of an equalizer in this situation. "What are you doing here?" he demanded. "And more importantly, whose side are you on?"

Interesting, Emma decided. *Sides.* She decided to let the boys have their fun and sort out the alpha. She took a step or two back, a slight smile on her face, but Castle was on her, his gun tracking her movements. To his credit he didn't look her up and down despite her outfit. His eyes were like flecks of ice.

"Not sure," Black Panther said. "That's what we're here to figure out."

"Let's hope it's the right side," Strange said, pointing at him. Emma couldn't work out the dynamic here. It was clear they knew each other; she was pretty sure that they'd worked together but they both seemed reluctant to give an inch.

"Let's hope there is a right side," Black Panther said.

Castle's gun twitched to Ant-Man, now.

"What did you find that led you here?" Strange asked.

Castle was a good choice for their shooter, the one dropping corpses all over Subterranea, particularly if he was backed by Strange. The Punisher certainly had the right skillset. All he would need was access to the correct level of technology and/or magic. The problem with that conclusion was that he didn't look at home here. He had the kind of on-edge look that she recognized as tactical awareness, and Strange sounded as confused as the rest of them regarding the tangle of events they were currently enmeshed in.

"Same thing I'm guessing you found," Black Panther said. "Lies and lots of bodies."

"Any idea who killed them?" Strange asked.

"All I know is where the lies began. So do you, or you wouldn't be here."

"I don't even know where here is," Strange conceded.

"Then how exactly did you find this place?" Black Panther asked, suspicion in his voice.

"I didn't."

There was someone else here, someone whose mind Emma hadn't detected. Then she looked around, aware of Castle tensing as she did so.

The shadows receded again, presumably at a command from Strange, revealing a third figure. Emma became aware of this new mind as well. It was a mess.

"He did," Strange said.

"Hello," the figure said. He was dressed in red and had a huge veiny eyeball instead of a head. Emma almost laughed at the incongruity of the three of them together. "I talk to eyeballs."

Of course you do, Emma thought, moving sideways a little so she could use Black Panther as a shield if it all turned violent. The plan was to leave Castle a drooling, near-mindless puddle on the floor and turn to diamond.

Ant-Man just stared with a *what-the-actual...* expression on what was visible of his face under the helmet.

Emma soft-probed this latest newcomer's mind. It was an open book, if said book was unfettered chaos. The inside of the walking eyeball's head was a tumbling gyroscope of sounds, some of them almost words, and colliding fractal images, all of which had a strong eye motif.

"Please tell me he's the killer, so we can wrap this up before it gets any weirder." Black Panther sounded as though he was starting to lose his patience.

"The Avengers found him in possession of the Watcher's eye," Strange explained. Emma noticed that he had moved between Black Panther and walking-eyeball.

"The eye is close. Don't you hear it screaming?" Eyeball asked. The whole thing was starting to sound very ocular. Emma wondered what eye the giant eyeball was talking about in his unpleasantly squishy voice. The Watcher's? Why was he in mental communication with the Watcher's eye? Was that why his mind was such a chaotic mess? She didn't want to dive any further into that particular mental maelstrom but communication with an alien... sensory organ could explain what she'd seen and heard when she had probed him.

And yet more curiouser.

"And where did you find him?" Black Panther all but demanded.

"He admits to being on the Moon when the Watcher was killed, but mostly he just speaks gibberish," Strange said, though Emma noticed that he had avoided Black Panther's direct question. If the walking eyeball had been a prisoner of the Avengers, then it held to reason that Strange and Castle had taken him from them.

"Judging by his mind, if you can call it that, gibberish is the best that he can manage," Emma told them. Then his mind lit up like a beacon. No, not a beacon—a receiver, as though the signal it was receiving was suddenly that much stronger, that much closer.

Ant-Man was asking a question, something to do with Doctor Midas, but his voice was lost in the wash of mental information. It was like a flipbook of all human history. Emma swayed on her feet, the others too intent on their exchange to notice. What she had experienced had been such a sensory overload that it rendered the information she was receiving meaningless.

"The eye, the eye is here," the walking eyeball said. "And oh—"

Emma almost missed it in the wash but two new minds suddenly appeared. One of them was the source of the mental broadcast, but there was something of the automaton about it, like a telepathic broadcasting machine. The other was cold, fractured, fragmented, traumatized and very human, though it seemed to be missing certain emotional frequencies.

"It's not alone," the walking eyeball added.

Emma detected the whereabouts of the two new minds a fraction before the walking eyeball did. Looking up she saw another dark-haired, well-built man, obviously armored, a bulky rifle slung across his back and a mask covering his eyes. He was crouched down on a support, amongst the machinery just above their heads.

She was trying to work out if anyone else had gotten here the hard way. The others just seemed to be appearing at random.

Emma thought the newcomer looked familiar, though she couldn't place him. He was, however, holding a giant eyeball trailing nerve endings. It was the transmission source of the confusing mental babble that was being broadcast. The babble she had detected filling Eyeball's head.

"Bucky?" Black Panther said.

"Just so you know," said the newcomer, whose name was apparently Bucky, "I don't trust a single one of you. I expect the feeling's about to be mutual."

He leaped from his hiding place. The thump of his boots echoed up and down the vast corridor. His left arm looked to be cybernetic. He was holding something in his metal hand: a severed head.

"Oh my god, is that Fury's head?" Ant-Man cried.

"This guy killed Fury?" Emma asked. It didn't feel right. Fury was a legend. It should take someone truly impressive to kill him. It seemed unlikely they'd be called "Bucky." He didn't even look like a Bucky. Though now she came to think on it, that name sounded familiar. She was struggling to think straight—a result of the babble being broadcast from the eye. Perhaps that was the point, to jam her telepathy. "Who is this guy again?" she asked.

"The Winter Soldier. Believe me, this was far from his first murder." Black Panther answered.

She had definitely heard the name "Winter Soldier." She recalled that Bucky Barnes had once been the wartime sidekick of that tedious moralizer Captain America. Barnes had, by all accounts, since turned assassin. Presumably he'd had enough of rescuing kittens from trees and helping old ladies across the road while standing in the good captain's shadow. Like Castle, he had the skillset to be the shooter they were looking for as long as he had access to sufficiently advanced weapons. Also, like Castle—who was now pointing his weapon at the Winter Soldier—Bucky looked out of place amongst the self-consciously super-heroic. She wasn't sure if she included herself in that list or not.

"Never liked you Barnes," Castle spat. Emma could hear the anger in his voice. "Now I know why. Get on your knees while you still got 'em."

It surprised no one when the Winter Soldier did not get on his knees. Emma noticed Ant-Man and Black Panther tense. Eyeball was cowering behind Strange while staring at the huge eye Winter Soldier was holding. He had no facial expressions to read but Emma could read the body language. The walking eyeball wanted that giant eye very badly indeed.

"I'm not some corner dope pusher, Frank, and I'm not afraid of a man who can't protect his own children."

Ow, Emma thought. She was surprised, perhaps even a little disappointed, that Castle didn't shoot Winter Soldier for that comment. She saw Castle tense, his finger tightening around the trigger. Even over the mental babble from the Watcher's eye she sensed the mingled rage and grief coming off Castle in waves. She almost felt sorry for the man. He may have been a mass murderer, but then who was she to judge?

"Stand down, both of you," Strange said. His ridiculous collar had started to grow on her. "There's nothing to be gained from us fighting each other."

"You sure about that?" Castle growled. Emma could practically taste his need to kill Winter Soldier like a lancing pain in her mind.

"Maybe you folks know something I don't," Winter Soldier said, ignoring Castle. "Like why we're all here."

"You're the one holding the eye, Bucky, why don't you tell us?" Strange demanded.

Emma could still feel Castle trying to calm himself, get himself under control. Perhaps this was what their mysterious puppet master wanted? Get all of them together and push them into a fight. Or maybe it was a scavenger hunt; with Nick Fury's severed head and the Watcher's eyeball, the Winter Soldier was already winning. Her team had turned up with nothing but a bag full of radioactive bullets, and Strange and Castle had just turned up with a weird guy. Either way, she was done dangling on the end of strings.

"Looks like you found your own eye and yours talks. I still can't get a peep out of mine," Winter Soldier told them.

"Forget the eye!" Ant-Man snapped. "What about the head?"

Winter Soldier raised the head up. The barrel of Castle's rifle followed every move. Blood dripped from it. Emma had been neither really for nor against Nick Fury until he had revealed her whereabouts—and the whereabouts of those in her care—to Ant-Man and Black Panther. She hadn't been particularly happy about the blackmail he had used to coerce her into joining this particular travelling circus either, but she hadn't wanted to see him like this. It was a sad end for the black ops mastermind, the cyclopean superspy. The expression on the decapitated head's face was one of surprise more than anything else.

"The head is why I'm here. The head is the—"

A deafening metallic clang resonated through the entire superstructure. Everyone flinched, looking around for the source of the noise. Everyone except Castle: he never took his eyes off the

Winter Soldier, nor did his gun waver. Emma suspected he was waiting until they had what they needed from Barnes, then Castle would "punish" the Winter Soldier.

"Another ship just docked in a hurry," Black Panther said.

"The eye would know what was happening if you'd just let me hold it one more time," the walking eyeball said, his unpleasantly squishy voice saturated with desire as he edged closer to Winter Soldier.

Castle finally took his eyes off Winter Soldier, grabbing hold of Eyeball.

"If you've led us into a trap, eye-face, I promise you won't live to see it through," Castle told him.

"Actually, this one might be on me," Winter Soldier admitted.

A rage-filled scream echoed through the satellite.

Emma sighed. She couldn't shake the feeling that everyone just needed to calm down. Although, after what Barnes had said to Castle, she could see how the Winter Soldier might rub people up the wrong way.

Whatever Emma had been expecting, it wasn't a green lady in an armored spacesuit dual-wielding swords and charging at them.

"Gamora?" Strange sounded equally surprised to see the green lady.

"*Winter Soldier!*" the green lady yelled. She sounded angry enough to have been on the receiving end of a previous conversation with Barnes.

Gamora charged the Winter Soldier. He just managed to throw himself out of the way, narrowly avoiding bisection from one of the furious green lady's blades.

"Die, you traitorous bastard!" she shouted at him. Winter Soldier had definitely made an impression on this Gamora.

"This is madness, we've got to stop this," Strange said.

"Might want to sit this one out, guys." This last comment came from a figure clad head to toe in white. He had a crescent moon symbol on his chest, his face masked, a white hooded cloak billowing out behind him. "Bucky's got it coming."

Emma briefly wondered if he was the Hellfire Club's new White Queen.

"Moon Knight," Black Panther said. "What happened?"

Apparently he was not the new White Queen.

Gamora was still making an impassioned, and Emma assumed not unreasonable, bid to do unto Winter Soldier what he had done unto Nick Fury. Winter Soldier was struggling to stay out of the reach of her swords, having to use every acrobatic trick in the book.

"Winter Soldier blew up my ship. Left me and Gamora stranded in deep space," Moon Knight told them. "We had to catch a ride with a friend of hers."

Emma followed Moon Knight's eye down.

"What in the hell?" she snapped.

There was a three-and-a-half-foot tall bipedal raccoon carrying a large gun standing next to Castle.

"Nice popgun, skull-boy, now step aside," the raccoon said, because of course it did. The raccoon was cute in a "would-make-a-nice-shawl-if-skinned" sort of way.

Castle looked as bewildered by events as she felt. He was, however, clearly happy to stand aside and let the green lady eviscerate the Winter Soldier.

Emma glanced back to the fight. Winter Soldier was insisting he was not Gamora's enemy as he punched her in the face with Fury's head. Perhaps the explosive destruction of their spaceship was a simple misunderstanding as well?

"Believe it or not, I was trying to protect you," Winter Soldier protested.

Ah, the old "it's not you, it's me," Emma thought. She wasn't convinced. Neither was Gamora, it seemed, as she renewed her attack with a pleasingly murderous vigor.

"Is that what you told the man whose head you wield!?" she cried, feinting with one blade while trying to drive him into the other, which Winter Soldier only narrowly managed to avoid.

Emma could have used her telepathy to switch them both off, give them a mental time out until everyone had calmed down. Or she could turn to diamond and punch the green lady. She wasn't convinced that this Gamora was at fault, but calmer heads needed to prevail until they could get to the bottom of this.

"Gamora's your partner, Spector. Rein her in or I will do it for you," Black Panther told Moon Knight.

"Hey, I just met the lady but I already trust her more than you. Back off, Panther," Moon Knight—his real name apparently Spector—replied.

The weirdness of the day was starting to piss Emma off. She needed some relief.

"If this is a joke, you picked the wrong guy to pull it on," Castle told the raccoon.

"You and what army, pal?" the raccoon demanded.

It was the last straw for Emma.

"So, does this mean we're supposed to..." Ant-Man asked Strange.

"I'd really rather not," Strange said, arms crossed. He did not look happy.

"Okay, good, awesome, cooler heads it is," then Ant-Man was talking into his helmet microphone. "All space ants stand down, I repeat, stand down!"

The whole situation was ridiculous. Emma turned her skin to diamond. The mental babble filling her head mercifully ceased. Her cold, diamond-hard focus returned.

As Gamora passed by, Emma sucker-punched the green lady in the face. "Calm down, green cheeks." Gamora staggered back but didn't go down. "Interrogation first, execution later. Let's hear what he has to say first." Emma hoped that the punch to the face, the busted nose, and the realization that there was nothing she could do against Emma's diamond skin, would knock the fight out of Gamora.

But it didn't.

They weren't moving in those kinds of circles.

Gamora head-butted her in the bridge of her nose. The diamond didn't break but the force of the blow took Emma off her feet.

"Diamond!" Gamora spat. "You fight me by turning into diamond!? I chewed on diamonds in the crib!"

Brilliant, Emma thought, *now we sound like the guys.*

Then Winter Soldier was standing over her, bizarrely waving Fury's head at Gamora.

"Gamora! Trust me, you really don't want to—" he started.

"Oh, but I really do!"

Her sword was already coming down. It hit Fury's head. There was a grating sound of metal-on-metal and the sword lodged in the head in the way that sufficiently strong and sharp steel, wielded with enough force, really shouldn't if Fury's skull had been made of bone.

"What in the name of Thanos?" Gamora said, staring at the head as it fizzed, letting off small electrical discharges.

Emma pushed herself to her feet and leant in to examine the severed head more closely. It was undoubtedly a very sophisticated android: flesh and blood wrapped around metal and electronics.

And yet even more curiouser, she thought.

"It's an LMD," Winter Soldier said. "A life-model decoy. One of the most sophisticated I've ever seen." Having pretty much just stood and watched the fight, the others were drifting over to join them. "I used the chip in its head to track where it came from," he continued. "That's how I ended up here."

"Wait, so how long was Fury an LMD? And where the hell's the real Fury?" Ant-Man said, voicing the same questions in Emma's head.

Walking-eyeball staggered up next to her. His presence was not exactly comforting. He was bent over, clutching his stomach.

"I don't feel so good…" he squished. "If I had a mouth… I think I might…"

Emma stepped away, unwilling to see someone vomit through their tear ducts.

"At this point how do we know there's a real Fury?" Moon Knight asked, his arms crossed in a way Emma suspected he thought looked heroic. "How the hell do we know anything?"

It was clear that everyone was just ignoring the walking eyeball.

Emma was tired of this. Too much duplicity, too many lies and secrets, and too much manipulation. It was all too clear that they were dancing to somebody else's tune.

"This started with Fury," she held her finger up in Black Panther's face. "That was what I was told by you." The mushroom treatment was stopping now.

"None of us were told the truth. Look around you; you think we're all here by coincidence?" Black Panther sounded just as confused as she was. "We thought we were chasing secrets. We were wrong. We are the secret."

"What the hell does that mean?" Emma demanded. It was the kind of nonsensical rhetoric that sounded profound until you stopped and thought about it for a moment. "You said we were working for Nick Fury!"

"You were, Emma dear." The voice came from the crack in a now-opening blast door at the end of the corridor. It carried a tone of patronizing superciliousness that she equated with patrician entitlement.

As the doors slid open, she made out a silver-haired, craggy-featured old guy leaning on a cane. Behind him were five Nick Furys, all young, all in S.H.I.E.L.D. uniforms and all heavily armed.

"And you still are," the old guy at the front said. Weirdly, he had an eyepatch as well.

CHAPTER TWENTY-TWO

WILL THE REAL NICK FURY PLEASE STAND UP?

WELL, I had their full and undivided attention. All sorts of hard men and women, some with inherent power and some supremely skilled, some with a mixture of both. Black Panther, Ant-Man, Emma Frost, the Punisher and Doc Strange with the Orb as their ocular bloodhound, Bucky, Moon Knight, Gamora, and an uninvited Rocket Raccoon for some reason, all waiting to see what came next. They probably felt manipulated, used, gamed but that wasn't what this was. I didn't play games and I tried to minimize the threat where I could. I had five of my LMDs with Badoon-made energy assault rifles to back me up. My audience knew me well enough to know that, even as old as I was, Nick Fury never did anything without a few tricks up his sleeve.

Nineteen eyes watching me, a mix of expressions: angry, guarded, faintly amused and one big eyeball just staring at me. Yeah, they were pissed, they had reason to be, but they'd listen. Whether they knew it or not, they owed me that at least.

"What's going on here, Fury?" Strange was just wary enough of me that his question wasn't a demand.

"The truth this time. No more games." T'Challa, on the other hand, wasn't.

"You want the truth," I began, leaning hard on my cane, "You gotta go back to 1958, and of all places Kansas." I'd always wondered what the connection was between Kansas and alien invasions.

"Give 'em hell boys! Take the bastards down!" I wasn't sure whether I was happy or supremely pissed off. I'd thought I was done with this nonsense when the war had finally ended in '45. Now, here I was, .45 in hand again, fighting a pitched battle. No Howling Commandos this time: instead their brethren from the 5th Ranger Company were taking the brunt. I wasn't in battle dress either—I was wearing a suit, and the thump of rifles and the rattle of automatic weapons weren't echoing out over some European battlefield or Pacific island. Instead the battle was being fought amongst the ruins of Mainstreet USA, some tiny Kansas town I'd never even met anyone from, and the invaders weren't Nazis or even Communists. Humanity wasn't doing so well.

"I was with army intelligence back then."

It wasn't entirely true but even now I never tell the whole truth. Old habits die hard, I guess.

"An eager young spy who still thought the world was a fairly simple place."

They had come through a portal lit with the same purple energy that their weapons fired. It had been generated by a sophisticated piece of technology that looked a bit like the iris of a camera.

"A place where the price of freedom was nothing more than the occasional war, some dead friends and a nightmare now and then."

There was naked cynicism in a few of their faces upon hearing the word "freedom." It's so easy to place so little value on what we take for granted. But if that was the case, then what were they all fighting so hard for?

They poured out of the portal and laid waste, moving more like a horde of locusts than a military force—but then, for all I knew, their strategic and tactical aims may have just been to have themselves a fine old time. They looked like robots in medieval armor. Each of them had some kind of Gatling gun-like energy weapon grafted on at the elbow of their right arm. It'd be a while before I'd learn words like cyborg, power armor and dimensional gate.

"Way I saw it, something like Iwo Jima or Berlin in '45 was about as hairy as things could really get."

I knew Bucky knew what I was talking about, maybe Castle as well. Fighting in a war is a very different experience to wielding super-powers in battles with super villains.

"Turns out for a guy who still had two working eyes, I sure couldn't see worth a damn."

It was the speed of the attack, without any visible plan, rudimentary tactics or even any kind of unit cohesion that I could see, that shocked me the most. They had devastated this town in a matter of minutes and our weapons weren't doing a thing.

We were crouched down in the rubble trying to figure out a way to not make our deaths utterly pointless. I wasn't coming up with much.

"Colonel Fury!" one of the Rangers shouted at me. He was just a kid, not even old enough to have fought in Korea. He'd been given a

Browning Automatic Rifle and told he was a man. "They see us!" I could hear the panic in his voice. I'd heard it so many times before in so many places. "I think they're—"

"Incoming!" I screamed, trying to shove him out of the way as one of the invaders threw a purple sphere at us. I hit the ground and tried to bury myself under the debris. I knew a grenade when I saw one. The explosion leaked through my eyelids in strange spectrums of energistic color. Waves of alien force battered human bodies. If I hadn't been on the edge of the squad I would have died as well. Instead the squad had taken the brunt of it, by which I mean they had died and somehow I still lived.

"We'd seen aliens before," I tried not to look at Gamora as I said this, though I sensed her eyes boring into me. To her we were the aliens.

"Small groups here and there. We'd captured our share, even killed a couple."

I was lying under a pile of bodies. Several were still burning from the energy of the strange grenade. It was as though their flesh fueled the fire. Their skulls glowed like grizzly jack-o'-lanterns. They deserved better but then almost every single dead soldier I'd ever known had deserved better than they'd got.

"But we'd never seen a full-scale invasion. Not like this. Not that I knew of, and I was still young enough to believe that I knew just about everything."

"Harden? Tolliver?" I just about managed to push myself back onto my feet. I felt pulverized, like I'd been beaten by a sack full of hammers. "Anybody?"

Kansas is flat. Really flat, as in it gives anyone used to actual landscape agoraphobia. That meant I could see the appalling destruction for a very long way. The burning horizon looked like a violent sunset.

No humans moved. The portal still glowed and armored inhuman feet powdered the rubble to dust as they poured out of it.

"Anybody?" I asked.

"They'd wiped out the whole town by the time we got there and it took 'em a whole ten minutes to wipe us out, too. I figured the rest of the world had a few hours at best. I planned on spending those last few hours dying as best I could."

I knew how this sounded: hyperbolic at best, self-aggrandizing at worse. Who knows, maybe it was. What I was looking for, however, was someone amongst my current audience who understood the kind of abject hopelessness I'd experienced there, in Kansas of all places. I needed someone who knew that feeling but was still capable of doing what needed doing.

The portal was glowing even more fiercely and kicking out some not-insignificant energy discharges. I'd managed to find my .45, and I had a faint idea of getting some of the Rangers' TNT and as many grenades as possible and trying to shut the portal down.

"Bring it on then you ugly bastards, let's see what you—"

"I suppose you could say I've been trying to find a way to die as best I can ever since."

Not long now.

He appeared from the sky in a shroud of white lightning, flying towards the portal, some kind of energy pistol in each hand, cutting down the invaders. He was an old guy but heavily built, muscular, wearing a golden helmet and breastplate—and, of course, he was mercifully human. He fought his way through the invaders, doing to them what they'd done to my Rangers, to this town. Making his way inexorably towards the portal.

"If he was one of ours then he was way above my pay grade."

Nobody smiled. They were still listening at least. Letting me tell my story.

I'd walked with gods. I'd fought shoulder to shoulder with Captain America, but I'd never seen such an awesome display of power. Only on a very few occasions since have I seen its equivalence. He obliterated the invading army. On his own. All I could do was watch; my useless .45 still in my hand.

Something launched itself from his armor and flew through the portal.

"Package delivered and I'm clear!" I heard him cry. "Do it, Howard! Do it now!"

He had moved away from the portal but the invaders were concentrating their fire on him now. A wash of violent energy broke over him, momentarily obscuring him from view, but it was as though he had some invisible shield protecting him.

"What the hell…" I'd just about managed to regain the ability to speak. I had the presence of mind to reload my .45 and then empty the magazine into the invaders in a bid to either help this stranger or draw attention to myself so I could get properly dead. They didn't pay me the slightest bit of attention. I may as well have been spitting at them.

I wasn't sure if he'd been hurt or his armor had been damaged, but the mysterious figure plummeted into the largest mass of invaders, firing both pistols right up until the moment of impact. He hit the ground hard enough to make a dent. The force of it took me off my feet, again.

I half crawled, half staggered to where the man in the golden armor had fallen, making my way through the broken bodies of the invaders. Glancing at the portal, I could see massing shadows through the purple light in the portal's iris.

The guy in the golden armor was lying at the bottom of the crater, his weapons scattered around him.

"Nice flying, pal," I told him, "but there are more of those things coming. Looks like a whole army's about to pour through that portal. You got any more—"

Then I realized he'd hit the ground hard enough to drive a spike of metal through his midriff just under the breastplate. The spike must have been part of a support for the building that had been here before the invaders had turned up.

"Oh hell," I said, "Don't try to move, all right?" I cradled his head.

"Can't move," he managed. "Guess that tells me what I need to know. Your face tells me the rest. Is it that bad?"

"I've seen worse," I told him. I omitted that when I had seen worse wounds they'd belonged to dead guys. There wasn't much I could do for him.

He laughed. It was a wet, rasping noise. He was drowning in his own blood.

"Haven't we all." It wasn't a question. His white beard was spattered with a red froth. "Always thought it would be the Skrulls who got me. Not these bunch of nobodies. Watch out for them Skrulls, you hear me? One of these days they're liable to—" Then the pain was too much for him.

I had no idea what a Skrull was.

"Listen, if there's somebody you want me to get a message to, somebody special, you'd better tell me now," I told him to make him feel better. Despite his efforts, the "bunch of nobodies" was about to empty out of the portal and scatter our constituent parts all over central Kansas. But hey, at least they weren't as dangerous as the Skrulls… "Pal?" I asked, thinking he'd gone to his reward, or punishment.

"Won't have to worry about that, kid," he managed. "Only folks waiting on me I'll be seeing myself, most directly, in Hell."

Then the portal blew. It kicked out what looked like liquid white fire and then sucked it back in. It came as such a surprise that I came closer to soiling myself than I had at any time since my first firefight against the fascists in Spain.

A few of the invaders made it out of the portal. They were burning with that strange energistic fire. There was something insectile about their cries—and no, I can't explain what I mean by that.

"And so there I was, in a ruined town in Kansas, with a dying man strapped to a jetpack, watching a whole world burn through an alien portal. I saw an entire race of creatures die screaming. I saw everything they ever were swept away in flames and I figured well… they must have had it coming."

I looked for a sign that any of them understood. What I saw was eight stony faces, a huge eyeball and a raccoon staring back at me. Then there was Gamora. She was looking at me with undisguised disgust. I realized how much I must have sounded like her father.

"Tell me it was worth it," the man managed. He was sounding weaker and weaker: not long now. "Tell me in the end it was all…"

Regardless of the truth of the matter, I opened my mouth to tell him it was worth it because what difference did it make now? But he was gone. I laid his head down. Another dead soldier on another battlefield. His body lit by the portal burning with strange-colored flames as it collapsed in on itself.

"Holy Toledo, did you see that?" an excited voice cried. It took me a moment to realize that someone was moving towards me and talking to the dead guy. "That bomb is going to make me a mint. C'mon, Woody, let's get—"

I brought the guy up short with my .45. He skidded to a halt. He was wearing a much nicer suit than the one I was wearing. He had a moustache, was handsome and clearly rich. I knew that my old friend Pinky, whom I'd served with in the Howling Commandos, would have described him as a "spiv," but then the British had a way with words. The newcomer seemed both too excited about the death of a civilization, even if said civilization was hostile, and vaguely familiar. I couldn't shake the feeling that I'd seen him somewhere before. Perhaps during the war?

"That's close enough," I told him. I wasn't even sure I'd reloaded the .45 or why I was suddenly so protective of the body. The newcomer had called him Woody, so it seemed likely he knew the dead guy.

"Whoa! Ease up there, friend," he said. His voice sounded familiar as well, but there was just something too smooth about him, too slick. "I'm on the side of the humans. Trust me, aliens can't grow moustaches." They probably didn't use as much moustache wax as this guy, either. "Hey, wait a second, aren't you—" Then he saw "Woody." That was when I worked out who this newcomer was. "Oh god, he looks really dead."

"He is dead," I said, not sure why I still had the .45 trained on him.

"Tribellians," he said like it meant a damn thing. "I can't believe it was the Tribellians who finally..." He almost sounded sad. Or like he was trying to sell someone on him being sad. Then he looked up at me. "Sorry, Colonel Fury, isn't it? I'm Howard Stark, I believe we've—"

"I know who you are, Stark." I pointed down at Woody. "Just tell me who the hell this man was who just died to save the world?"

I'd come to realize that Howard wasn't a bad man, he was just too... enthusiastic about his world of technology. Too blinkered. It would take having a family before he really started to understand things like human empathy. Some people are just late bloomers, I guess.

Minutes later, I was flying somewhere over the Rocky Mountains in a late-model Cadillac reconsidering my adult lack of interest in science fiction. We must have been moving at incredible speeds—the landscape under me was little more than a blur—but I'd barely felt the acceleration.

"This isn't the first time we've almost been invaded by aliens, Colonel," Stark told me as I tried to keep my breakfast down. Speaking as someone who used to be part of a wing-walking act, Stark was a flamboyant if not very attentive pilot. "Not even close," he added.

We were heading towards the solid rock wall of a mountain. A moment of trepidation, and then the rock shimmered and I could see what looked like a poured concrete hangar entrance protruding from the rock.

Stark was silent for a moment as he took us into the cave-like hangar. The wheels folded back into their normal place as the Cadillac touched down.

Stark got out. Other than faint daylight from outside, the cave was mostly in darkness. I had an impression of vastness and machinery, but that was all as I followed Stark.

"For every encounter like the one we experienced today, there've been dozens more where they never even got boots on the ground, because of men like Woodrow McCord."

That name also sounded familiar. I vaguely remembered something about an officer in the 2nd United States Sharpshooters, one of the regiments that had formed the Iron Brigade during the Civil War.

"McCord was the gentleman you had the honor of watching die today," Stark told me.

"He was what, some sort of top-secret G-Man?" I asked. We'd crossed the hangar to a concrete wall, pipes running down and along it. There was a humming sound coming from the pipes.

"We may be in the Rocky Mountains in the good old US of A but down here there are no governments, Colonel. This is the domain of one man."

I couldn't make up my mind if Stark was talking like one of the anarchists I'd fought alongside in the International Brigades, or just some kind of corporate version of the same tyrants I'd spent my whole life fighting.

Stark had led me to a hefty lever switch mounted on the wall. It was clear that this was his big reveal.

"The man who guards the wall between us and annihilation." He pulled the lever and lit the huge cave up in a silvery light. I saw vast incomprehensible machines, strange vehicles, weapons, armor *and what looked like a rocket ship. It reminded me of the Buck Rogers and Flash Gordon stories I'd consumed as a kid—before I'd "grown up." More fool me. Something about the trove of strange technology made me think that it had come from numerous different cultures, different species. I'd later come to understand that it was the spoils of war, cobbled together and made usable for humans—one human— by Howard Stark and the other technologists who'd provided support for the Man on the Wall before Howard.*

I walked out into the secret base hidden in the mountain, footsteps echoing. It was so still, so empty. Strangely sterile and somehow unwelcoming, as though you had to earn your right to be here. Still... there was something about it. I belonged in this strange, alien place.

"There are those of us who paid for all this, who helped scavenge the technology, who set this up in secret long ago," Stark told me. His hands were held up high, gesturing all around, as he showed me his— Woody's lonely kingdom. "Those of us who knew of the dangers that were out there and that were coming." He sounded strangely in awe of it all, despite his own part in this facility's existence. "But the man who uses all this doesn't work for us. He doesn't work for anyone. No government, no organization."

As we walked past a pillar of alien technology, I couldn't shake the feeling that I was at a job interview.

"He works for the Earth. He works for us all. He's the first and last line of defense against those who would prey upon this planet. He does whatever is necessary to protect all of humanity from the horrors that are out there, and to ensure that no one who walks the Earth need ever know he even exists."

No. It wasn't a job interview. Stark was trying to sell me on this. We came to a stop by the gleaming rocket ship and he turned to me crossing his arms. Here it comes, I thought.

"Or at least that's what we used to do. Now he's dead. Same way he's died so very many times before and yet, there must always be a man down here. There must always be a man guarding this wall." It was a good sales pitch. I remembered keeping my face as expressionless

as possible. "Tell me, Colonel Nicholas Joseph Fury of Hell's Kitchen, New York, just how much do you love your planet?"

I almost laughed at this. The last time I'd been asked that question the word "planet" had been replaced with "country." I hadn't gone to war for my country as much as I loved it. I had gone to war for the same reason I'd joined the International Brigade in Spain. To deal with a threat. A global threat. Tribellians, fascists, Nazis. In the end it all just led to suffering and extinction.

The scale of what Stark was offering was terrifying. At the same time, it was what I'd thought I'd been doing all along.

I turned and looked at the rocket ship. I could just about remember the sense of wonder I'd had as a kid, sitting on the stoop, a hot July in Hell's Kitchen, clutching the yellowed pages of a pulp magazine that Liebman, the barber, had given to some poor Irish kid.

I gestured towards the rocket ship with my thumb.

"This thing, can it actually fly?"

CHAPTER TWENTY-THREE

THE MAN ON THE WALL, PART ONE

I WAS still standing in the doorway, my LMDs behind me. They were ready to respond to any threat. My guests were still gathered around the blast door, still prepared to listen. For now.

I saw incredulity on several faces. That was understandable, though I suspect a few of them got it. The rest—the likes of Black Panther and Doc Strange—wanted, no, *needed* to know my secrets. To know things they didn't already. That was fine. I could work with that.

The aliens looked like bipedal warthogs wearing armor.

"Harvest time will soon be upon us, my lords." They were sat at a long table in a pillared circular chamber. The place looked like a conference room designed by the architects of Imperial Rome. "Tell us, Grand Procurer, what succulent new fruit have you found for us, hanging among the branches of the cosmos?" one of the seated aliens asked. Ten of them sat along either side of the table, an eleventh, the "Grand Procurer," at the head.

I was listening to them from my concealed position on a device called a "phased entanglement transducer." The reason I knew about this threat to Earth was the result of an "algorithmic threat portent analyzer." I swear to God, Howard just made this crap up.

The Grand Procurer stood up to speak.

"A newly ripened one, my lords. With barely a billion years of multicellular evolution. Their interplanetary capabilities are primitive. Their greatest weapons are projectile and fission-based. They've barely manifested any preternatural mutations, let alone enough to constitute any sort of viable super-powered defense system."

As I watched the Grand Procurer through my scope, listened to his strangely high-pitched, piping voice, there was something about the phrase "super-powered defense system" that resonated with me. I kept listening.

He kept droning on, "In short, I predict a quick and thorough harvest."

I don't think so pal, I thought.

"And these are carbon-based life-forms, my lords, which as we know, given the proper seasoning, can be quite delectable." The Grand Procurer touched the glowing screen that was the surface of the conference table and a spherical hologram of my blue and green homeworld appeared floating in front of him.

It was confirmation enough. I squeezed the trigger. My weapon didn't have any discernable recoil. I was firing from such a distance that the bullet would take a not-inconsiderable amount of time to reach the target. The scope used some kind of predictive aiming system. I hadn't been paying attention when Howard had briefed me on it. In short, the Grand Procurer still had time to talk.

"So if it please my lords, I give you the official menu for our upcoming season."

I had time to reflect on what the Grand Procurer was saying as I tracked the progress of the bullet. I kinda got where he was coming from. If I looked like a bipedal warthog, I'd want to be the one doing the eating rather than being ate.

"I give you, the Eart—" His big announcement was spoiled by

a hypersonic tungsten-cored penetrator going through the asteroid habitat's dome and bursting his head like a melon hit with a, well, a high-velocity bullet.

I stood up on the piece of rock I'd been using as a firing position, backlit by red nebulous space. The rock was in a slightly lower orbit over the gas giant than the Grand Procurer's asteroid habitat. It had been a tricky shot, but not that tricky. The low gravity had meant I'd been able to fit the already heavy rifle with a ludicrously long barrel.

No matter how difficult looking like a warthog might be, they didn't get to eat the population of my home world.

"I took the job without hesitation."

Again, it wasn't entirely true, but they didn't need to know that.

I wore the gold armor. I stood on the wall.

"I'd been a soldier and a spy for as long as I could remember. I figured this was the same job I'd always been doing, just a bit bigger in scope. Instead of being sent to destabilize a Southeast Asian country that some desk jockey worried was a potential threat to our way of life. I was taking down aliens who wanted to eat us," I told them.

Which wasn't to say that I hadn't been involved in destabilizing Southeast Asian countries, but my real job had always seemed more about dealing with clear and present dangers rather than responding to perceived ideological threats.

I ran through the tunnels in Subterranea, the Moloids guiding me.

"This the guy? The one who said he was gonna 'Stomp the surface world into bloody mudholes'?" I asked them. I could hear the creature roaring in the cavern ahead. He didn't sound like much of a planner. Moved quickly though. The grey-skinned thing loomed out of the darkness. It was entirely too big, with entirely too many fangs and claws. Not unreasonably, the Moloids had fled. I'd only just got my gun up fast enough.

"Never mind. I got my answer." I put round after round into it until it fell over.

"For every subterranean monster who tried to invade Manhattan, there were ten more you never heard of. 'Cause they never made it outta their cave."

I looked at nine significantly unimpressed-looking faces and a giant eyeball. At least I thought Rocket was unimpressed. I'm no expert in raccoon facial expressions.

I also wondered why monsters were so attracted to New York.

The dimension of hungry shadows had a "proper" name. By proper, I meant a name given to it by Howard that was mostly in Latin and that I mostly ignored. Our idea had been to use the dimension to dispose of bodies in the hope that the living shadows that inhabited it were carrion eaters. They weren't but it was still a convenient dumping ground.

The first time I'd lured a demon there had almost been my last. It had chased me through the dimension's nerve system, hunting me as much as I was hunting it.

Even as it swung down through the branches, the shadows bearing down on me, I'd only just managed to put enough bullets in the demon to bring it down.

"Note to self: Need bigger bullets." It had been a close-run thing.

Had Castle and Strange enjoyed their time in that particular dimension?

"Monday through Thursday I'd spy on hippies and commies for the CIA, but come Friday it was into the Netherworld to see which of the Old Gods was looking to use the Earth for its nesting ground, or into space to discover which interstellar empire wanted to dine on humanity." And this was the problem with my job in a nutshell. My audience could understand what I was telling them intellectually, but the scale of it was so large, even for the most powerful of them, that it was an almost abstract concept.

"Eventually my day job changed," I told them. S.H.I.E.L.D. was formed and I was made its first director. It seemed that I hadn't just caught the eye of Stark and the other invisible backers. God knows why: I must have seemed like a complete flake in those days.

I was sat at the head of the table, the S.H.I.E.L.D. logo emblazoned on the meeting room wall behind me. In a suit but unshaven, listening to a briefing, arms crossed, because all things being equal I would much rather have been out in the field.

"As you requested, Director Fury," Gabe had told me. I felt no more comfortable being called "Director" than I had "Colonel." In my heart I still thought of myself as a sergeant. *"I have the latest reports from all field agents regarding known Hydra activity."*

Hydra needed dealing with. There were no doubts in my mind about that. I took their existence, the continued threat they posed so long after the war, as a personal affront. I had hoped that we mopped up the last of them and their Werewolf SS allies in '47. Though we hadn't helped ourselves with Operation Paperclip, of course. My mind, however, was on other things—threats more serious than even Hydra.

"We've also managed to gather more information relating to the recent gamma bomb accident in New Mexico, including the possible involvement of Tony Stark," Gabe continued.

Tony Stark was proving to be every bit as gifted as his father but an even bigger screw-up. Howard had confided as much in me before his untimely death. Now this, tampering with Banner's gamma bomb experiment no less. I couldn't shake the feeling I was going to have to have a chat with Stark Jr.

"And I've compiled dozens of eyewitness accounts of the supposed man-spider, who's mostly been seen in the Forest Hills neighborhood of—" Another of my long-suffering agents was cut off by the intrusive bleeping from my pager. This was a good ten years before pagers were a thing but hey, I wasn't just a superspy, I was *the* superspy.

"We'll have to postpone the briefing. Gotta run. Forgot it was… my Aunt Matilda's birthday."

Then I was out the door, jumping into the 1964 DeVille convertible, taking off from the helicarrier's flight deck and Bettie and I were on our way into orbit.

I was amazed I didn't get fired early on.

Why was I a lousy husband? A worse dad? I was the Man on the Wall and running an international spy agency at the same time. Who had the time? That doesn't mean I don't still have regrets.

"I never told anyone at S.H.I.E.L.D. about my other job. All those years and I never told anyone at all. When it comes to being the Man on the Wall, I never trusted anyone but myself."

As the decades passed, the surface of the world came under too much scrutiny. There were too many eyes in the sky looking down. The Rocky Mountain base was no longer tenable, so we moved up into the sky. The satellite base and the LMDs of yours truly were Howard's final legacy, to me anyway.

I remembered fleeing that briefing only to be met by Andrew and another of my LMDs just outside the airlock. Bettie was parked on one of the satellite's external landing pads. I didn't recognize the second LMD, despite him looking exactly like me. I guessed he must have been fresh off the production line.

"We picked him up in orbit, sir," Andrew told me. He was talking about the prisoner.

"We called you as soon as we brought him in," the second LMD said.

I strode past them, making my way through darkened industrial corridors, heading towards the interrogation chamber. The words of Woodrow McCord from that day in Kansas were still echoing in my head. What he'd told me about who and what the real threat to Earth was.

"Has he said anything?" I asked.

"Several curses in his native tongue. Nothing else," Andrew told me.

"Unit K-17 was destroyed during the subject's apprehension. Request permission to requisition a replacement," the new LMD said. Both of them were following me through the guts of the satellite.

"Which one was he again?" I asked.

"You called him Marty, sir," new guy said. It had been years since I'd felt weird dealing with my LMDs as subordinates.

"Right, Marty was a good one." It was, however, odd how they'd all become kind of individual. Or maybe it wasn't. Their programming was pretty sophisticated: they were supposed to learn from their experiences and be able to pass, convincingly, not just as humans but as me if they needed to. More than once, an LMD had been the director of S.H.I.E.L.D. for a day or more while I was busy with my other activities. As the Infinity Formula had started to fail and I'd started to age, the LMDs had taken over my real-world responsibilities more and more, but I'm getting ahead of myself.

"You're new, aren't ya?" I asked the new LMD. Then, not waiting for an answer: "We're gonna call you Matilda. I'll see him alone," I said, meaning the prisoner.

I'd never been comfortable being watched when I was torturing somebody.

The Skrull was a green-skinned, rib-chinned, muscular alien with huge ears. He was wearing a purple and black one piece. The LMDs had firmly secured him to a pillar-like piece of alien tech salvaged from some particularly sadistic members of an advanced species.

"I demand my rights!' the Skrull protested. "I know your planet and your pathetic Geneva Conventions."

"Those only come into play if you're on Earth," I explained. Besides, I couldn't remember the Skrull Empire being signatories of the Conventions. "You ain't on Earth and it's my job to make damn sure you never are. So, you're gonna answer my questions, Mr. Skrull. First question: does it hurt when I do this?"

I flicked the switch on the agonizer. I swear his screams were loud enough to be heard in the cold vacuum.

"Good answer," I told him.

These weren't the kind of people to quail at stories of torture. A number of them had used similar tactics themselves. That didn't mean they liked it. Some of my audience members' looks of distaste had been promoted to looks of disgust. I didn't care. I knew who I was. More to the point, I knew what needed to be done.

"Being judge, jury and executioner came rather easy to me," I told them, surprising precisely no one. "So easy… maybe I should've been worried."

Some years after I'd averted the first Skrull invasion of Earth I was on top of a building in Midtown, New York. I'd never liked operating in the real world when I was doing my "real" work. If they were on the surface then I'd failed. I'd let the potential threat get too close but this was a new phenomenon.

"He should be coming into view now, sir," one of my LMDs said across the comms link. They were monitoring it all from the control room of the satellite, currently held in a geosynchronous orbit over New York.

"Yeah, Matilda, stop jabbering. I got him," I said, my one good eye peering through the rifle's scope. "These new bullets better be as good as you say," I said. I missed Howard.

"We used Banner's own Gamma Bomb designs, sir. They should be able to put a hole in even someone as strong as Thor," Matilda told me.

I had to admit I wasn't overjoyed about wielding a weapon with a magazine full of radioactive bullets, even if the magazine was supposedly shielded.

"Well, let's hope we never have to test that particular theory," I said. I didn't want to go toe-to-toe with someone who, according to the intel I'd seen, was a genuine member of the Norse pantheon, but humans needed contingencies when they walked with gods. Anyway, it looked like Thor had fallen for Steve's charm offensive.

I lowered my rifle.

"Sir?" Matilda asked over comms. "Has the gun jammed?"

"You know what?" I paused for a moment or two to gather my thoughts. Sure, he was on the threat register but as I looked for the "clear and present danger" I just couldn't see it. "There's something about this one. Call it a gut feeling. Sure, he's weird and radioactive but let's give him a bit more time, see if maybe he doesn't turn into something special."

As I watched this guy—later I'd learn he was really just a kid—swing through the sky on webs over the Manhattan skyline in his blue and red pajamas, I remembered the words of a talking warthog. Something about a super-powered planetary defense system. After all, a second line of defense couldn't hurt.

"I was never a madman. I was never out of control," I told them. "I did what I had to do and I was damn good at it." I was wondering whom I was trying to convince. Them or me. Besides I knew that Castle, at least, wasn't going to be impressed by a story of me sparing Spider-Man way-back-when.

"Years went by. Howard Stark was long dead. As far as I knew so was anyone else who might've ever known what I was doing. More super-folk came along faster than I could keep count. I thought they might make me irrelevant, but well…" And here I lowered my head and damned my friend for how he made me feel just because I had lived in the shadows. "I love Steve Rogers like a brother." Because I had gotten my hands wet, left bloody footprints in my wake. "But not every job is for Captain America."

I'd never quite managed to suppress the resentment I experienced because I could do the things he couldn't. No, not couldn't: *wouldn't*. I knew it was a messed-up idea but it was the soiling of my soul that allowed him to be who he was. To sleep so well at night. Then again, I slept well. Most nights anyway.

I hung in space in the golden armor, the rifle configured for maximum destruction, and I looked at what I had done.

"Sir?" Andrew asked over comms. "Has the mission been a success?"

"I'd say so," I replied, bathing in the molten light.

I knew I was being watched. Normally that feeling triggered a threat response well learned on the streets of Hell's Kitchen before I'd ever picked up a gun. It was different when he watched me, however. I'd never noticed any particular expression on his face when he did so, but somehow I still felt judged, shamed. Perhaps it was all in my head.

I confirmed the kill, by which I mean I hung there in space and watched the living world, a creature, a sentient being the size of a planet, burn. I had done it. I had killed it. Put bullet after bullet into it until I had triggered a chain reaction in its lava-funneling veins.

It had strayed too close to Earth. Its psychometric readings pointed to psychosis on a vast and terrifying scale. Its mere presence in the Sol System could have resulted in the social collapse of a nervous planet with a truly suicidal nuclear capability.

"I've killed more times than I can count," I told them, not meeting any of their eyes. "I've burned worlds, destabilized galaxies, dethroned gods—and I did it without any of them even knowing my name."

"I'm done. Come and pick me up." I told Bettie.

"That's what it means to be the Man on the Wall. To be the invisible monster who keeps the other monsters at bay," I managed through gritted teeth.

I had no idea this was going to be so hard. I wasn't sure if it was remorse, though it seemed unlikely: I had never not believed in what I was doing. I suspected that I was struggling to wrench out all these dirty secrets for even this small audience. They had all been locked away deep inside for so long.

Bettie wove her way through the chunks of the no-longer-living world's flesh.

"Forever unnamed, unknown."

I swung myself into the flying coupe's driving seat. Aware, but not looking back at those two fiercely burning eyes that saw all.

Now I looked up at them.
"Unseen."

I still didn't turn around, but I couldn't help but glance in Bettie's rear view mirror. There he was, standing on a piece of planetary debris, in his toga, with his huge bald head. Expressionless, but I knew he judged me for my crimes.
This, I left out of the story I told the others.

○━━━━━○

THEY WERE watching me now—Black Panther, Ant-Man, Emma Frost, the Punisher, Doc Strange, the Orb, Gamora, Moon Knight,

Rocket and Bucky—all sensing that my story was over. Waiting to see what I'd do next.

"And I suppose that, in a nutshell, is why you're all here," I told them. I shuffled closer, leaning maybe a little heavier on the cane than was strictly necessary. Matilda and one of the other LMDs moved with me, flanking me, moving to the side for a better shot if any of our guests became excitable. "So… any questions?"

It took a moment and then the babble began.

"Only like a thousand," Ant-Man said. "Starting with, 'why are you so old?'" Poor Lang. So intelligent, so lacking in basic common sense—but then would he be a "super hero" if he had any? Why did I look so old? The fool, I was born in 1920. I didn't even look my age but Infinity Formula—that had slowed, but not stopped the aging process—notwithstanding, all flesh is frail and ultimately decays.

"Nick, what you're confessing to here," Doc Strange started, "this can't be true. This isn't you."

I truly believed that Strange was every bit as ruthless as I was. He understood how surgery worked after all, understood triage. The scale of it may have gone beyond his remit but that he didn't recognize me in my story was damning. It meant that he didn't truly understand himself. It was a check in the cons column.

"Isn't it?" Emma Frost asked, because she knew. A check in the pros column.

"I don't see a problem," Castle said. He'd effectively done the same work as I had on a smaller scale when he'd worked with the CIA's Special Operations Group. My issue was with his motivations. What I did had nothing to do with revenge. Rage only made you less effective, no matter how cold it burned.

"He's still not telling the whole truth." I almost flinched as the Orb said this. "He's still not telling you about—" I had made the decision to kill him right there and then when he started screaming and collapsed. Despite being surrounded by "heroes," everyone just watched.

"What's the matter with him?" Moon Knight asked.

"His body is still absorbing what he stole from the Moon," I said before turning to Matilda. "Put him in the interrogation room. The clock is ticking. We don't have long to find the others."

"This is crazy," Ant-Man said as my LMDs dragged the Orb back through the blast door. Nobody stopped them, which was good: I needed the Orb to shut up. "What the hell is happening?"

"What's happening is we have work to do. The same work I've been doing for all these—"

"Nick, I have a question." I had been dreading this; of course, it had been T'Challa who had spoken. "What happened to the Watcher?"

I felt the question in my chest. I didn't say anything but I knew the answer was etched into every line on my face.

"Nick?" T'Challa said.

"He died." I just needed them to trust me for a little longer. "And now… now I suppose it's my turn."

CHAPTER TWENTY-FOUR

TRANSATLANTIC MOONSHOT

NOT EVEN killing the crew of the trawler had cheered Exterminatrix up. On the evolutionary scale they may as well have been ants in comparison with her. The closest she'd come to improving her mood was using some of the fishermen as chum. She liked sharks. Perfect hunters, no need to evolve. However, the pleasure of seeing the sharks only lasted for a little while. Eventually she was sat on one of her victims, a golden gun in each hand, looking out over a choppy ocean filled with dorsal fins, raucous gulls overhead. She was still struggling with her defeat at the hands of every so-called super hero on the East Coast *and* the trawler stunk of fish. Honestly, it was the worst day ever.

"We never should have come back to Earth," she groused. To make matters more complicated, if not worse, her father seemed to be recovering well—notwithstanding the fact he still looked like a soft-baked Thing with fissures of light running through his flesh. Exterminatrix was not sure what she thought about that. Probably the usual bit of familial/paternal programming mixed with the need to kill and usurp him. "Once we left the Moon we should've kept going. You have a summer house on Saturn, don't you Daddy?"

He didn't answer. Her father was standing on the bridge looking out at the Atlantic. The terrified captain of the trawler, and the crew's only survivor, was simultaneously trying to steer the ship and not expire from sheer terror. His constant shaking and smell was irritating Exterminatrix.

"Instead, here we are running from the Avengers in the world's crummiest stolen fishing boat," she continued, "with nothing to show for our efforts but a bunch of angst-ridden Mindless Ones."

Exterminatrix could see the Mindless Ones in the eating area set behind the bridge. They seemed to have less bulk, as though they were instinctively able to adapt their bodies to surroundings and situations. They were, however, still freaking out like the most performatively angst-ridden teen. On the plus side, they had at least stopped telepathically projecting incredibly overwrought indie rock lyrics.

"And whatever the hell it is that's happening to us, that's changing within us, it's probably killing us for all we know." The changes hadn't stopped. She had sensed it as actual physical movement within her body. She was now so aware of her own physicality that she could feel every single tiny biochemical transformation. Evolution was fun, as long as the base matter was up to such sudden changes. She glanced back at the Mindless Ones freaking out and began to understand how they felt. "Daddy, this may seriously be the worst murder we've ever been a part of."

If she had expected a response then she was disappointed. He just stood there wrapped in the tarpaulin they had used to cover him in the Midtown loft back in New York. Exterminatrix tried willing the fault lines of light in his face and the rest of his body to crack and rupture, tried to make him burst through sheer force of will. Nothing happened.

"Daddy!" A bit more force in her voice. He ignored her.

"This is it, sir," the trawler captain said. He was covered in a sheen of stinking sweat; Exterminatrix was very much aware of the extent to which the man wanted to soil himself to death. "These are the exact coordinates you gave me."

Exterminatrix looked out at the empty, featureless ocean.

"Yes. It would appear so," her father said.

Exterminatrix threw her arms up into the air. He'd ignore her but was happy to talk to this non-entity. It beggared belief.

"You said," the captain started, his voice shaking, "if I brought you here, you wouldn't hurt me and that you would even pay me for my trouble." For a man whose livelihood involved strenuous physical work in dangerous and difficult conditions, this was undoubtedly the single bravest thing he'd ever done. Exterminatrix sighed. It was all so predictable.

Her father turned to the captain and regarded him as though noticing him for the first time.

"I did," he finally said. "And Doctor Midas is a man of his word." Then he reached out. The captain tried to flinch away but Midas's arm elongated and stretched out to touch him. "I assume you take gold."

Exterminatrix watched the cosmic energy alchemy that her father wielded as he turned the very base flesh of the trawler captain into solid gold. There was a heavy-sounding thump as the man hit the deck, now far too dead to appreciate his promotion up through the periodic table.

She stood up, and made her way off the bridge and out into the sea air.

"Daddy, I thought you said you had a safe house hidden nearby. We're in the middle of the ocean. There's nothing here." She headed down the steps and onto the main deck, trying to ignore the stink of dead fish violating her vastly improved olfactory receptors. "I think these changes we're going through may be affecting your mind." His powers as well. She had never seen him turn an actual person to gold before. Still, the more power he acquired, the greater his fall and the sweeter her eventual victory.

Her father had followed her down onto the main deck, before climbing over the rail, using the ladder on the side of the trawler to clamber down towards the water.

"You forget who I am, girl. I am Midas, the man who turns things to gold with a touch. The man who turns everything to his advantage." He stepped off the ladder. Water turned to gold under his foot and supported his weight. "But you were right about one thing."

The seas were getting rougher now as Exterminatrix leaped over the rail and landed on the golden path spreading out in her father's wake.

"We never should've come back to Earth," her father said, continuing his monologue. "We have been changed, Oubliette. We have been touched by but a fraction of the Watcher's immeasurable power. We never should have left without taking all there was."

The sea was ferocious now; huge waves were kicking up all around them. The wind drove stinging salt spray into Exterminatrix's eyes and against her exposed skin, but the sea directly around them remained calm enough for her and her father to walk the golden path. It was as though they walked through a valley surrounded by heaving, ever-changing mountains of water. She heard the crash of the trawler capsizing behind them, breaking under the sheer force of the heavy sea.

A spacecraft the size of a tower block burst through the waves, rising up from the sea.

"Welcome back, Doctor," the spacecraft's AI said over comms. "I am space vessel Midas 17. Where shall we fly today?" The voice was pleasantly neutral and unobtrusive, yet still grated on Exterminatrix.

"To the Moon!" her father cried. He seemed to be enjoying himself, at least, and very much recovered. "You will take us to the Moon and, after that, perhaps to immortality." He paused. "And also… I suppose at some point we're going to need to find those damn eyes."

Exterminatrix just sighed.

CHAPTER TWENTY-FIVE

...AN LMD OF INFINITE JEST...

I HAVE always found silence difficult to come by. I grew up in a tenement in Hell's Kitchen. Then I went to war and pretty much stayed there. It's the humming that eventually gets to you, though. Whether in a helicarrier or a satellite, there's a particular sound that comes from the energy generated to keep such machines working that never goes away. It's always present: the last thing you hear as you go to sleep in whatever institutional berth you find yourself sleeping in, and the first thing you hear before you open your eyes. Perhaps it was a comfort. The few times I'd managed solitude—just me and the tinnitus from too many gunshots, explosions and blows to the head—the noise of my own thoughts had been worse. I had to keep working, keep moving, or it would all catch me and overwhelm me. All of which made me wonder why I was looking at the severed head of an LMD. Gamora's sword had unevenly bisected the android's face down to the metal endo-skull. Slashed the eyepatch to reveal the red eye underneath. This was just a machine, like a toaster, that had served a purpose, so why did I feel as I did?

"Damn it, Andrew. You didn't deserve to go like this," I muttered. "I assume you knew it wasn't really me before you cut his head off?" I asked Bucky.

"I had a pretty good idea," Bucky said, no trace of remorse in his voice—but then, why should there be? He didn't know what I did: that all the LMDs had developed individual personalities of their own despite being originally based on me.

"How do we know this is the real you?" Ant-Man asked. "Since when are you so old?"

"I don't make LMDs of myself as a withered old man," I explained with a lot more patience than I felt, if for no other reason than to shut him up. I handed Andrew's skull to Matilda. "I'm the real Nick Fury, or at least what's left of him. As for why I look like this, well… that's because I'm—"

The Orb's cries cut through my words, echoing through the satellite's corridors even as he was dragged deeper into the bowels of the satellite behind me. For someone without a mouth, he could make a hell of a racket. Anyone would think that we were torturing him.

"God, it burns!" the Orb screamed. Two of my LMDs were taking him to the interrogation chamber.

"What the hell is happening to the Orb?" Doc Strange was in my face. It was clear that he hadn't understood my story, else he would be less intent on a confrontation. He was not nearly the threat to me that he thought he was. "Where are you taking him?" the Sorcerer Supreme demanded. "He's an eyewitness to murder."

Bucky had shifted, bringing his rifle up, because our default conflict resolution in this world was always violence. Matilda and the other LMD that had stayed with me by the blast door changed position as well, ready to act if Bucky tried anything.

"Bring him back. We need some straight answers," Bucky growled,

"Put the gun down, Bucky," Moon Knight demanded, also tensing. "The guy who blew up my ship is in no position to make demands."

I sighed.

"I didn't know who was working for whom at that point, Moon Knight," Bucky growled. "Matter of fact, I still don't."

I leaned heavily on the cane. This time it wasn't misdirection. I'd never been more tired.

"I think you all sound nuts," Rocket said helpfully.

T'Challa still hadn't taken his eyes off me.

"From what I can read of his mind, which isn't much," Emma said. "He seems genuine enough to me. He's the real Nick Fury all right. So that's one question answered." I was impressed despite myself. The Kree countermeasures I'd had cybernetically implanted were supposed to be proof against mental probes from telepaths of even Emma's power.

"I would still like an answer to my question," T'Challa said quietly. "Fury, what happened to the Watcher? Why was one of your gamma bullets dug out of his skull?"

"That, T'Challa, isn't an easy question to answer," I lied. "You see, me and old Uatu have always had what you might call a 'complicated' relationship."

○──────○

SOME WEEKS AGO

MY BERTH *on the satellite was more like a cell than anything else. I'd given up on comforts sometime during the '80s. Comfort was a distraction. Besides, I didn't have time to shop for soft furnishings and I didn't know any interior decorators with a high enough security clearance. Still, it meant that when I'd thrown myself out of bed, coughing up blood, I'd hit a cold metal floor.*

"Not... not yet. Still... so much work to do." I could feel it, you see. The Infinity Formula crapping out, age and all its attendant issues rushing back in at once. The devil always gets his due, after all. "I can't die yet." I was begging. After all there was no witness, nobody to see me there, lying on the metal at my lowest ebb, at my weakest. Nobody to hear desperate words spoken through bloodied phlegm.

Except him. Of course he was there, because he always was, watching.

"No, oh no..." *I sobbed as Uatu stood over me, his eyes burning like dying suns in his huge bulbous head. If he was just supposed to watch, then why could I see judgment on his face?*

I knew I had done awful, terrible things. My hands dripped with the blood of entire civilizations, but each time it had been us or them. Would the extinction of humanity have been better? Was I such a monster that I alone deserved the Watcher's scorn?

"If you're here... then that must mean... that I'm..." *I actually had my hands held up in front of my face, as though to ward him away.*

The Watcher just stared down at me, a strange and awful malevolence upon his infantile features.

"No. I'm not dying like this." *You can forget yourself, who you are, in the moments when you come to the realization, the surety that you're dying.* "Not at your damn feet." *Stand up, Sergeant Fury! I told myself. Gasping for breath, I stood before him. Stared up at those implacable burning eyes.* "You just keep doing what you do!" *I was coughing blood down myself.* "Which is nothing, am I right?" *He did not reply. He never did.* "Me. I got a world to protect." *I turned and staggered away from him.* "No matter the damn cost."

He was just a fading presence in the shadows behind me. Just like everyone else I'd ever met.

―○―

UATU'S EYE was in my eyeline. Staring at me. Accusing me as I bent over my cane. Bucky was holding the eye. Had he meant to show it to me? I couldn't read his expression. I'd never been able to, even when he was a kid. What had Steve seen in this murderous bastard?

"I'm dying," I told the assembled candidates and Rocket. "The Infinity Formula that's been keeping me young all these years is gone. Used up. I'm aging rapidly now. Every morning I wake up a little bit older. At this point I don't think I've got many mornings left." It was the first time I'd said it out loud. The admission had tumbled out of me all at once.

"So this is what—your way of making a deathbed confession?" Strange demanded. "You recruited us to uncover all these murders you committed, these years of assassinations all over the known universe and beyond. All because you knew what you'd done was wrong and you wanted to get caught before you died? This is just some weird cry for help, isn't it?"

I wanted to laugh in his face. It wasn't so much how poorly the great Doctor Strange understood me. That was irrelevant, though it suggested that he was a much poorer judge of character than I'd thought. It was his near total lack of self-awareness. His desperate need to sit in judgment of me, I suspected, stemmed from his own guilt. His crimes may not have been as extensive as my own, but he was here precisely because he did not hesitate to use, manipulate and sacrifice when he believed—no, knew—it was for the greater good. He just wasn't prepared to face up to who he was, which put him out of the running. It was a shame. I had initially thought him to be a frontrunner.

"Not exactly, Doc," I said, both hands on the cane now. "None of you are here by chance. Well, except for the raccoon."

"You wanna lose the other eye, pal, just keep it up," the heavily armed raccoon snarled. Perhaps he would make a better candidate than Strange.

"I chose each of you quite carefully." I shuffled along in front of them, feeling every minute of my nearly hundred-year-long lifespan, making the effort to look each of them in the eye. "Some of you are friends. Others I know only by reputation. Some of you owe me debts from long ago. Some of you don't owe any damn thing to anyone." I came to stand in front of T'Challa. He towered over me. I knew that I was using up his not-inexhaustible reserve of patience. "Some of you are without doubt… the smartest, most capable people on the face of the Earth." He remained quiet. I was relieved that he didn't ask his question again as I turned to face them all now.

"I wanted you each to see what I've been doing all these years. Yes, I wanted you to follow my trail, but not so you could stop me." They must have gotten it by now. Even the raccoon. "It was so you could replace me." I shuffled back a little.

"When I die… one of you must take my place."

CHAPTER TWENTY-SIX

CAPTAIN AMERICA IS TIRED OF YOUR @*$@!.

STEVE ROGERS was not happy. First the Orb's secret bomb had shown him his betrayal at the hands of people he trusted, and now this. He was looking down at the dissected body of a highly sophisticated android that he had thought was one of his oldest friends. Things like this could give you trust issues.

"Belay the obituaries!" Tony cried. Once again, Steve reflected on how much he didn't care for the timing of Stark's sense of humor. They were in the Tower's cybernetic lab. Tony was wearing his black and gold armor, using finger lasers to dissect the Nick robot.

Stark's humor was particularly grating now Steve knew about how the Illuminati, including Tony, had betrayed him. While he couldn't let that affect how he dealt with the current crisis, it didn't stop him going over the recent revelations again and again in his head,. It was as though his memories were on fire. Steve's anger was such that he felt he could burn through the Iron Man armor with a hard stare. He was surprised Tony couldn't feel it but then understanding other people's emotional state had never been Tony's strong point.

"This isn't Fury," Tony told them, more serious now. "It's a life-model decoy. The most sophisticated one I've ever seen."

"An LMD? We had dinner with this thing the other night! Damn it, how long has Nick been fooling us?" Steve demanded. He knew enough about the world that Nick lived in, a world that Steve only occasionally dipped a toe into, to cut his friend some slack. It hurt that Nick hadn't clued him in. Hadn't asked for help. The thing that got him the most, especially after the Bastogne story at Meat Night, was that Steve didn't know his friend well enough to realize that he'd been replaced with a robot.

"And if he's not dead, where is he?" Natasha asked. Steve was sure that she was just as upset. Nick was her friend as well. But she remained the consummate professional. "I've got a dozen different emergency numbers for Fury. He's not answering any of them. All known safe houses are empty. He could still be in danger for all we know. This only raises more questions."

"Not for me it doesn't," Logan growled. Definitely a pro, not so consummate. "Bucky, Doctor Strange, and the Punisher have all gone off the reservation."

Steve had read the files and was of the opinion that the Punisher hadn't even been near a reservation since he'd first arrived at boot camp on Parris Island. Frank Castle was a sick individual who needed locking up; Steve was tired of his colleagues treating the mass murderer otherwise. Steve also wanted to have a very serious conversation with Strange. It had been the good doctor he'd seen altering his memory when the truth bomb had gone off.

"They stole the Watcher's eye, kidnapped the Orb and shot the Hulk through a damn wall," Logan continued, pointing in the general direction of the hole in their tower. It may have been Steve's imagination, but he was sure that Tony flinched at Logan's mention of the Hulk. "That sort of operation has got Fury's fingerprints all over it."

He wasn't wrong. It was far from the first time that Nick had cut him out. Somehow it didn't get any less painful, even now. Normally Nick did it when he was going to do something that he knew Steve wouldn't approve of.

"Working on it," Tony said in answer to Logan. He was plugging various cables into the LMD's circuitry, connecting it up to the cybernetic lab's systems and tapping away at a holographic keyboard. Steve watched as code, meaningless to him, cascaded down the holographic display, presumably telling Tony what he needed to know.

"You think you can track this thing back to where it came from?" Steve asked.

"I've been doing this a lotta years, Steve, and I've never been outsmarted by someone who wears an eyepatch."

That wasn't true. Nick had outsmarted all of them at one time or another. It was sort of what made Nick… Nick; what made him so good at his job. He might not have been smarter than Tony, but he was certainly a lot more cunning.

"There's some weird tech in here," Tony finally said. "This wasn't made by S.H.I.E.L.D., that's for sure. It's a mix of all sorts of alien cultures and—"

It was instinct more than anything. Steve managed to get his shield up in front of his face just as the LMD exploded. The force of the blast caught him and battered him against the wall.

Steve hadn't been happy before: now he was angry. He checked around the wreckage for Natasha. It wasn't his—apparently outdated—sense of chivalry, or "residual sexism," as Natasha liked to call it. Or so he told himself anyway. Steve knew Logan's mutant healing meant he'd be fine and Tony was in a suit of armor. However, Natasha might be very fast, physically fit and extremely skilled, but she was ultimately just a normal human. He was relieved to see her kick a screen off herself and stagger to her feet shaking off dust.

The cybernetic lab had been an isolated freestanding structure in a much larger space within the tower, but the explosion had taken it apart. Parts of the surrounding area were burning. The fire suppression system hadn't yet kicked in yet.

"Is everyone all right?" Steve asked.

"What the hell was that?" Natasha demanded.

"Self-defense mechanism," Tony told them. "It knew it had been breached." He shook off some pretty heavy-duty debris that had landed on him.

"Sure can't track it now," Logan muttered.

"Not so fast," Tony said. "It sent out a signal before it blew." Steve recognized the distracted quality to Tony's voice. He was reading information from the complex heads-up display in his shell-shaped helmet. "Pack your oxygen tanks, people. We're going into space."

Steve had had enough. He headed off across the rubble. He had no idea what was going on but he had a pretty strong suspicion that Nick was caught up in the middle of it. With Doctor Strange and the Punisher acting up, it felt a little like the opening skirmishes of yet another Civil War.

What was Bucky doing? Steve asked himself. Logan had smelled Bucky all over the decapitated LMD. Steve knew he'd been lying to himself regarding his old sidekick. Bucky Barnes and Winter Soldier were clearly not the same person. Whatever was going on needed to stop now. These were the kinds of games that the powerful liked to play; more often than not, it was the innocent that paid the price.

"Call in everyone. I don't care where they are or what they're dealing with. This takes priority. The lies and the secrets stop now. For all of us." There was just the briefest pause before he said it: "Avengers, assemble."

CHAPTER TWENTY-SEVEN

THE JOB OFFER

THESE WEREN'T stupid people. I wouldn't have brought them here if they were. Most of them had more than enough tactical acumen to be aware that, just on the other side of the open blast door, I was slowly assembling more and more of my LMDs. Gamora, Castle, the Punisher, Emma, and Bucky: I'd seen all their eyes flicker past me. The rest had masks that made it difficult for me to see their eyes; I suspected that Strange, who was definitely out of the running, was too arrogant to care. I shuffled amongst them to try and draw their attention, leaning heavily on my cane. I was coming close to the limits of my remaining endurance.

"So you want me to go kill aliens and underground monsters? Are you sure you've got the right Ant-Man?" Lang asked.

"Don't kid yourself, Lang. You've got it inside of you, even if you're not ready to admit it." I told him, though he was one of the weaker candidates. "You all do, or you wouldn't be here."

"Nick, this is insanity," Strange started. "Your physical condition must be affecting your mind. There was no need for this, for any of this. We save the world every day. All of us. Without killing anyone."

Castle cleared his throat. He wasn't the only one who'd killed in the room either, including, I suspected, Strange himself. The sorcerer's lack of self-awareness was staggering.

"Most of us," Strange continued. "If the world is in danger, we'll protect it, the way we always have. The right way."

I turned and fixed him with my one good eye.

"Someone who has literally walked through the netherworlds shouldn't be this naïve, Stephen. The fact that I was always out there, doing a job you never even had to know existed gave you the freedom to be this naïve. To keep your pretty little hands clean. You're about to lose that freedom, whether you like it or not."

I had known that monstrous egos were going to play a part in this discussion. Perhaps I underestimated the extent to which their arrogance would have them deny the existence of the problem, of the sacrifices I'd made, of the crimes I'd committed in their name. I'd also underestimated just how angry this would make me feel. I could have had a life instead of eighty years of murder, war and genocide.

"I can see his point but this is a lot to take in," Emma said.

"It truly is a wonder you Earth people haven't been conquered already. You all strike me as thoroughly incompetent," Gamora said. In many ways she was the best choice. She already had the skillset and already knew the major players. The problem was that she wasn't particularly for or against Earth; I suspected that she might see things from the perspective of the alien invaders I'd been forced to wipe out.

"Nick, this is the last time I ask you politely," T'Challa said. He wasn't going to let this go. Matilda knew it as well. He shifted, readying his weapon. "Who killed the Watch—"

Matilda's comms link started beeping.

"Ah hell," I said. "That would be the self-destruct on Andrew's body. Means we don't have much time. We need to hurry things along here, I'm afraid." The Avengers were on their way and I could never explain all this to Steve in a way that he would understand.

I ceased my shuffling, coming to a halt close to Bucky. He didn't even tense. I wasn't sure whether to be offended that he no longer considered me a threat, or pleased that I was still able to deceive with the best of them.

"Sorry, Buck," I said. I wasn't really. I hit him with the stun cane. He cried out as electricity coursed through his body. He hit the ground, a twitching mess. It wasn't a great way to treat one of the front-running candidates but needs must… My LMD reinforcements flooded out the blast door, weapons at the ready. With some difficulty I stooped to retrieve the Watcher's eye. I was level with Rocket. He was just watching me. I couldn't read his expression because he was a raccoon.

"Fury, you really need to stop and think about what you're doing here," Strange said. It appeared that he had decided that he was in charge. He still hadn't moved. There was no fear. His arrogance really was astonishing.

I noticed nobody had rushed to Bucky's aid. Kid really knew how to make friends.

"Believe me, I have, for a very long time now." I grunted as I straightened up. I was going to feel this in the morning. Assuming there was one. "Until I'm actually dead, I've still got a job that needs doing." I held up the eye and stared at it with my own. I could almost hear the secrets contained within, so eager to be free. "I've got a world to protect and that's what I aim to do." I turned my back to them and started hobbling back through the blast door. I knew they'd make a move but they were now well covered and outnumbered by my LMDs. "I hope, before this is through, at least one of you will see the truth in what I've done here."

"He's just an old man with a satellite full of old robots. We can just take him down without anyone getting hurt," I heard Moon Knight say the words, but I could hear the doubt in his voice. After all, I was *Nick Fury*…

"Those guns are Badoon-made. I wouldn't be so certain about no one getting hurt." This from Gamora. Seemed even Thanos's daughter knew what I was capable of.

"If this is the way it has to be, then this is the way it has to be," T'Challa said. I glanced back at him. "Just remember, Nick, you had the chance to come along peacefully."

I was disappointed. I'd never known peace in my life. I had at least expected T'Challa to understand that.

A spinning kick from Black Panther caught one of my LMDs in the face. I'm not sure which one—maybe Dean? The kick nearly took his head off. Then it was on. Energy blast after energy blast burst from the Badoon-weapons, set to stun. (Honest!) Gamora had a sword in each hand. Black Panther's claws opened artificial flesh and rent metal bones and plastic circuitry. Moon Knight seemed to flow around my LMDs, his cloak billowing, and then they would drop, strange weapons embedded in them.

"Don't hurt them, Matilda," I said. He was right behind me, putting himself between me and the candidates.

"Yes, sir. We understand, sir," Matilda said.

"I'm sorry it had to end like this," I told him, and I was.

"It's been an honor, sir."

I cursed the sentimentality of old age. I had water in my one good eye. I didn't have time for this. The roar of Frank's ridiculously oversized rifle filled the satellite. He was fighting back-to-back with Rocket. Each time they squeezed their triggers, another one of my LMDs went down.

Gamora roared with berserker rage. Both she and T'Challa had nearly reached the closing blast door.

"Fury!" Even over the roar of Frank's gun, I could hear T'Challa's electronically amplified voice. "There's nowhere else to run!"

The door closed behind me.

"Who's running?" I asked the empty corridor. I was more sort of shuffling along on my cane still looking at the Watcher's eye. The blast door cut off all sounds from the fight.

I made my way, more slowly than I would have liked, to the interrogation room. The Orb was strapped upright to a slab of metal. Two of my LMDs were monitoring his biometrics as I shuffled unsteadily across the catwalk towards them.

"I feel like… my skin is on fire," the Orb said in his squishy voice. There was no fear that I could discern, despite his situation. If anything, there was a kind of wonder in his voice. "I'm changing, aren't I? I'm like a caterpillar with an eyeball for a head. But what am I changing into?"

The grim expression on the LMDs' faces and a quick glance at the Orb's biometric readouts on the holographic display told me that he was right. He was changing, though somehow I couldn't see him becoming a beautiful butterfly. Also, I didn't have time for this.

I struck him with the handle of the cane across his eye. Face. Whatever.

"How did you open it?" I demanded. "How did you get at its secrets?"

He stared at me for a moment or two. I suppose that was all he really could do.

"It… likes me," the Orb whispered as though sharing an intimate confidence. It made my skin crawl. "It wanted me to see."

I hit him with the cane again.

"We don't have time for games! Midas is still out there! How did you open the damn eye?!" I was screaming now. Choking back a coughing fit.

"Can't get yours to work, can you? That must be frustrating." He was mocking me. From Spain to the Netherworlds and all points in between, I had extinguished entire species. Here I was, being mocked by this Z-list super villain.

One of my remaining LMDs appeared at my shoulder.

"Commander, they'll be here soon. We should get you suited up. Commander?"

I stared at the Orb, trying to catch my breath. I turned and hobbled away.

"It likes you, huh?" I shot back at him. "The fella this eye belonged to certainly never liked me." I reached the lockbox and held my hand to the side of it. The box confirmed my biometrics and failing DNA, and clicked open. "But he's dead now and I don't see why his secrets oughta die with him."

I looked down at the content of the box. The Watcher's other eye looked back up at me, glowing with its own internal light.

CHAPTER TWENTY-EIGHT

AN OUT

THE LMD had a tear in its fake flesh, exposing the metal and circuitry beneath. It was the last LMD standing.

"You have to see the truth. All he ever did was save the world," it said.

"Doesn't mean he has to be such an ass about it," Ant-Man replied. He was in his tiny, you-really-want-to-step-on-me mode as he leaped up and punched the LMD. The android hit the ground and didn't move again.

The raccoon, who Frank was starting to like despite himself, used his ray gun to disintegrate the head of another of the LMDs. Frank decided that he needed an out.

These things, these so-called "team-ups" had a momentum of their own. He was standing amongst the bodies of the LMDs. Bucky was back on his feet. Gamora, a sword in each hand, was checking that the androids weren't going to get up and start fighting again.

Frank hadn't particularly wanted to fight the LMDs and he didn't particularly disagree with Fury. He'd just been defending himself when the androids started shooting. Nor did he want the job. He respected Fury as a realist if nothing else. That, and the way he'd always been able to manipulate the other costumed clowns to achieve the ends he wanted. Fury, however, had made the same mistake that the rest of them made. Fury's first line of defense was a system. Frank Castle wasn't a hero, a villain, a soldier, an assassin or any of the other things he'd been called over the years. He was what happened after the system broke down. He was the last line of defense. If Daredevil, Captain America, or any of these other so-called super heroes really wanted him gone, they would work to fix the systemic ills that caused the symptoms that he dealt with on the street. But that was too hard, too big and scary. But fighting Galactus when he showed up on Main Street? Now that was something they could get their heads around. They chose to lock themselves into a cycle of constant capture and release that, while pointless, worked as an endlessly recycled excuse to justify their existence.

Frank had played his part in this latest nonsense and now he needed to get back to work. He was momentarily amused at the raccoon picking the LMDs' eyes out of their metal skulls.

"Open that door, Stephen. We're not letting him get away with this," Black Panther said. He was standing at the blast door next to Strange. The sorcerer's arms were raised up as he traced glowing symbols in the air.

Frank just watched and shook his head. They were so convinced of their own relevance, moment to moment. That was when he realized just how tired he was. It had been a long, strange day.

"The door appears to have magical safeguards," Strange was explaining, "How in the world did Fury—"

"We have to get into that room."

Frank wondered how well the Wakandan had known the Watcher.

"Actually, Panther, I do believe someone is about to beat us to the punch," Strange said. Frank could see the third eye in the center of the doc's face again.

There was the sound of metal impacting on metal. Something had just attached itself to the outside of the satellite.

Frank closed his eyes and leaned against the corridor wall. He couldn't imagine anything about this situation that would be helped by the presence of yet more costumed clowns. He suspected that his day was about to become even more tedious.

CHAPTER TWENTY-NINE

ASSEMBLED

LUKE CAGE, Black Widow, Wolverine, Hulk, Thor, Falcon, Spider-Man, Captain Marvel, and Iron Man. It was a solid roster, Steve decided, even if both he and Thor had to get between Tony and Hulk in the Quinjet on the way up here. He, and the other Avengers that couldn't inherently work in space, were wearing armored space suits.

The satellite looked advanced. It was surprisingly large to have avoided detection all these years but then that's what Nick Fury did. He kept secrets—some of them pretty big.

They'd hit the satellite hard. Stealth had seemed pointless. The signal sent from the booby-trapped LMD in Avengers Tower meant that Nick already knew they were coming.

Thor and Hulk had wrenched the airlock doors open between them and then they were in. All of them racing through the corridors looking for answers. Looking for Fury.

What they got were more LMDs. The LMDs tried to ambush them in a split-level loading bay. Steve deflected a blast from one of their weapons with his shield. He took the gun from the LMD, smashed it, and flung his shield at another android on the next level up, hitting it hard enough to knock it down to the ground where it was still.

Hulk was tearing LMDs into pieces; Wolverine was ripping into them with his claws. Neither held back. Iron Man flew through the loading bay, jettisoning submunitions that sought out and destroyed the remaining LMDs. The other Avengers didn't get much of a look in.

"Where's Nick Fury?" Steve demanded of the android he'd just disarmed. It was disconcerting how closely it resembled Nick. "The real Nick Fury. Tell him the Avengers are here." Steve caught his shield as it rebounded back to him. "Tell him Captain America says 'no more damn secrets!'" It was only then he realized how angry he was. It had just been one betrayal after another.

Hulk lumbered up to stand by him. Spider-Man landed at Steve's other shoulder.

An alien light, a color that Steve didn't quite recognize, washed over them. It was so bright that he brought his shield up, turning away. Spider-Man and even Hulk were covered their eyes, flinching from the light.

"No more secrets. I agree, Steve. So do they, apparently."

Steve recognized the voice. It sounded amplified.

"Nick? What the hell?" Steve cried.

"Maybe it's because they're together again. Or because they know that this is the end," Fury continued. Steve could just about make out a bulky figure silhouetted in the bright light. "Either way, all that really matters is that now, at long last…"

The light subsided but didn't completely disappear. Now Steve could see the bulky figure more clearly. It was Fury: older, white-haired, a cybernetic implant where his eyepatch should be. He was wearing power armor that looked considerably more sophisticated than Tony's. The armor bristled with weaponry that Steve was not even remotely familiar with. In one hand Fury held a monstrous-looking cannon-sized rifle. In the other, he held both of the Watcher's eyes by their nerve endings. It was grotesque. The strange light emanated from the eyes.

"…all my eyes are open," Fury said.

Old friend or not, it seemed pretty clear that whatever was going on with Fury wasn't going to be settled with a conversation.

CHAPTER THIRTY

THE ECSTASY OF GOLD

A FEW DAYS AGO

EXTERMINATRIX BROUGHT the golden corsair, Midas 12, which was mostly made from "salvaged" Kree-tech, in to land on the Blue Area of the Moon. She was out of her seat, the space suit's helmet growing around her head.

The Orb's spacesuit made him look even more ridiculous: the glass of the helm had a magnifying effect on his eyeball-head.

Exterminatrix joined her father and the Orb. Midas was wearing the Iron Man armor he'd stolen from Stark Enterprises many, many years ago. He had, of course, plated it in gold and made his own improvements, much of it with stolen alien technology. As they strode through the hold, the Mindless Ones stood to attention as her father passed by and then they fell in behind him.

"I hope you know, Orb," her father said as they made their way down the hatch's steps and out onto the surface of the Moon. "If you cannot deliver on what you promised me, I will literally tear that ridiculous head off your shoulders and hurl it into orbit."

Exterminatrix decided that she would quite like to see that. In fact, she could imagine a number of sporting uses for the Orb's head.

"I didn't come here to die, Doctor Midas. None of us did," the Orb replied. She could still hear the pretense at confidence in his voice. He was self-aware enough to know that he was in over his head. She was pretty sure that he didn't know the degree to which he was in over his head, however. Had he realized the true extent of the danger he was in, the things she could do to him, he would've been terrified beyond speech and movement

"We came to be reborn," the Orb said.

They crested the top of a large crater and their strange crew made their way down towards the alien citadel that lay at its center.

"I thought we came to rob the Watcher," Exterminatrix said. Even to her own ears she realized that she sounded like a somewhat sulky teenager. She was not happy how this was going down, or about the Orb's part in it. They should have just torn his knowledge, his secrets, from his broken, sobbing form. Their approach to the domicile of an entity with the power of the Watcher's should have been so much stealthier. Instead they were exposed, just casually wandering towards the citadel.

"That too, Exterminatrix. This way—follow me," the Orb said.

There's nothing quite like being patronized by a fool, Exterminatrix thought.

◦─────◦

THEY MADE it to the citadel's front door without Exterminatrix killing anything. It was a closed and extremely solid-looking door.

"Um... hi," the Orb said. Exterminatrix closed her eyes. She could feel a tension headache building. Now this fool was talking to a door. "I'm the Orb. I've had dreams about this place. I think that means I was invited...?"

Her father's shell-like armored head turned to look at the Orb. Exterminatrix found the prospect of seeing the proposed "head tearing off and throwing into orbit" plan actualized quite stimulating.

"Strange," the Orb mused. "It doesn't seem to be letting us in." As last words went, they lacked poetry.

"You imbecile," her father said with the kind of quiet precision that she had come to realize from years of experience meant that he was really angry. "I will flay you alive for—"

The door slid open.

"See?" the Orb said cheerfully. "I told you I wasn't crazy."

Exterminatrix couldn't shake the feeling that he was as surprised as the rest of them that this had worked. She didn't wait to question their good luck. She headed into the citadel and started up a broad set of stairs clearly sized for a humanoid far larger than even the Mindless Ones.

"Spread out," she told them. "Find anything that looks like a vault or an armory. We have to move fast. He's the Watcher. He sees everything." She would have much rather have planned this herself. Trusting the Orb had turned this into a farcical smash and grab. Her father was getting sloppy. "We won't have long before he—"

She all but ran into him. Exterminatrix looked up at the Watcher. She took a moment to appreciate his size, his sheer physicality, the palpable power radiating off him.

"I see you."

She felt his words as much as heard them.

The need to kill him, to slay the Watcher, overwhelmed her as a physical sensation. Those weren't golden guns in each of her hands. They were extensions of her will, purpose given form.

"Plan B," Daddy said, the repulsors on his golden armor already glowing. "Kill the bastard."

Then the dome of the citadel tower exploded.

CHAPTER THIRTY-ONE

NICK FURY VS. THE AVENGERS

THE HULK hit the surface of the Moon hard enough to make a new crater. Nick Fury, an aged Nick Fury no less, had flung Hulk through the hull of his satellite base and at the Moon. He'd done so with sufficient force that Steve had seen the impact through the rent in the satellite's hull. Not even Tony in his Hulkbuster armor was able to do that to Hulk.

Luke Cage, who Steve had previously understood to be unbreakable, was floating unconscious in space, perfect spheres of blood escaping into the void while his suit's self-repair system tried to close the hole Nick's gun had made. Even though Steve was in the midst of the battle, even though he was fighting for his life as LMDs—who seemed to have a pre-programmed understanding of how he fought—swarmed him, he was still struggling to get his head around what had happened. It felt like betrayal after betrayal after betrayal. He wanted it to stop; he needed to take a moment to try and work through what had happened here but he knew he couldn't. He had a responsibility to everyone who'd followed him to Fury's satellite. He could mourn all the friendships—if indeed that's what they'd ever been—when this, whatever this was, had been dealt with.

"Avengers priority alert: this is Captain America, requesting backup from any and all space-faring operatives," he said as he went down under a pile of Fury-droids, trying to get his shield between himself and the pounding they wanted to give him. "We are engaged in battle in Earth's orbit," as he kicked, punched, gouged and tried to free his shield. He felt like he had when bullies had jumped him on the way home from school back in Brooklyn, before the war, before the Super-Soldier serum. "The target is Nick Fury." The words were sour in his mouth. Everything about this was wrong.

Even buried under the LMDs, Steve could just about make out flashes of light from the battle. Fury had taken the fight outside, exiting through the hole he'd used the Hulk to make. He could hear the others over comms as Fury—a normal man—went toe-to-toe with Earth's most powerful heroes.

Steve burst free of the LMDs. He was hitting androids in the head with his shield, splitting their faces, bisecting their skulls until they stopped moving. It wasn't right that they all had the features of his friend.

"Nice armor, Fury. Where'd you get the alien tech?" Iron Man asked over comms.

Steve fought his way towards the hole in the satellite's hull. He needed to get eyes on the battle. Try to get some control over the situation.

"And why are you an old man all of a sudden? Did I miss something?" Tony continued.

"You've missed a lot of things over the years, Stark. More than you could possibly imagine. Me though…"

The spacesuit covered Steve's head and he made it out the satellite with the escaping atmosphere just before the hull repaired itself. He clung to the outside of the satellite desperately trying to achieve some kind of tactical awareness, as nothing was making sense.

"...I don't miss," Fury finished.

Steve saw the flash from the shot. Worse, he heard Tony screaming. Nick had just one-shotted Iron Man. Steve checked the tactical display in his suit's HUD. Iron Man was floating inert in space, unmoving.

Fury had shrugged off some of the most powerful Avengers as though they didn't matter. Leaving them hanging, unconscious—at least Steve hoped that they were only unconscious—in space. The only thing they had to show for it was that Nick had dropped the Watcher's eyes. They were floating away from him, their lambent glow acting like an eerie beacon.

Steve bent his legs and then launched himself off the satellite towards Fury's position. His erstwhile friend had anchored himself to a bit of orbiting space rock. He was a shooter after all. He'd always want something solid underneath him.

"And what'd I miss, Nick?" Falcon demanded. Steve could hear the pain, the betrayal in his old partner's voice. "What'd I do to deserve being lied to? Other than watch your back for years."

Steve used the spacesuit's propulsion system to increase his speed as he flew at Fury. He was close enough to see Falcon fly into Fury's legs, tearing him from the rock. Falcon hit him low and Wolverine hit him high.

"We trusted him," Wolverine snapped as he clawed at Fury's power armor. "That's where we went wrong. Won't happen again. You violated the sanctity of Meat Night, you sonuva..."

As he closed Steve could see that even Wolverine's adamantium claws couldn't pierce the alien tech power armor that Fury wore.

"Nick!" Black Widow said loud enough to drown out Wolverine's furious and now mostly incoherent rant. "Just tell us what's happening. Help us understand this." She was all but pleading with him. Steve could hear it in her voice, in all their voices: the desperate need to understand this betrayal.

"I wish I could, Natasha," Fury said, and that was the thing: it was definitely Fury. No copy, clone, LMD or any other trick. Steve recognized the remorse in his friend's voice. He did not want to be doing this. He clearly thought that he didn't have any other choice, but then Nick had always been one for unilateral action. "I wish there was time," Fury continued. He shrugged Falcon, Wolverine and Black Widow off, flinging them away with sufficient force to put them into new and unstable orbits. Fury triggered the propulsion system on his suit and used it to maneuver back into position, to re-anchor himself to the rock.

"There is time, Nick," Steve said as he flew at him, shield outstretched, increasing velocity. "Time for you to stand down but it's running out."

Steve hit him hard enough to shake his own bones, once more knocking Nick off the rock.

"Even if I could explain things, Steve, you'd hate me more than anyone," Nick told him.

Steve went cold. What had Nick done? What was bad enough to cause this level of destruction? And why was he sitting on all this advanced tech?

"Damn it, Fury! I've always known who you are and I've always respected you," Steve told him. "Don't cross a line you can't come back from. Not after everything we've been through."

They wrestled high above the Earth. Fury had all the power but Steve had all the moves. He was practically crawling around all over Nick's armor, looking for a way in.

"I crossed that line a long time ago, for all the right reasons," Nick told him even as he grabbed for him. "Look behind me, Steve. In the days to come, as you start to understand what's happening here, I want you to remember this view."

Fury finally managed to get hold of him. The armor's strength was incredible. It was like trying to wrestle the Hulk. Fury held onto the struggling Steve and showed him the world. Steve stopped fighting, just for a minute, and looked at the planet that he helped stand watch over.

"Know that I'm not sorry for anything I did," Nick said quietly. "Except this."

Nick threw him away; just discarded him.

"I'm sorry too, Nick," Steve whispered as he flew through space looking down on his home planet. "Sorry it had to be like this. Thor..."

They had needed time. With even the heaviest of hitters, like Captain Marvel, unable to take Fury down, they'd needed to think of something else. Steve had been the distraction while Thor had used the Earth's gravity to slingshot himself around the planet; the Norse god was now headed towards Fury, hammer first, at a ferocious speed.

"Aye, Captain," Thor said over comms, "this will take but a moment!"

Thor collided with Fury like a stellar event. Cracking Fury's helmet. Steve heard his old friend cry out.

"I'm sorry I didn't see what was happening here sooner, Nick." Steve said. "You've been manipulating this investigation from the very start and I'm afraid to find out why." Though he was starting to have some very unpleasant suspicions. "But I will. No matter how much it hurts us both."

Thor had hold of Fury now and was beating him with Mjölnir, trying to increase the size of the crack in Fury's helmet.

CHAPTER THIRTY-TWO

SIDES

EMMA HELD two fingers to her head and concentrated. The hull of the satellite seemed to inhibit psychics and wielders of magic. Inhibit, but not stop. She could also hear a background babble similar—but slightly different—to that which she'd heard emanating from the Watcher's eye. Despite both these factors, she was able to get some idea of what was happening with the battle outside. It appeared that Fury had been giving the Avengers a pretty significant beating.

"They're fighting," she told the others, still stuck in the corridor behind the blast door with her. Emma grimaced as she received new information. "Thor's involved. It shouldn't be much longer."

Strange was still standing in front of the blast door, drawing arcane patterns in light on the structure as he attempted to bypass the satellite's magical defenses. Black Panther was next to him.

"We should be helping them," Ant-Man said, meaning the battle outside. He had been an Avenger: his loyalty to them made sense.

"We should be getting the hell out of here," Emma said, wincing as she did so. The background psychic babble was getting louder. "This could look bad for us. Like we've been working for Fury." She knew she was thinking like a "villain," but part of thinking like a villain involved the understanding that "heroes" were often of the "punch first, think second" mentality.

"We have been working for Fury," Moon Knight correctly pointed out.

"Some of us may still be working for him," Black Panther said. He looked at Barnes.

"Me?" Barnes demanded. "I'm the one who cut off his head, remember?"

"Yes, and also brought the real Fury the Watcher's eye."

"Maybe you missed the part where he shocked me with his old man cane and took it?" Barnes pointed out.

"What about the part where you blew up Moon Knight's ship?"

"What about you, Mr. High-and-Mighty Panther-Man? You're the one who recruited us all into this!" Barnes was in Black Panther's face now.

Emma could feel the anger and frustration pouring off Winter Soldier. He'd had more than enough but he definitely wasn't working for Fury, though he was sympathetic to Fury's offer. She could have offered this up to the group. He was practically broadcasting his emotional state after all, but she suspected that Black Panther wasn't terribly interested in hearing it. They'd both rather work off some steam tearing at each other.

Barnes wasn't the only one who could see Fury's perspective. If he wasn't completely and utterly mad, if half of what he had said was true, she got it too. The crime scene evidence and the fact that he could bounce the Avengers around like toys also seemed to back his version of events.

She knew that hard decisions sometimes had to be made to protect what you held dear. When it's a genuine choice between us and them, it always had to be "them" that suffered. She also knew that sometimes those so-called hard decisions were used as an excuse to justify atrocities. Things almost never came down to that strict a dichotomy. Perhaps when it genuinely did, that was when you found this "Man on the Wall" waiting.

It may have been moral cowardice on Emma's part, but it was all too big. Just the very idea of her travelling to exotic places, wearing unflattering armor and toting vastly overcompensating weapons to kill insanely dangerous creatures was clearly utterly ridiculous. Besides, in the realms of us and them, she still had the "us" of mutant-kind to think of—particularly her students. They'd come a long way in terms of acceptance in her lifetime but there was still work to do—and there were still forces at work in the world that wanted to tear down any form of social progress in the face of their own, often externally stoked, fear.

"Are we still picking sides?" Ant-Man asked Moon Knight. "Because that's an easy call. I'm siding with the Avengers."

Emma wished her world were that black and white. Unlike Fury, she didn't believe that Ant-Man had it in him. He was like a lamb amongst wolves. Perhaps he was just here because he could turn himself small enough to crawl around in gunshot wounds.

"I honestly don't know anymore," Moon Knight replied. "Fury has gone to some insane lengths but he's done it for the right reasons. Hasn't he?"

Emma smiled coldly. Would they have reacted the same if it had been Magneto pulling their strings—or even the master manipulator Professor X, easily Fury's equal with the ability to read minds to boot? Would they still be so conflicted if it had been a job offer from a mutant? Perhaps they were all just so sure of themselves, of their righteousness, that they were struggling with the moral ambiguity of the situation.

That was when she noticed they were missing a few people. Looking around, she saw the Punisher, Gamora and the weird raccoon creature walking back towards the airlocks where the ships were docked.

"Where the hell are you going?" Black Panther demanded.

"Someplace where I don't have to listen to you people," the Punisher told him. Whatever else he may have been—mass murderer, psychopath, terrorist vigilante—Emma couldn't shake the feeling that he at least wasn't a hypocrite.

"I am on the side of the man who wears the skull," Gamora added. The green lady had been a bit too fast off the mark in attacking Bucky, as much as Emma might understand the urge to do so. In retrospect, however, Emma suspected that she probably shouldn't have hit Gamora. It had been a sign of her own frustration with the situation. In another time it would've been nice to have a martini with Gamora, see what she was about.

"I'm still not even sure why I'm here," the raccoon creature said, "I just know I hate all of you."

Emma couldn't really blame him either.

The psychic babble was increasing in volume, as if whatever was causing it was getting closer.

"Nobody's going anywhere!" Doc Strange shouted.

Another control freak who presumably didn't feel that they were getting their due, Emma thought.

"We are in this whether we like it or not," Strange continued, his face illuminated by the glow of his own magic. There was a somewhat disturbing third eye in the center of his forehead. This investigation had been entirely too ocular for Emma's taste. "All of us together are going to decide our course of action. Regardless of Fury's reasoning, he's still a mass murderer. I vote we fight to take him down. Who else wants to be on the right side of history?"

Emma shook her head. She wasn't sure she'd ever heard someone so significantly misjudge their audience. The Punisher was a mass murderer; she was pretty sure that Barnes was as well. Gamora and even the raccoon had that vibe too. It seemed like a speech designed to kick off a fight. She prepared to turn to diamond and go and lean against a wall until it was over.

She flinched as pain lanced through her head and the psychic babble nearly overwhelmed her. It was getting louder. The source was getting closer.

Then the blast door slid open.

"Do I get a vote?" the Orb asked.

Emma had to tamp down her telepathy as much as possible. The chaos of his mind was screaming at her. Strange's coruscating magical energy changed color as the Orb walked through it. It was almost as if the eyeball-headed "villain" had psychically hacked the sorcerer's magic. Emma didn't want to think about that too much. She was too busy trying to avoid a telepathically induced migraine.

"Because I vote we kill him," the Orb continued. "And take every last one of his eyes." He was dragging along the head and torso of one of the LMDs. It looked as though the Orb had worked out some of his aggression on the android.

"By the Hoary Hosts," Strange said. "What did Fury do to you?"

"I don't think it was Fury," Emma told them, wondering what a Hoary Host was and if a Renaissance fair somewhere was missing its wizard.

"What did he mean when he said you were being changed by what you stole?" Black Panther demanded. "What exactly did you steal, villain? Other than eyeballs."

"Secrets," the Orb answered. "I stole all the secrets. Including this one."

Emma saw it too late. She raised her hand, instinctively, defensively. She started to shout a warning, even as she tried to shut down the Orb's now disturbingly alien mind, but it was too late. The psychically hacked energy washed over them all, taking them down, and the Orb's memories poured into her mind.

IT WAS *raw mental energy. It shielded the Watcher from the Mindless Ones' concentrated energy blasts even as he used waves of concussive psychic force to knock them back through the central chamber under the tower. The power on show was astonishing. The Watcher could have laid waste to them all with a thought. The Orb assumed that he* was holding back because he was an observer, because presumably there were unknown prohibitions regarding the amount of force he could use to defend himself, his home and his possessions.

"Look at that." The Orb could not tear his eye away. He could feel the energy awash around him as a palpable force. It was like standing in the eye of a storm.

Exterminatrix ran past him, her arms full of advanced alien weaponry.

"Can you imagine having power like that?" The Orb's voice was full of awe.

"We found the armory! Grab all you can carry and let's go!" Exterminatrix shouted. It was clear to the Orb that she didn't understand.

"I wonder what it's like to be him." The Orb was staring at the huge alien as it held off the Mindless Ones. "To see what he sees. I wonder..." That was when he saw it. Understood the emotion that the Watcher was experiencing. "You're scared, aren't you?"

In the Orb's expanded peripheral vision, he saw Exterminatrix drop some kind of portable cannon-looking device. The Orb moved towards it, never taking his eye off the Watcher's battle with the Mindless Ones—a tempest of powerful and destructive energies. The Orb leaned down and picked the cannon up. It was surprisingly light.

"You're holding back because you saw..." Whatever the Watcher had seen, it was just out of view for the Orb, just a little beyond the limits of his sight. It was as tantalizing as it was frustrating, like having the answer on the tip of your tongue. The Orb wasn't sure he had a tongue. He was bathed in the light of the energy from the battle. It washed out the surroundings. The Orb could no longer see the alien citadel for the light all around him. "What did you see?"

The Watcher swung around to stare at the Orb.

Then it was obvious.

"You saw your own death, didn't you?" This moment. "Yes, I can see it myself in your eyes." The weapon in the Orb's hand. A weapon taken from the Watcher himself. "Oh, you poor, poor Watcher."

Inevitability.

"I can help you, I can make sure..." The Orb didn't really have a choice. The weapon in his hand was some kind of cannon. It looked powerful enough to slay a god. "...you never have to see anything again!" He depressed the trigger stud. A blast connected the weapon in the Orb's hand to the Watcher's head for the tiniest instant. The Watcher went down like a felled tree.

○─────○

EMMA FELT as though her head had been split open. She was lying on the floor, crying blood through the pain in her skull, but at least she had an answer for the others now. There couldn't be the slightest doubt just who had killed the Watcher.

However, the Orb was no longer anywhere to be seen.

CHAPTER THIRTY-THREE

NICK FURY VS. CAPTAIN AMERICA

"**UM... I'VE** got the eyeballs," Spider-Man said over comms. "Just curious, what happens if I throw up in my space helmet?"

Regardless of Spider-Man's coping mechanisms, Steve didn't need to hear this over group comms right now. Every second counted here, even if Steve was out of the fight. He was perched, in his spacesuit, on what he suspected was an old Soviet-era spy satellite. The Avengers were scattered in various orbits but Thor was still in the fight. Steve had faith in Thor, which was perhaps ironic for a Christian.

"Also, guys, these things are really glowing like crazy," Spider-Man continued. Steve searched the star-filled night over the planetary horizon. It was difficult to see anything between the vast darkness contrasted with the reflecting light from the Moon and the Earth. The best he could hope for was to spot movement and the glow of the Watcher's eyeballs. *There!* Two balls of light, close together, like shooting stars. That had to be Spider-Man and the eyes. Now Steve just had to work out who was left to intercept them, because as far as he could tell Spider-Man was just trailing behind the eyes, holding on to them with webbing. This suggested that the eyes knew where they were going. He tried to work out if he could use his suit's own propulsion to intercept, but orbital mechanics were not his forte.

"You remember what happened the last time one of them did that, right?" Spider-Man asked. Steve did. That had been when he started to realize just how compromised they all were. "Bomb full of secrets anyone?"

And that was the problem when someone you knew and who knew you turned against you: they could wreak irrevocable damage just by knowing your business.

It didn't matter, Steve told himself, *you have to be able to trust.* He knew too well his own fallibility, his own weaknesses, his trusting nature. But you had to try—you had to hope for the best in people, didn't you?

Then, out in sublunar space, Steve saw the spark of a hammer born of magic and technology hitting a suit of armor, and lightning in space. Thor and Fury.

"Yield, Fury!" Thor cried, the loudness of his voice distorting the comms link. "The time has come to explain thyself!" Everything Thor did, he did at volume. "Thy metal suit is failing! I do not wish thee harm!"

"Same to you, big guy, but I'm afraid this is going to hurt." It was Nick. He sounded so old, so tired, but no less determined. "I see you've got a sister…"

Since when? Steve wondered.

"You have access to the Watcher's secrets? How?" Thor demanded.

"Learn from this hurt, Thor. Learn and be better for it," Nick told Thor.

Alarm bells were ringing for Steve. It sounded as though Nick was about to do something awful. Steve knew that Nick didn't dislike Thor; rather, he was uncomfortable at the power the god wielded. Nick had decided, after the first time he'd met one, that gods needed reminding that humanity mattered as well.

"Never forget that it wasn't a punch that took you down," Nick continued. "That despite all your strength, in the end when you were beaten all it took was a whisper."

Steve's blood ran cold.

"What…? What didst thou say?" Thor demanded. Whatever Nick had told him it had been on a closed comms band, a personal message between him and Thor.

"Anybody have eyes on Fury?" Steve asked, trying to force the desperation out of his voice. Trying to be the calm he needed to be to lead, although this was a mess. "Thor? Thor, come in!"

Something hit the surface of the Moon, hard. Steve could just about make out what looked like an explosion of electricity from his vantage point, riding the old satellite. A huge mushroom-shaped cloud of regolith rose from the Moon, close to where Hulk had landed. It was lit from within by neon electrical discharges.

Was that Mjölnir? Had Thor lost his hammer? He saw Iron Man's comms come back online. Regardless of how he felt about him right then, he was very pleased to see Tony. There had been a few moments where Steve was worried that Nick had actually killed him.

"Tony, any sign of Thor or Fury?" Steve asked. He could make out Iron Man's suit burning hard against the backdrop of the Moon's bright white light, trying to get back into the fight.

"Negative, Cap, all I see is…" Whatever Nick had done, Tony wasn't making jokes now. He sounded pretty shaken up. "Wait a minute, something just hit the Moon."

Steve knew that the Iron Man armor had all sorts of sophisticated sensors, not to mention excellent optics. They'd all now be pointed at the impact area on the surface of the Moon.

"I must be seeing things," Iron Man said over comms. He sounded scared. "It looks like Thor is trying to…" The last part of the transmission disappeared in a storm of static.

Had Tony been trying to tell him that Thor couldn't pick up his own hammer? Steve could understand Thor dropping his hammer, particularly if he had been rendered unconscious, but being unable to pick it up? That didn't make sense.

"Say again, Tony?" Steve said over comms, hoping against hope. "Sounded like you said trying to pick up his—" Too late. Steve realized that the static coming in over the comms was jamming. Then suddenly comms was clear as a bell again.

"Stark override code, Hdgk(X)=H2k(X,Q)∩Hk,k(X). Return to Earth." It wasn't Tony's voice. It was Nick's.

"Oh hell, how did you know…?" That was Tony's voice.

From his vantage point on the satellite, Steve got an excellent view of the torch from Tony's boot repulsors as he headed back down towards Earth as fast as the armor could travel.

"Tony? Where are you going?" Steve asked. "Tony…" He knew it was useless. "Anybody out there read me?" He asked. "Avengers, come in." He was more than a little worried that Spider-Man, who'd last had control of the eyes, was no longer answering. "Anybody?"

Steve was very much alone as the satellite he was holding onto crested the Earth high above the Americas and showed him the Pacific. It was breathtakingly beautiful. Steve closed his eyes and tried to work out what to do next. The problem was that Nick had always been there. Always. He knew so much about them, even before factoring in the Watcher's knowledge.

"He was a robot." It was Nick's voice over the comms link. "But he wasn't a liar, Steve." Quiet, reflective. Steve could hear the remorse in the voice. "Bastogne, best steak I ever had." But Nick had never let remorse stop him.

"Nick, what in God's name have you done?" Steve asked.

There was no immediate answer. Then, after a few moments:

"All I see is truth now, Steve, ever since I opened the eyes. That's what I showed them. Truth." From anyone else it would have sounded like madness, but Steve knew his old friend better. "Did you know Wolverine once murdered his own children?" Steve could hear the weight of it all bearing down on Nick. Fortunately, Nick was talking to him over a private link. Steve didn't want Logan to hear this. "And Natasha. She'll never understand why

I didn't choose her. It's because she's a lot more like you than me these days. I was hoping she could stay that way." Steve could hear affection, the pride in Nick's voice, as he talked about Natasha.

"Nick, whatever you've done, there's still time to stop. Just talk to me…" Steve said as he pushed off the satellite. It was a forlorn hope. Steve knew it had already happened, was a done deal. Nick wasn't a super villain. He was a spy. He understood operational security. He didn't talk about a thing until after the fact.

Steve knew he had to find someone, anyone else. Spider-Man's suit transponder was closest. Steve triggered his own suit's propulsion system.

"You don't have to try and forgive me, Steve. I'm not asking you to. Years ago, I watched a man die: a man who'd given his life to a greater cause and with his last words he asked me if it had been worth it."

We watched millions die for a greater cause, Steve thought, *then we decided that it could never be allowed to happen again. We decided that together, Nick, after we had truly come to understand what the Nazis had done.*

Steve searched the heavens, looking through the helmet of his spacesuit. He felt like a goldfish in a bowl, but he was pretty sure he could make out the blinking light of Spider-Man's suit beacon.

"I didn't have time to answer," Nick continued.

Steve couldn't be sure, but he suspected that there was a figure alongside Spider-Man's unmoving form. A stealthed suit?

"I wished now I'd said yes. I wish I'd told him how sometimes the worst of us have to walk point and do whatever it takes to clear the way for the best of us to follow."

No! Steve thought. *That's how we make the monsters, because everyone always thinks they're the ones who're right.* He almost opened his mouth to tell Nick this, but he was more concerned with getting to Spider-Man, getting to the eyes. Steve was willing his suit to move faster. He was using the highest level of magnification that the suit's optics were capable of. He could now make out the dark shape over Spider-Man. He was pretty sure it was Nick. Steve had no idea what he was going to do if he caught up with his old friend. It was clear that he was no match for him.

"I wish that man had met you, Steve. I'm sure glad I did."

"Nick, don't you—!" Steve cried but Nick's next words overrode Steve's comms as though they didn't exist.

"Goodbye, Cap."

Steve saw the torch from Nick's suit as he jetted away from Spider-Man's unconscious body. Nick held a glowing alien eye in each hand.

"Nick!" But the private comms link had gone dead. Steve was just crying out into the vacuum.

CHAPTER THIRTY-FOUR

ASCENSION

THERE WAS a golden ship within the Blue Area of the Moon. Midas. The Orb remembered how he… No. How the person he had once been had been so afraid of Midas and his daughter. As he dropped through the sky towards the lunar surface, protected by his own burgeoning psychic power—a gift from the Watcher's eyes—he realized how ridiculous that had been. Even as Midas looked now—a man of clay, rents of light in his body—the Orb saw nothing to fear. Midas had changed, evolved, as had Exterminatrix. But the Orb knew them intimately now. He could see their lives as afterimages stretching out behind them in their wake. He perceived matter and time differently. He had not quite reached the Watcher's omnipercipience. He could not see all things at all times, but he was certainly much more aware on many different levels, in many different spectrums of light and thought.

After this, you make us mindless again, yes? A telepathic broadcast from one of the remaining not-so-Mindless Ones who still followed Midas. *You take away the thinking? Just like you promised?*

Yes, the Orb thought as he looked down on them from far above. *In thought there is only pain; seeing, however, seeing is all*, he mused.

"Trust me," Midas told the creature—unaware that he was being observed by the Orb—as he walked towards the Watcher's citadel with its broken tower once more. "After this I'll take everything."

The Orb remembered that he'd once spent the better part of an hour practicing a maniacal laugh in front of a mirror with a bag over his head just so he could sound more villainous. Now he chuckled squishily as he touched down on the Moon's surface a little way from the golden ship. He was genuinely amused. The need for pretense had been peeled back. He knew exactly what he was and none of it mattered.

He had, however, landed between two of Earth's mightiest heroes.

Thor was tugging at his hammer, unable to lift it out of the impact crater.

A groaning Hulk was staggering to his feet.

"Hulk… Hulk will smash. Hulk will…"

The Orb struck the Hulk with a discharge of psychic energy. The huge creature hit the Moon's surface once again, like a sack of green potatoes.

"This is what my dreams were about all along," the Orb said out loud as he strode past the Hulk's smoking, glowing body. "This is why I was meant to be here."

Thor ignored the attack on his fellow Avenger, too focused on trying to pick up his hammer.

"To see the Watcher's last secret. The secret that killed him," the Orb said. Then it unfolded in his mind's eye like a sepia-toned movie as he followed Midas, Exterminatrix and the Mindless Ones from a distance. The Orb remained unseen.

○─────○

A FEW DAYS AGO

THE ORB *looked back through time and saw Fury as he brought his '64 Cadillac DeVille in to land just outside the Watcher's citadel. The* tower was burning like some ancient beacon. The Orb listened in on the comms message that Fury was receiving. He knew instinctively that the message came from Matilda, one of Fury's LMDs.

"It sounded like he said 'I can see you.' Then there was an explosion and the line went dead," Matilda told him.

"And that's it?" Fury asked. The armored spacesuit he wore was supported by an exoskeleton, tiny servos effectively making the suit into power armor. However, Fury looked as though he was having trouble moving. His advanced age and subsequent weakness were evident.

"Yes, sir," Matilda confirmed. "All moon-based listening devices are currently offline."

"I knew it was a good idea bugging this place," Nick replied. "I'm going in."

"Sir, are you sure about this, given your condition?" Matilda asked. "And your past history with the—"

"You know what to do if I don't come back, Matilda." Fury drew his pistol from the holster on his hip. "You've got the list. Call them. Tell them everything."

"Everything?" Matilda asked as Fury crossed the threshold into the technological ruins of the Watcher's citadel.

"Every last damn thing," Fury said, looking around at the wreckage of what had been probably the single most advanced structure in the Sol system. "Show 'em the Unseen. That's an order. Show 'em why it had to be this way." Fury picked his way through the rubble. "There's definitely been a break-in here. Helluva fight, too. Can't tell what was taken yet but I'm guessing there was—"

The Watcher lay amongst the debris, psychic energy discharging from an empty eye socket like a fallen power line. At first it looked as though the Watcher was dead. Then the huge, bald alien moved, pushing himself up onto one knee and staring at Fury with his remaining good eye. The power of the cannon notwithstanding, it seemed as though the blast had done little more than stun the Watcher. Though it had done so sufficiently that the Orb had been able to remove one of his eyes while the powerful alien was unconscious.

"Oh hell," Fury said. *"I'm guessing you didn't do that just to mock me. Tell me what happened here. Tell me what you saw."*

◦─────────◦

NOT YET, the Orb decided. Now more than ever he was starting to truly appreciate just how destructive the truth was. It was clear to him that each and every human being was made of lies. You unraveled the lies and you unraveled the person, you left them naked and screaming, like being born. Besides, the Orb was aware of Fury, now, in this moment. His sight had seen Fury land before the door on the other side of the citadel from the Orb's own position.

"You saw it all back then, didn't you? Even this, I bet."

The Orb wasn't sure to whom Fury was talking. Himself? The ghost of the Watcher? The eyes that Fury held in either hand? Or was Fury talking to him, the Orb? Did he know? After all, he could surely see as well as the Orb could. *Interesting*, he thought.

"You big bald sonuvabitch," Fury said, answering the Orb's question.

The doors of the citadel opened for Fury, as though greeting an old friend. "At least this time there's nobody watching." He walked forwards into the dark citadel.

He was wrong, of course. Fury couldn't see all, it transpired. The Orb was watching. As were seven Watchers, projecting themselves into space high above the citadel from somewhere else that even the Orb couldn't see, but he knew he would, one day.

Almost everyone was here now. The end was in sight.

CHAPTER THIRTY-FIVE

THE MIDAS TOUCH

I MADE my way through the darkened citadel like the ghost I very nearly was. The surveillance devices I'd planted in the citadel were all gone, destroyed in Midas's initial raid. Uatu's eyes let me listen in on Midas and his team as they returned to the scene of their crime, however. They let me watch them as they strode amongst the ruins. Midas looked like an energy-scarred Ben Grimm; Exterminatrix, a golden gun in each hand; the Mindless Ones, all telepathically begging for their self-awareness to end. *You and me both*, I thought.

"Yes, there is great power here," Midas said. I was making my way through the badly damaged alien halls towards the citadel's broken tower even as I watched Midas and his crew in my mind's eye. After all I couldn't miss the "villain's" triumphant monologue. It just wouldn't be right. "In the walls, in the air," he continued. "Enough power to enslave worlds." Somehow, even the warthog-guy who just wanted to turn Earth into an all-you-can-eat buffet had more vision than Midas. "To put galaxies to the torch." *Been there, done that*, I thought. "Enough power to change the course of creation: this time, we will take it all." He stretched his arms out in an expansive gesture. Midas was just another dictator to knock over. Another tin-pot Caesar to take down. The thing was, he was walking amongst wreckage as he gave his speech, with his only audience his poor daughter and creatures literally known as Mindless Ones. Midas may have been the ultimate alchemist, but he was no master of irony.

Even as I concentrated on Midas's crew I tried hard not to think about the last time I was here. I failed.

A FEW DAYS AGO

INTERROGATING A *wounded alien on the Moon. It didn't even strike me as odd anymore. I could barely remember the man who would have found it strange. Maybe that was the problem.*

"You've been robbed. How the hell does that happen?" I demanded. Uatu was crouched in front of me, his eye socket venting bubbling energy like a deep-sea vent. His other eye, still glowing, was staring at me. "You know what, never mind that for now. Just tell me who did it."

Nothing.

"They may have taken your eye, but I know you still see everything. You know who they are, where they come from, and probably where they're headed right now. Just tell me and I'll take care of the rest." That bald bastard just stared at me like inscrutability was a superpower. "Damn it! There isn't time for this, Watcher!" He just crouched, still, amongst the ruins of his previously sterile home. "Look at this damn place! It's been looted! And we both know what trinkets you liked to keep here!" It must've been nice being the ultimate observer, able to claim neutrality, but I knew the artifacts that he stored in his citadel. Each one was an existential threat to humanity, my oh-so-fragile world. "If just one of those things has fallen into the wrong hands, the entire Earth is in—"

"You are correct, Nicholas Fury. I do see all things," he said, his voice mellifluous and calm, even if I could hear the pain behind it. The pain and the judgment. "Even the Unseen."

He lifted his hand and the bubbling energy from his eye socket coalesced into visions of my crimes: the assassinations, the mass murders. He showed them to me as though he didn't think I knew what I had become. I just stared at it as it all unfolded in front of me. Close to a century of a life, a life of service, reduced to the absolute worst of me. But unless you make a real effort to redeem yourself, that's how we should be judged for crimes of this magnitude. I knew I was damned. Trying to redeem myself at this juncture would have been obscene. I was a monster. I had also done the right thing.

Hadn't I?

"You son of a bitch," I said quietly.

I WATCHED as Midas picked his way through the debris in the central chamber to the makeshift bier where Uatu's body lay. My ill-fated LMD Andrew, Steve, and the others in the initial investigation team had placed it there.

"There is power in the Watcher's flesh as well," Midas continued. "Take him apart, so I may drink his blood and consume his knowledge, one bite at a time."

Oh hell no. I flew through what remained of the tower's superstructure.

"In life, all this fool did was watch." Midas wasn't wrong about that at least. "Through his death… all we shall do is conquer."

I touched down on a pile of rubble in the central chamber, unseen. I held both the eyes by their nerves in my left hand, but I didn't need them to show me Midas anymore. I saw him reaching for Uatu's body. I couldn't let his alchemical touch defile the alien corpse. Whatever else Uatu might have been, he didn't deserve that.

"Not with that hand, you won't," I growled, raising my own hand. Tony Stark would have killed for the blaster technology built into my armor. It had more than enough power to blow Midas's hand off. His cry of pain was satisfying.

One last fight. I'd killed gods and demons. This bunch didn't strike me as much of a challenge.

"Fury." Midas's voice sounded like rocks shifting. He was cradling his newly made stump. "I will gladly trade you the hand in exchange for all your eyes." Then to his Mindless crew: "Kill him."

There were five of them left. They charged me. They moved with surprising speed. I was close to death.

Still, one last fight. There's always one last fight.

The Mindless Ones were broadcasting all the way:

Fury is the bringer of sin.

Yep.

Fury is the Master of Secrets.

Guilty as charged.

Kill the one who made us know.

Seemed like I was responsible for everything.

The one who damned us.

"I thought you Mindless Ones were smarter than this," I said.

Kill the killer of God!

Smoking slits in their half-formed faces shot lines of red force, staggering me, but the armor held despite the battering that Thor had given it. Then they were upon me. Huge four-fingered fists pummeling me, denting sophisticated alien alloys. I could feel it through my armor. I was letting this happen. It was something I deserved, a punishment. *What are you doing, Nick?*

I held my hand up, changed the frequency on the hand blaster and sent a particle beam charge lancing out like forked lightning in all directions.

◦——◦

"DON'T YOU dare look at me like that. Who the hell are you to judge me?" I was practically snarling now, good and pissed, pointing at Uatu's newly ruined face. At least the eye socket had stopped leaking energy. "What have you ever done but stand around and watch?"

That his face was a scarred mess, that his eye socket was now empty gave me a kind of grim satisfaction. It was nice to see someone as pointlessly hands-off as he was getting roughed up a bit. Getting his hands dirty like the rest of us.

"Watch as I fought to save the world. I won't make apologies for how I did it. Especially not to you." I was working up a good head of steam now. "You had the power to stop me if you wanted. You had the power to stop it all." Which made him complicit in my books. "But all you ever did was nothing." I'd heard his justification for his inaction before. "I know, I know… you're bound to bear witness and not interfere. Part of some crazy cosmic order of Peeping Toms." I was only just starting to realize the degree of contempt I had for Uatu.

"And you like to brag about how you've broken that vow, more times than anyone can count, right? Because what? You show up and shout a warning?" Setting off a series of events that he got to watch like a favorite soap opera! "I've been down there day after day after day in blood up to my knees." Long suppressed resentment was all pouring out of me now. "You wouldn't have an Earth to stand above and stare at if it wasn't for me and I'm not going to let you throw all that away now!" I was shouting at him. "So long as the Earth is still spinning, everything I did was worth it!" Which is true, but who was I trying to convince? "So tell me what you saw!" Because my soul is an open wound.

"TELL ME WHO I HAVE TO KILL NEXT!"

I was shaking like a leaf, despair and… fury.

What had I done?

What had I still to do?

He just watched, because of course he did.

"You already know," he said so very quietly.

I was running out of secrets and shadows to hide in.

CHAPTER THIRTY-SIX

THE EXTERMINATRIX INTERLUDE

THE AGED Fury, in his power armor, threw the Mindless Ones off him in a storm of particle beam energy. Oubliette sighed at the tedium of it all. She wondered how much more successful her father would be if he spent less time on being a "super villain," with the grand schemes and the monologues, and more time just consolidating his already existing power.

She'd also found her father's severed hand.

"I will turn this to my advantage. I always do," her father said, as he moved away from Fury's battle with the Mindless Ones. He was practically rippling with his recently acquired power, yet there was something pathetic about the way he staggered through the rubble, cradling his stump. "I will grow a better hand. Nevertheless, we should probably save the old one just in case."

He sounded weak.

Oubliette bent down to pick up the hand.

Fury was more than holding his own against the Mindless Ones. Not even Noh-Varr had done that. There was an almighty crash as a Mindless One slid through a huge pile of debris sending it flying into the air. Fury and his foes were giant shadows projected on what was left of the walls of the ruined citadel, silhouetted by flickering exchanges of powerful blasts of energy.

"You're right, Father," Oubliette said as she stooped to pick up his hand. "There is power in the air here. With every breath it tells me that if we stay, we're going to die."

"Oubliette, I want you to put a golden bullet in that old man's skull." He didn't even look at her as he issued the order. "And then I want you to bring me…"

Oubliette took the hand and ran. She had the codes for the ship, the bank accounts, access to their various facilities and all his stolen technology. She would have to avoid the various traps he would have set for her in case of his demise but in time she would be able to take control of all the fruits of his inter-dimensional piracy operation. And she had his hand.

"OUBLIETTE!" It was a rage-filled scream. She knew that he wouldn't be angry at the betrayal. Her father had quite literally programmed the importance of betrayal into her from an early age. No, what he wouldn't be able to understand was why she wasn't doing as she was told. She knew that it may have seemed contradictory to people who hadn't grown up in her family, but her father understood that she was loyal until she was strong enough to usurp him. What he presumably hadn't realized was that her time had come. Her father had lost. He had failed again. Now she had to salvage what she could. It wasn't as much of a usurpation as she had hoped for, but she suspected he was too arrogant to see it for what it was.

"Goodbye, Father," she said as she ran through the wreckage, making for the ship as fast as her recently evolved body and high-heeled boots would carry her. "I'll always keep you close to my heart." She clutched his huge, still-glowing hand to her chest. They had an army of scientists and technologists but he had never allowed much in the way of research into himself, into how the cosmic ray bath had changed him. He didn't want it replicable. He didn't want anything to challenge his advantage, his edge. It was all in the hand: both his cosmic ray-induced transformations and his recent evolutionary alchemical changes. She would vivisect the still-living hand, plumb its transformed DNA and mine all its secrets. That was her real usurpation, her real victory. That and her freedom.

CHAPTER THIRTY-SEVEN

IF THY EYE OFFEND THEE…

I WAS beating on the Mindless Ones with one hand. Running energy into the suit's gauntlet and using its incredible strength to pound on them. I knew the likes of Tony, for example, got off on this kind of power. I never had, but sometimes there was just something deeply satisfying about delivering an extensive beatdown. It was a shame that they just wouldn't stay down.

"You can't win this fight, boys. Believe me, I know," I told them, taking three of them off their feet with a haymaker that would have made Rocky Marciano envious. "With these eyes I can see all things." I held both of Uatu's eyes by the nerve endings in my free hand. They were showing me the Mindless Ones' moves before they happened.

I took another of them off its feet with a shot from the suit's palm blaster.

"Yes, but you're not the only one." I recognized the disquietingly soft, liquid tone of the voice.

I turned around casually, blasting another Mindless One as I did so.

The Orb was striding across the rubble towards me. This was not the same Orb that I had known. I could tell by the way he carried himself; I knew the difference between total confidence and false arrogance.

"I've been touched by those eyes as well. Would you like to know what they showed me about you, Nicholas Joseph Fury?" he asked. Something about his tone suggested his confidence bordered on psychosis.

"Not particularly." I'd had enough of my privacy being flensed to last a lifetime, as hypocritical as that may sound.

"They showed me where your soul is weakest," he said, and then he hit me with a blast of raw, undiluted psychic energy. It didn't matter that it was stolen power from the Watcher; it hit me like a concussion grenade, slamming me into a pile of alien masonry.

"As well as your armor," he added.

The force of the blast had opened rents in the suit and battered my frail, elderly flesh beneath. I dropped both of the Watcher's eyes. Not long now. But die at the hands, or rather the eye, of the Orb? The damned Orb! I don't think so.

"No," I managed after spitting the blood out of my mouth.

"You don't deserve so many eyes," he said as he closed upon me. Good. I played it weak, as though struggling to stand. I didn't have to do too much acting. "Not when you couldn't even keep all the ones you were born with."

Harsh, but if he just moved a little closer...

I swung at him with every last bit of exoskeleton-amplified strength I could muster. I hit the Orb's big eye-face and snapped it round.

"You took the first eye! You started all this! It's your fault he's dead!" I was shouting now. I was dimly aware of one of the Mindless Ones pushing itself back up on to its feet as I coughed up more blood and tried to catch my ragged breath.

"I thought you could see the truth?" the Orb said. I'd hit him with the power of a Mack truck. Not only had he not gone down, he was still able to engage in witty repartee. Not a promising development. "You still don't understand the biggest truth of all, do you?" He turned his back and walked away from me. In many ways, that was the most disrespectful thing. He clearly didn't see me as a threat. He moved to where the eyes had landed, their nerve endings intertwined. "We didn't start any of this. We didn't choose him or his eyes."

I was thrown into shadow as a Mindless One stood over me. The casual backhand sent me tumbling through the air, hitting the ground again, hard. I was largely being kept alive by the alien medical technology contained within my armor. My flesh was well and truly broken. I was living on borrowed time.

"He chose us," he told me.

I was vaguely aware of the Orb now holding both of the Watcher's eyes as the rest of the Mindless Ones started to pound on my prone form. All I could see was an avalanche of fists filling my vision.

⸻

I FELT *as tired as the Watcher looked. No, not tired. Weary. My pistol hung limp at my side. I knew where this was going. The answer to my question: who was next? Because there's always one more, isn't there? Violence is cyclical: there's always another body to drop when you "know" you're in the right. I took a deep breath.*

"Why did they take your eye?" I asked. It was relevant but I suspected that I was trying to put off the inevitable, put off what Uatu already knew because he'd seen it. I looked around at the ruins of the citadel. Everything was coming to an end. "I know this place. I've searched it myself. When you were passed out in one of your fugue states. I've had the whole place bugged for years. You've been watching me? Well, guess what—I've been watching you too, pal."

I remembered when my counter-voyeurism would have provided me with a sense of satisfaction, of getting one over on someone who deserved it. But now all the righteous indignation, all the anger, was just bleeding out of me.

"And you never write anything down. All your secrets, everything you see, and you don't record any of it. Or do you?"

He still towered over me, even while sat cross-legged. Just looking at me.

"The secrets are in the eyes, aren't they?" I asked.

Nothing. This was someone you didn't want to play poker with. There was no tell. (Steve, on the other hand…) Maybe inscrutability is a super-power after all.

"You know how many lives I could save with those secrets?" I demanded, the righteous indignation and anger returning. This was the thing that'd always got to me about the Watcher: with his power, I could prevent atrocities before they happened, minimize the damage from accidents and natural disasters. Where was his sense of responsibility?

"You know how many lives could be lost or ruined if they end up in the wrong hands?" My detractors might think I am the wrong hands but then, with the kind of knowledge we're talking about here, there was only one person I trusted with it. "Who was here? Who took your eye?!"

Inscrutable or not. I couldn't shake the feeling that he was of the opinion that I just didn't get it. If anything, that made me angrier.

"Damn it. Answer me!" I would put the pistol into his eye socket to get answers if I had to. "WHAT DID YOU SEE?"

He continued to stare at me. I swear that his expression didn't change, but somehow he seemed angrier. Maybe the glow in his remaining eye intensified. Or there was something in his expression, or lack thereof. Then it was gone. The tension in his face seeped away and his head dropped as he took his last remaining good eye off me. The rivulets of black ichor running from his empty socket made it look as though he was crying.

"I have seen… too much," he finally said. "It is time for someone else to watch."

He raised his hands, palms up, and summoned flames of intensely burning psychic energy.

"What are you doing?" I asked. "Put your hands down." He didn't.

"I'm not the enemy here! I'm trying to protect the damn world! You will not stand in the way of—"

I was just talking to hear myself say things now. I saw what was coming. It sickened me.

He turned the palm of his hands towards me.

"Damn it, no! Don't you make me!"

I brought my gun up.

○─────○

MY REALITY had been reduced to constantly falling fists. My armor was holding up—just—but that didn't mean the body underneath wasn't getting some of the punishment as four of the angry Mindless Ones pounded me into the rubble. They seemed to hold me accountable for their self-awareness, as though I was God and they were my creations, and as such they were properly pissed at me. Like Nietzsche-level pissed.

"There are so many things we're going to see together. I can't wait to get started." The Orb was talking to Uatu's eyes. My awareness of this must have been residual power left over from my own handling of them. It wasn't helping. I didn't like the way he was stroking them, rubbing them together. I was worried that he was going to start juggling them. The weirdest things cross your mind when you're being beaten to death by four over-muscled, extra-dimensional henchthings. "Yes, I feel you stirring, you like that idea, don't y—"

I was praying for death now. I didn't want to see the Orb getting it on with two giant alien eyeballs. Then, the nerve endings trailing from both eyes wrapped themselves around the Orb's neck. Strangling him. It was probably the best thing that had happened all day. I particularly enjoyed the choking noises that the guy with no mouth made as he sank to his knees.

The Mindless Ones were so surprised that they stopped beating on me. I used the opportunity to try and crawl away. I was missing a lot of my armor now; it had been torn away by brutish, extra-dimensional strength.

"Can't die. Not until I know it was worth it. Until I know this isn't the end." I hadn't even realized that I was talking to myself.

Looks like the end to us, one of the Mindless Ones broadcast. In many ways, they were the real victims here.

I was pretty sure that I was hallucinating. I could see a raccoon toting a huge gun. It took me a moment before I recognized Rocket.

"They may be mindless but they're not wrong. This ends now." It was Doctor Strange, his cloak carrying him over the heads of the rest of the candidates, hands glowing with mystical energy. He sounded as angry as he did self-righteous. He must have teleported everyone here. Castle and Bucky were both armed with the same Badoon rifles that my LMDs had carried back on the satellite. Along with Rocket, they were putting bolt after bolt of energy into the Mindless Ones, forcing them back. Moon Knight was throwing glowing crescent-shaped projectiles.

Black Panther sprinted ahead of the pack, across the debris, and reached me first, delivering a sidekick to a Mindless One that was about to tear my head off.

"Thank God," I managed as T'Challa pushed the Mindless One away from me with a further flurry of kicks. "Thank God, you're—"

"Here to see you answer for your crimes?" he said, finishing my sentence for me. "Yes, we are. Now stay down."

It seemed that he hadn't understood the importance of the work I was doing at all. Punished for my crimes. They had better get to that quickly, then.

"You're here because you've seen the truth in what I said and for that I'm sorry." I was lying in the dust. I may as well have been talking to myself. "I'm sorry I have to pass the burden on. It ain't an easy road. Wasn't for me, won't be for one of you." I looked around at what the rest of the candidates were doing. As close to death as I was, this was still a job interview.

Emma looked cold and beautiful, a human-shaped diamond, as she straight-up slugged one of the Mindless Ones. Gamora was fighting at her back, her twin swords biting deep as they tasted the henchthing's extra-dimensional flesh.

"But it's a road somebody's gotta walk. For the sake of us all." And that was the thing, for all their judgment. I knew that came with the territory when you put a costume on. They wouldn't be here but for my actions. A number of them wouldn't even have been born.

Castle and Rocket were laying down a punishing hail of fire from their energy weapons. Moon Knight caught one of the Mindless Ones high in the face with a kick, unbalancing it, taking it down to the ground.

My residual connection to the eye, and through the eye to Uatu, and through Uatu to his home that was more than a home, was trying to tell me something. There was some kind of energistic disturbance, beyond the battle, within the citadel. I pushed myself to my feet, barely able to stand now. I had been fighting for way too long.

Doc Strange was backing himself towards me, both wrists wreathed in scarlet arcane energy as blasts of eldritch power flew from his outstretched hands.

"We're not here to redeem you, Fury. We're here because there's one last sin you haven't confessed to," he cried.

What a fool. Redemption. There was nothing left to redeem. Why were they fighting so hard? Just so they could sit in judgment over me? They weren't holding back with the Mindless Ones, like they would have if they'd been fighting humans. I guessed self-awareness didn't matter when the other sentient creatures in question looked so different to you. Hypocrites. At least I was honest about my killing.

"One last sin…" I managed. Trying to stagger towards the other source of disruption in the citadel.

"Damn it, Fury, say it!" Strange screamed at me.

He was a self-deluding fool, but then what difference did it make now?

"Yes. I… I did it."

I remembered squeezing the pistol's trigger.

"I killed the Watcher."

○─────○

THE RECOIL *traveled up my arm. I saw the explosion of flesh as the gamma-hardened bullet burst the Watcher's bulbous alien skull. He collapsed to the ground and I found myself standing over the corpse.*

○─────○

"I KILLED him and then I..." That was when it slithered up to me. The nerve ending wrapping around my leg and climbing me like a constricting snake.

"God help me."

Then the ghost of Uatu was watching me, again, through the gouged-out eyeball that I suddenly held in my hand.

The candidates were still fighting the Mindless Ones, kicking up dust amongst the rubble, the clouds illuminated from within by blasts of eldritch light and alien weapon fire. It was like a German opera. Gods and monsters. I tried to remember which one I was. That was it. Human.

Then Bucky, the kid I'd suspected of enjoying killing maybe a little too much, was standing in front of me, pointing one of his many guns in my direction.

"Nick, put the eyeball down. This is finished."

Hadn't he been there, somewhere close to the start? Hadn't we eaten steak together in the snow one Christmas a long time ago? I had to say I was disappointed. If anyone was going to get it, what I'd been doing all these years, I thought it would've been him.

Except the eye in my hand had told me what the disturbance was. The latest violation of the citadel, of Uatu's home, a more significant violation than even this battle.

"No, Buck. Not quite yet it ain't," I told him. "Midas is still inside and growing stronger. I can feel it. Somebody's gotta stop him." Because now, finally, I could see what I needed to see. "I'm the only one who can. I gotta save the world one last time or else..."

It would have sounded so stupid if it hadn't been my life's work, I guess. I staggered away from him, towards where I knew I would find Midas.

"Nick, you're going to die if you don't give this up," he said. Hell, I was pretty sure the only thing keeping me up was the psychic energy from Uatu's eye. "Let us finish it. We can save the world too."

I looked back at him, fixing him with my one good eye and my implanted cybernetic targeting monocle.

"Yeah, I sure hope you can." Then I continued on my way.

"Nick, damn it, don't…"

Some people just don't appreciate a good exit.

"I can do this, Bucky. I got one more sin left in me." Except this wasn't going to be much of a sin. "Just get everyone out before—"

Something hit the already-crumbling citadel hard. The force of the impact sent more supports, and chunks of masonry that had been old before Christ was born, tumbling down the central tower. It was as though the Moon itself was shaking. Electrical energy wreathed the entire complex. The bright blue neon threw us into harsh relief, rendering us as shadows—but then, I'd been one of those for a very long time.

"Nick, what the hell is going on?" Bucky called after me. "This whole place looks like it's gonna come down around our…" I ignored him as I staggered towards the nexus of light. "Nick!"

I found Midas at the base of the tower, suspended in a nimbus of energy like a three-dimensional version of one of Strange's pentagrams. It looked as though the tower itself was trying to collapse and he was holding up its constituent parts through sheer force of will. Midas was still missing his hand: that at least gave me some sense of satisfaction.

"All this power and all he ever did was stand around and stare. Such a pathetic waste."

I mean, I felt the same way but this guy really liked the sound of his own voice. I staggered into his presence, holding one of the

Watcher's eyes. I could see Uatu's body on the makeshift bier they had made for him.

"I'm glad you killed him. Now give me his eye. I promise, old man, that you won't have to watch what comes next."

I'd done business with this guy. Sat across the table from him but it was like he didn't even know me at all. The eye in my hand was radiating anger. It showed me all.

○――――○

I SAW the judgment of the Orb as witnessed by Ulana, Uatu's wife, and the other Watchers high above the lunar landscape against the night sky. He screamed and screamed and screamed as he got exactly what he wanted. Funny how that works.

"It burns… help… help me, please!" he begged.

The eye was forcing its way into his chest, fusing with his flesh, the nerve endings whipping around like furious eels.

"We cannot interfere. Such is our sacred vow," Ulana told him as he continued to scream. "All we can do is observe." Her objectivity was merciless.

See, the Orb's judgment wasn't at her hands or the hand of the other, silent Watchers. He had judged himself. In the end we all do.

○――――○

I SAW the candidates, locked in their seemingly endless battle with the poor Mindless Ones, who just wouldn't stay down.

"Pull back! We'll regroup outside!" Doc Strange shouted.

"We can't! Fury's still in there!" yelled Bucky. Bless him.

"Something tells me Fury is right where he belongs," Black Panther replied.

○――――○

I WAS looking at the body of the Watcher I had murdered—so yeah, maybe I was where I belonged. At least T'Challa knew me that well. I had done this. I was responsible. If there was a court over and above my own conscience—such as it was—then perhaps it was self-defense, or perhaps Uatu had pushed me to kill him, but it was irrelevant in the end. Midas didn't get to defile Uatu's resting place. The Watcher had never been a friend, far from it, but he was the only other living creature who knew the full extent of the things that I had done. That had to count for something.

Didn't it?

○────○

"I HAD no choice. I..." *I had nothing. I stood over Uatu's body, yet another corpse I'd made, wondering why the death of this ineffectual, judgmental bastard bothered me so much. Why I was trying to justify myself to him?*

I had my knife in my hand. I pushed it into his other eye socket, cutting his remaining eye out because I needed it. I needed it to find the other eye and the things stolen from the citadel. I needed it because it would help me do my job, protect the Earth, protect humanity. It was an early warning system. I wanted it because it could facilitate pre-emptive attacks.

"It'll all be worth it in the end." I lied. "I swear. I swear." And like every other lie I'd told, I meant it.

I wished the revulsion I was experiencing was because I was holding a gouged-out eyeball in my hand.

○────○

"I HOPE I was right, big guy," I said to Uatu's corpse.

"I'm still not quite sure how you did it," Midas said.

This guy.

I turned to look at him.

He was walking towards me, still surrounded by the nimbus of energy.

"He had the power to kill you a thousand times over," he said. "So why didn't he?"

"Because Uatu wasn't a murderer." I wasn't sure that this was a concept that Midas could grasp. "Unfortunately for you, Doctor Midas, I sure as hell am."

"You're going to kill me? With a dead man's eyeball? Apparently the years have turned you senile as well as—"

Then he was howling with pain and impotent fury as I thrust the eyeball through his nimbus and into his cheap, Ben Grimm-knock off, clay-like flesh. I'd listened to him for about as long as I was going to.

It lit up the tower; it lit up the entire structure and most of the Blue Area of the Moon. I could see clearer than I ever had before. I saw every last single blood-soaked moment of my life, from cradle to rapidly impending grave, with perfect clarity.

But regardless of what I'd told everyone, despite all this knowledge—no, not knowledge, *sight*—I still did not know if I was right or wrong.

I damn well knew that Midas was wrong, though.

I SAW Bucky, T'Challa, Castle, Emma, Strange and the others. They were out on the surface of the Moon. They watched the lightning storm engulf the citadel.

"Whoever comes out of that, we take down," T'Challa said, "hard."

"We can't just stand here and watch!" There was desperation in Bucky's voice. Maybe I'd misjudged him. Maybe he wasn't such a cold fish after all.

"You sure about that?" Emma asked. She was looking up.

The others followed her eyes. Ulana and the other Watchers floated in the sky as they observed the Orb getting exactly what he wanted.

UATU'S EYE was a sphere of lava in my gauntlets. I could feel the alien alloys melting, running, burning my flesh even as they fused with it. Pain was irrelevant: another piece of information to be recorded. I continued pushing the eye deeper and deeper into Midas's flesh.

"You wanted power…!? Take it all, you sonuvabitch!" I cried.

"No!" he cried out. "It's too much! Too much! I can't…!" This from a man for whom nothing was ever enough.

He became an outline in light, an energy ghost. The eye had a life of its own now, burrowing deeper into what was left of Midas. I staggered away, my gauntlets molten, and hit the ground. I managed to roll onto my back. I was staring up at the neon night through the tower, now more hole than structure. Every single inch of me was agony but that was just more data to be processed.

"Heh, death by eyeball." I wasn't sure if I was talking to myself or Uatu's corpse. Didn't really matter. Nobody could hear anything over the noise Midas was still making. "He looks like he's finally getting what he deserves." I turned to look up at Uatu on his bier. "We all do sooner or later, don't we?"

"Get it off! Get it off!" Somehow Midas was still capable of using language. It proved my suspicions as regards the love he had for the sound of his own voice. Then his energy ghost-form collapsed in on itself.

"Damn. What I wouldn't give for a shot of good whiskey right about—"

CHAPTER THIRTY-EIGHT

SECRETS

THE CITADEL exploded as though it had just had enough.

"Goodbye, Uatu," Ulana said against the bright white light of the blast. There were tears in her eyes. For all that they saw, the Watchers also felt: hate, joy, fear, love. Every. Last. Thing.

"DAMN IT, Nick," Bucky said, out on the surface of the Moon. They'd never been friends; their bond had run deeper than that. They had been to war together. Fury had been one of the few remaining who remembered. Bucky guessed he had gone out the way he would have wanted to. He was pretty sure that Nick had never gotten comfortable with all the awful things he had done. Fury could justify it but hated having to do it all.

Bucky hoped that Fury had found peace either in the afterlife, if that was a thing, or in oblivion.

STEVE WAS so angry he had gone cold. He was striding through one rubble-strewn crater after another under the star-pricked lunar sky. He was sick of the Moon. One of his oldest friends was dead after going berserk and kicking the Avengers' butts. He couldn't shake the feeling that he knew less than half of what he should about what was going on and liked absolutely none of it. Least of all was the involvement of Doctor Strange and Black Panther. The secret bomb that the Orb had unleashed on them in New York had shown him just what they were both capable of. That would be dealt with another day, however.

"Nick Fury is dead," he said as he reached them. Logan actually flinched at this. Steve was pleased that it was Logan and Hulk with him. He wanted them there in case it turned nasty. Once he would have counted Strange and Black Panther as allies, if not friends. No longer. Steve was even more pleased that Natasha was there. Natasha would be at least as ruthless as he felt if they didn't like the answers they got regarding Fury's death.

"I've seen the sack of bloody stew that proves it." Someone had dropped an alien citadel on his oldest friend's head. "And we've got another sack they tell me is Doctor Midas. What we don't have is a reason why." It was more a scattered energy signature, a spectral ghost fused with the debris, but sack had sounded better.

He gave Strange and Black Panther a moment to see if they wanted to say anything.

Nothing.

"Fury's satellite full of LMDs disappeared the second he died. There's no sign of the Orb or Exterminatrix, and all the Mindless Ones that were so chatty before are suddenly mindless again." Which was probably a good thing. "Whatever the Watcher and Fury died for… It's gone now."

Strange and Black Panther just looked at him.

Logan shifted dangerously.

Natasha let her hands drop down by her sides. Her face a cold mask. She was ready to kill. Steve knew she would go after Strange first. Put a bullet in his head before he could cast a spell.

Black Panther looked around. He could feel it. He knew what was in the air.

"There's nobody left who can tell me why one of my oldest friends suddenly went crazy and died." Steve paused, giving them another chance to speak. Still nothing. "Unless there's something you gentlemen would like to add?"

Strange looked around, finally understanding that he was in danger, and that, by God, Steve was ready to beat what he wanted to know out of them.

It was Logan of all people. Logan, who put a hand on Steve's shoulder and said it all with a look: *Maybe you don't want to know.*

○─────○

CAPTAIN AMERICA turned and walked away. Wolverine, Iron Man, Hulk, and, with a final glare, the Black Widow followed him.

"Why didn't you tell him?" Strange asked.

"I don't tell anyone anything." Black Panther said. "Why didn't you tell him?"

"I don't know. I still might, I suppose, but with the way things are after all this…" Strange paused for a moment, apparently choosing his next words carefully. "No one trusts anyone now. With so many of our secrets dragged into the light, somehow it has made us all more secretive than ever. For now, I think we've all suffered enough for our sins. Maybe this one should die with Fury."

As they picked their way through the ruins, all of this was observed and recorded, as all things must be.

"Then let us hope that it is actually dead," Black Panther said.

Despite their supernatural and technologically advanced senses, neither of them saw the wretched figure clad in rags watching them from a nearby pile of rubble.

CHAPTER THIRTY-NINE

HAPPILY EVER AFTER

EXTERMINATRIX HAD crashed Midas 17 into what looked like an ochre John Ford landscape. The golden spaceship was burning against the backdrop of Monument Valley on the Utah and Arizona border. Sitting on a rock, she was struggling to appreciate the majesty of manifest destiny and a thousand westerns, despite having a gun riding each hip.

Her father's hand, the rents in the clay flesh still glowing with an inner light, was lying on the dusty ground next to her.

"The power's gone," she said to herself. She would miss that. She was now back to being just one of the smartest and most physically capable human beings on the planet. She had enjoyed being so highly evolved: it had felt right somehow. "My father's gone." Mixed feelings. She loved him, but sooner or later you have to grow up and murder your parents. "Without him, his empire will crumble." She would also miss their empire. She had enjoyed being rich and powerful. She would still be rich and powerful, just not "that" rich and powerful. "The world as I've always known it is finished."

All-in-all… "This was not one of our more successful capers."

Had she remained as evolved as she had only so recently been, she would have been aware of the diamondback rattlesnake slithering across the desert towards her. The heat and ongoing death spasms of her father's severed hand had attracted the snake.

"You got too greedy, Daddy, wanting the power of a god all to yourself. You should have known you can't take over the world in a day. You've got to do it the old-fashioned way…"

The snake struck. It went for the hand, but its fangs did not penetrate the strange flesh. Instead, the diamondback turned to gold.

Something glinted in Exterminatrix's peripheral vision. She turned to look down at the snake. She picked it up, delighted.

"…One golden bullet at a time." She examined the golden diamondback. "So begins the New Midas Empire."

After all, she mused in the dry, dusty heat, there was no situation that she couldn't turn to her advantage.

This was observed.

―――◦―――◦―――

HE KNOCKED on the tenement apartment door. It was wrenched open.

"Go away! You can't stop me!" the bloodstained woman with the kitchen knife screamed at him. If she was surprised at his appearance, it didn't show. Instead she stepped back into the sparsely furnished apartment towards the heavyset and bloodied man tied to the chair. She had all but invited him in, as far as he was concerned. The man was sobbing, clearly too frightened and in too much pain to be capable of anything resembling coherent speech.

"I've had enough!" she cried. "Enough of him treating me like a fool! Enough of his stupid eyes!"

I mean, we can't have stupid eyes, can we? he thought.

"Leave me alone!" More screaming. "You can't stop me from killing him!"

Tch, he was so misunderstood and always had been.

"Lady, I'm not here to stop you," the Orb said, stepping forward into the apartment's dim light. The Watcher's eye's nerve endings had grown into an entire external nervous system: covering his body, piercing his costume, lacing through his flesh and connecting to the enormous eye he had in place of a head.

"I just want to watch."

○――――○

EMMA WAS sat next to the raccoon as he piloted his ship towards Earth. Her arms were crossed. It had been an incredibly stressful and emotional day, and she was pretty sure that nothing had really been accomplished. A zero-sum game. There had, however, been a lot of blood and thunder.

She was thinking of trying to salvage a bit of her day by getting the raccoon to drop them in Manhattan and seeing if Gamora wanted to go for a drink. The only problem was the raccoon seemed to be a friend of the green lady, and he kept on side-eyeing her as though he were moments away from asking her to prom.

"They told Cap everything, I guess," Ant-Man said.

Emma rolled her eyes at the sound of Lang's voice. It appeared that he'd never learned that quintessential hero skill of brooding in silence.

"Must've been hard, hearing how his friend went crazy like that," he continued.

Emma supposed this day wouldn't be a total bust if she did actually telepathically spay Ant-Man.

"I mean we can all agree he went crazy, right?" Lang asked.

No, we can't, Emma thought, *that would have been far too simplistic and let us, all of us, off the hook far too easily.*

"Guys?"

Emma was a little disappointed that Castle hadn't punished Lang for not enjoying the silence.

"Um... aren't we missing somebody?"

Emma didn't want to give Lang the satisfaction of paying attention to him, but she did do a quick telepathic head count.

Interesting. It appeared that someone had taken the job after all. Emma smiled.

This too was observed.

○──────○

THOR CRIED out silently into the vacuum as the spacecraft soared overhead. His tears had frozen to his cheeks. Every single one of his muscles was strained to the point of tearing as he tried to lift Mjölnir, the hammer that he was no longer fit to wield, from the surface of the Moon.

This was also observed.

CHAPTER FORTY

THE MAN ON THE WALL, PART TWO

BUCKY TOOK the shot. It would take some time to hit, as he had to take the solar horizon into account. Even on the very edge of the Sun's corona, he also had to account for the effect of the heat on the electromagnetically driven projectile's ballistic properties. He knew he was pushing the railgun's predictive targeting algorithm to the very limits of its capabilities, even with the triangulated data from the solar-shielded stealth drones.

"It is just as we have heard," the reptile said. The LMDs back at the satellite had managed to break the reptiles' encryption with some stolen Skrull code-breaking software. This enabled Bucky to listen in on the cross-reality communications.

The visual feed from the drones showed a powerfully built humanoid dinosaur. He was riding a gravitational sled that doubled as a sophisticated sensor array. He was the point man... *point-lizard* for an invasion fleet from a Type II Kardashev civilization from an alternate universe. The reptile civilization had harnessed the power of their own sun to skip across alternate realities and sack them like dinosaur Vikings.

Not on my watch, Bucky thought and then permitted himself a grim smile.

He had believed Nick about the threats facing the Earth and even this reality. He wondered if the others would have been quite so dismissive if they had seen the things that he and Nick had seen during the war. While some of the other candidates had either the skillset or the inclination for this kind of work, Bucky knew that he and Castle were the only two real candidates. Well, maybe the raccoon too. He also knew that Castle was too tied up in his own thing and too psychotic. That left him.

"Their forces are in chaos. Their Watcher is dead. The Earth is ripe for the taking." Dino-boy continued his report, unaware of the inevitability of the bullet traveling through the haze of the Sun's corona toward him.

When things had calmed down and Bucky had enough time to think about it, he had realized that he was born for this job.

Back at Camp Lehigh, Virginia in 1941, Bucky had thought himself just about the luckiest kid in the world. The age at which you could volunteer had seemed completely arbitrary to him. He had felt like a coward as he had watched fathers, older brothers and sons sign up to fight the Axis powers. Then he had been picked to fight alongside Captain America himself! Excited didn't really cover it!

Looking at it now, with older eyes in more enlightened times, he realized that he had been a child soldier. There was precedence for it. There's a reason the word "infantry" contains the word "infant," after all. Because he was a kid, adults would say things in front of him and assume he either didn't understand it or it just didn't matter. He remembered one of the propaganda guys that helped promote Captain America saying that Bucky was "the wholesome all-American answer to the Hitler Youth." Even then, Bucky had asked himself if an organization as cynically manipulative and evil in purpose as the Hitler Youth needed an answer.

In a place called Achnacarry in the Highlands of Scotland, two ex-Shanghai policemen had taught him how to push a taper-bladed dagger up through the back of a human skull. That was the moment that he had first suspected he was going to enjoy this work. After parachuting into Fortress Europe and putting the training in to practice, his suspicions had been confirmed.

Nobody wanted talk about this, particularly Steve, and it had taken Bucky a while to come to terms with it himself. The Winter Soldier was not nearly as far removed from Bucky Barnes as people liked to think. The brainwashing had been about who he worked for, not what he did.

Being the Man on the Wall had taken its toll on Nick because, at heart, even after wading through all the blood and filth, Fury had just been trying to do the right thing. He had once been a good man. Bucky, however, knew that this work would take significantly less of a toll on him.

"We should attack now, attack and—"

The bullet caught up with the reptile and blew the back of his skull through his helmet. Bucky checked the drone feed and saw the creature floating away from his sled. He triggered his suit's propulsion system and sped through the corona towards his latest victim. He would take the sled. Its sensor array and cross-reality comms technology was worth stealing. Heat and gravity would claim the reptile's body.

Maybe this assassination would stop the invasion. Maybe not. If it didn't, the LMDs were pretty sure they had a way to collapse the inter-reality gateways and strip the invading fleet's heat shielding. The Sun would consume them. Or they'd find another way to stop them.

Because the people who came to Earth with ill intent had to understand that there will always be someone watching.

EPILOGUE

THE UNSEEN

THERE WILL always be someone watching. Someone who sees all things. All the beauty and horror. All the secrets and sins.

The figure moved through the rubble of the leveled alien citadel in the Blue Area of the Moon. The figure was clad in a hood, rags, and chains, and kept their head down as though bowed in supplication.

It was their sacred duty to record the life of the world, to observe from afar. To watch but never interfere.

The figure could only walk so far. The restraint around their ankle may have looked like a simple manacle, but it was made of an unbreakable metal that had been mined from an asteroid thousands of light years distant. The end of the chain was anchored deep within the bedrock of the Moon.

Never interfere. Before he had been reborn, his life had been one of watching and then interfering—steering and manipulating people, organizations, even entire governments. Now all he could do was watch.

The man who had once been Nicholas Joseph Fury looked

up at the distant Earth. His once-dead eye glowed with an inner light. He could see it all. He had all the information he could ever want and more. It was too much. It felt as though it would collapse his remade mind, but he knew it wouldn't. This was his burden now. His curse.

He was the Unseen.

ACKNOWLEDGMENTS

I WOULD like to thank Ed Wilson of Johnson & Alcock; Titan and associated personnel, Kevin Eddy, Paul Simpson, William Robinson, Adrian McLaughlin, Sarah Mather, George Sandison and Michael Beale (for an epic edit).

From Marvel I'd like to thank Jeff Younquist, Sven Larsen and of course Sarah Singer. Most importantly, however, I'd like to thank Jason Aaron and Mike Deodato and everyone who worked on the original Original Sin series, without whom, of course, this cover version would not have been possible.

Finally I'd like to say thank you to Edward Cox, RJ Barker and Tade "Always Wrong About Galactus" Thompson for their support, humour and advice.

ABOUT THE AUTHOR

EVERY TIME he has to write one of these things Gavin Smith has to look up his own CV to remind himself that he is the author and co-author of around fourteen books, a couple of novellas and several short stories (actually there are more than several but these are the ones he's prepared to share with other people). His books include (but are not limited to) *Veteran* and its sequel *War in Heaven*, the Age of Scorpio Trilogy, the Bastard Legion Series, *Spec Ops Z* and the novelization of the Sony Pictures *Bloodshot* movie. When not writing he is er... writing for the gaming industry whilst making sporadic attempts to break into scriptwriting. In his free time he likes to er... write, game, go for walks and travel.

For more fantastic fiction, author events,
exclusive excerpts, competitions, limited editions and more

VISIT OUR WEBSITE
titanbooks.com

LIKE US ON FACEBOOK
facebook.com/titanbooks

FOLLOW US ON TWITTER AND INSTAGRAM
@TitanBooks

EMAIL US
readerfeedback@titanemail.com

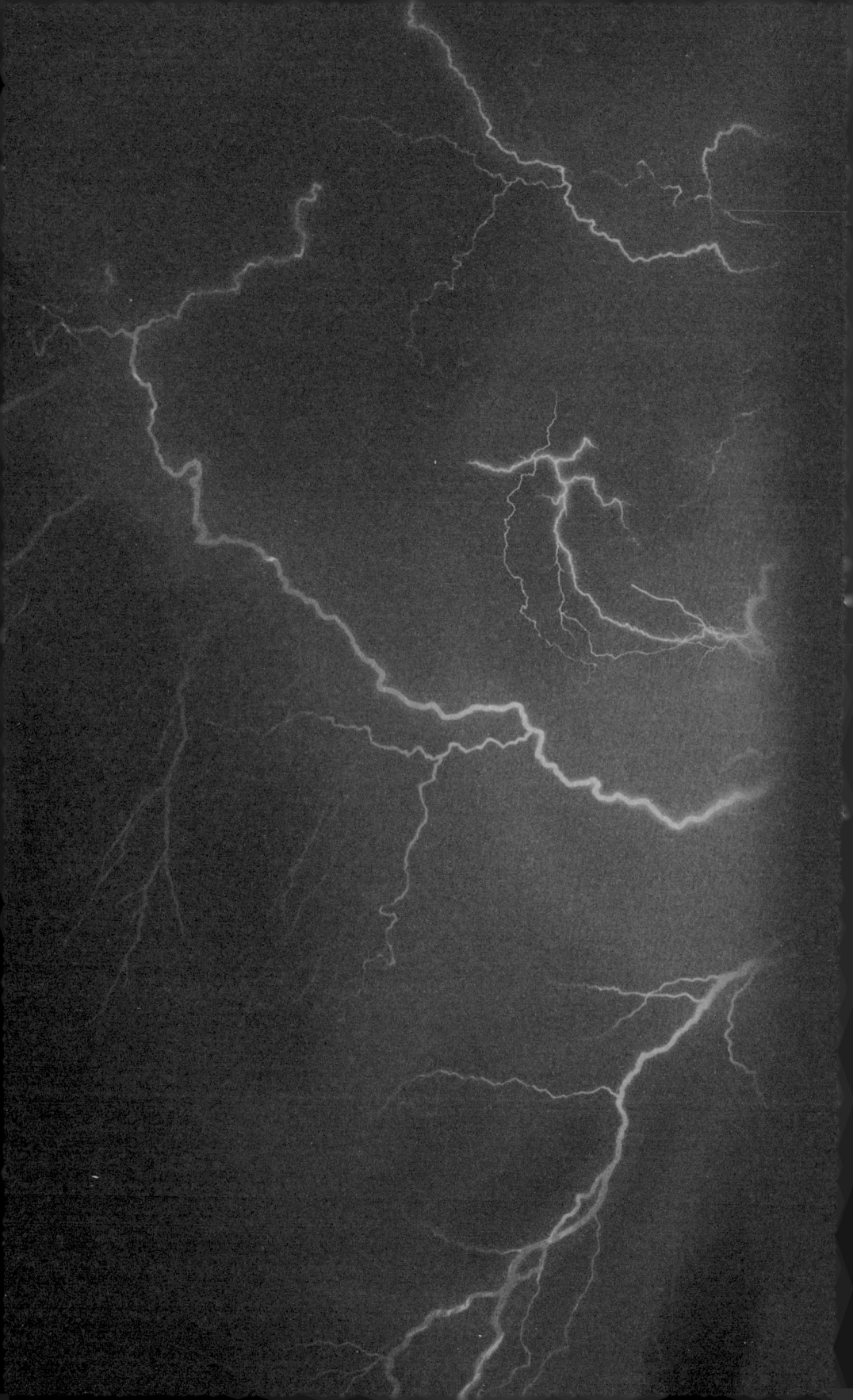